～ Fishing for Ghosts

Fishing for Ghosts

~ TWELVE SHORT STORIES

Richard E. Brown

University of Nevada Press

Reno ~ Las Vegas ~ London

The paper used in this book meets the requirements
of American National Standard for Information
Sciences—Permanence of Paper for Printed Library
Materials, ANSI Z39.48-1984. Binding materials were
selected for strength and durability.

Library of Congress Cataloging-in-Publication Data
Brown, Richard E., 1946–
Fishing for ghosts: twelve short stories / Richard E. Brown.
   p. cm.
Contents: A dream of flight—Fishing for ghosts—End of the war—
Bird song—Melting with Ruth—Storying you—Wise and foolish
virgins—Bootlegger's daughter—The devil you don't know—
Marked by the lamb—The Partridge place—The blue light.
ISBN 0-87417-229-2 (cloth : alk. paper)
1. City and town life—Missouri—Fiction.   2. Country life—
Missouri—Fiction.   I. Title.
PS3552.R6978F57   1994
813'.54—dc20   93-29446
                                                      CIP

University of Nevada Press, Reno, Nevada 89557 USA

9   8   7   6   5   4   3   2   1

⁓ Contents

⁓ Preface

My grandfather drove a truck over the back roads of northwestern Missouri to buy eggs, chickens, and beef hides from small farmers, which he sold to the poultry distributors in St. Joseph or Kansas City at the end of every day. His routes covered fifty or sixty miles apiece, not including the drive home at twilight. Still, there was often time for fishing in the streams he passed between towns, so he kept a couple of cane poles tied up under the truckbed. One of these fishing poles was intended for me.

When I rode along, he passed the time by telling stories—usually comical ones that ended in punch lines. However, his narratives contained full-fledged character portraits and explanations of land deals or other calculations, so they were genuine stories, rather than simply jokes. When I was six or eight years old I assumed that all the farmers my grandfather and I met on our rounds after the eggs and chickens had stories like this attached to them. I thought that was how you knew who they were.

Through these stories my grandfather encouraged me to draw certain conclusions that used to give each new generation comfort. He taught me that the place where we lived had been settled for a long time, and that most of the people who lived there were kin to one another, and that the land itself was a character in everyone's history.

The other great tale-teller of my youth was Uncle Bee, on my mother's side of the family. The narratives he told were about Platte County, while my grandfather's were mainly about Clinton County. Uncle Bee's were also different in that they dealt with a generation of people older than those my grandfather knew.

Uncle Bee's narratives might be called purely jokes, since they came to the surprise more quickly and did not involve such analyses of character and motive as my grandfather indulged in. Uncle Bee told the jokes to my father, who sat with him in my great-aunt's living room on Sundays. My father encouraged the old man by chuckling at appropriate points, to signify that he was still awake.

I did not care to listen to Uncle Bee, since the people in his jokes were not so real to me as the ones in my grandfather's stories. I had seen a few of my grandfather's characters in the flesh, and I knew exactly where some of his punch lines had taken place. Uncle Bee's Platte County was less explored, but it seemed to be a territory of more abrupt happenings, among a population never given to explaining itself. My father was old enough to supply the connections in these jokes for himself, so that he could understand them, but I was not.

My father admits with chagrin that he is no tale-teller of any kind, even though he has listened to thousands of good ones over his long lifetime. When I go back to Missouri now, he wants to drive me through the farming country north of the dense suburb where he lives, to point out objects to me. Most of these objects he has shown me several times before, although occasionally he will find something new on the same gravel roads we always take. There is a small concrete bridge that he remembers was built by the WPA in about 1935. There is a decayed, empty house where one of his high school friends used to live, or the churchyard where a group of our cousins is buried. My father uses the land to show me where he and I came from, since he cannot tell me any of the tales about it.

The stories in the middle section of this book were written in memory of those I heard early in my life. None of the particular stories here was ever told to me by anyone, but what I mainly owe to my grandfather and Uncle Bee are certain aspects of personality, certain nuances of voice that have made our family seem peculiar to people from other places.

The stories in the first section of this book are about the experiences of a first-person narrator whom it will be natural for the reader to confuse with me. Actually the stories are about me, but not about me, as is usual in such cases. The closest to a true story is "Fishing for Ghosts," yet no fishing trip in my family ever happened in exactly that way. For one thing, my father would not have stayed behind to work the hay; he would have wanted to come fishing along with everybody else. Similarly, there is no real Lassos' Hotel that I know of in Missouri, yet there is one in "Melting with Ruth," because for purposes of arrangement it was useful to invent one so that the larger truth could be told. There is no Ruth either, yet there must be a Ruth—and so on.

One of the larger truths I am trying to get at in these stories is the way the younger characters live under the shadow of the older ones. Another truth is the type of humor the characters employ. This humor may appear corny to some readers, but besides the corniness, it is distinguished in my mind by a continuous undertow of sardonic analysis that absolutely defines the sensibility of these people. Therefore I have risked a little corniness in order to express the other quality properly.

The last group of stories, portraits of solitary men in the landscape, seems to me by far the saddest. These stories are about a type of adult experience I did not share, since I left Missouri when I was twenty and have only been back since then on short visits. At first I was surprised to see that I was writing about the men this way. However, I realize now that certain figures who lived in and around the towns of Weston, Plattsburg, and Cameron were my models for these characters. Kindly, hard-working, they carried a touch of desolation about their faces. Perhaps they were only sons (as I was), used to spending much of their time outdoors alone, mulling over the problems that troubled them while they worked. It was a fine situation to encourage eccentricity—if that trait has any value, as I believe it does. Sometimes these men would make casual remarks that took my breath away.

One man especially comes to mind. He had charming manners—in the style of that country—and was better educated than average, since he had been a high school ag teacher for a decade before he turned to farming full-time. He also had a fantastic love of beef cattle. The look of a fine herd grazing in a field would always bring forth a sigh of admiration from him, if we took him out for a drive.

However, he was given to bouts of discouragement, deeper than the reasons he offered for his moods would seem to justify. He experienced periods of devastating loneliness, despite his love for his wife and daughter. There were times when the cattle, corn, and soy beans he raised were scarcely comforts enough to keep him alive. Now in his seventies, he is badly arthritic, mainly housebound, though he is still able to see his fields from the windows and porch of the modern farmhouse he built.

It is easy to imagine that he wants to be buried on his own land— the exact spot is in the corner of a pasture behind the house, shaded by a little stand of pines—but his wife fears that such a grave will be lost sight of in future generations. Everybody knows that if she outlives him (she is in somewhat better health), he will be buried in the cemetery in town, despite the outrage his ghost may feel. How heavily this subject must weigh on him! I think when I visit him. His pale blue eyes move away toward the window from which the chosen corner of the pasture can be seen. When our conversation comes to a momentary halt, I know that he is thinking about his last passion, in a terrible way that is impenetrably his own.

The final stories in this book are about men like him, in one way or another, although none of the plots is taken from their lives.

Readers of my novel, *Chester's Last Stand,* will recognize certain characters in these stories. Chester himself reappears as an old man, first in "Fishing for Ghosts" and later in "Storying You," where he is accompanied by his antagonists, the Wilson boys. Chester's unindicted coconspirator, Reverend Selkirk, appears in "Wise and Foolish Virgins," along with the lawyer Bill Beagle. The bootlegger in "Bootlegger's Daughter" is a very minor character in the novel. A figure of greater dignity, the newspaper reporter Johnny Acorn, is the protagonist of a story in the last section, "The Devil You Don't Know."

I am grateful to several readers who made suggestions for improvements in these stories. Three friends at the University of Nevada, Reno, were especially helpful: Robert Merrill, Elizabeth Raymond, and Ann Ronald. My greatest debt is to another patient reader, Larry Hillman. Whatever infelicities remain must be ascribed to my own stubbornness.

~ Part One

A Dream of Flight

Considering Rachel on these vacant spring weekends, I catch myself thinking of flight. My lover's forearms and calves extend maybe four inches longer than the upper parts of her limbs, making her whole body flap broadly, hips and shoulders rolling toward each other, head bobbing on its long stalk above her revolving breasts. Coming straight at me on her way from the bedroom into the kitchen, she looks aerodynamic and determined, like a great migratory crane cranking up for a slow struggling takeoff and a graceful fade into clear sky.

In these weekend visions, I sometimes glimpse myself as well: a terrified fledgling or a crumpled rodent, caught amid spiny tail feathers. My stomach sinks as I'm drawn skyward, hanging on for life, until I find myself suspended dizzyingly above some icy northern lake. Meanwhile Rachel's eyes are on the sun and she makes for it, stretching back her legs and waving those prodigious wings.

My lover's affinity with birds first struck me when I realized how often she's literally up in the air. Most weekends she whooshes away on a commuter jet to Portland, en route to some feminist conference or else to consult with action groups. By trade she's a sociologist, renowned for her books predicting where the postmodern woman's mind will turn next. Recently I've noticed that her dust jackets all feature the same distinctive photograph: narrowed eyes search intently for something beyond the camera's range, while tawny ropes of hair are swept back from the face by a violent head wind. Reading the words inside the covers is hardly necessary after a signal as blatant as that.

After I drop her at Eugene's small airport on Fridays, I return to the apartment and listen all weekend to the irregular silences between heartbeats. This time alone should actually be welcome—it should allow me to get to the bottom of certain things at last. But after I've summoned up the bird image and had my wicked laugh, it's round and round in my brain and then bang! Sunday night, and I'm no closer to a breakthrough than ever.

Sometimes I run over my history with Rachel, looking for clues about our problem. I first met her amid the clouds over northern California. She was striding down the aisle of a 737 when an air pocket threw her into my lap. I've been an eager flier myself during certain seasons, and that day I was returning from an academic convention where I'd failed to make the right impression on the department heads who were hiring new faculty. On the plane I was tossing back whiskey, trying to kill the thought that I wouldn't be able to move away from Oregon at the end of the school year. I'd never worked at the same place for so long before, and I felt sick of this low gray sky, the dull green or brown hills encircling the town: a landscape that reflects nothing inside me.

After our shocked laughter at her tumble, as I mopped up my spilled drink and she unfolded her long legs beside me in the aisle, we fell to talking about her latest workshop, at Stanford. Academic women from up and down the Coast had flown in to pick at watercress salads and discuss the next phase of their particular brand of feminism. Rachel led the avant-garde, who believed the new phase would leave feminism itself in the dust.

I listened eagerly, even though her slant on women's issues didn't move me very much. I saw that she was hurtling ahead at a speed I'd never dreamed of, along a tract of geography that was new. I'd only been nursing the tame ambition of shifting across the country from one university to another, hoping someday to land in a soft endowed perch. Listening to her at thirty thousand feet, I felt like a kid who's been pedaling his tricycle up and down a narrow strip of sidewalk, when out of nowhere a glorious teenager flashes past on a ten-speed, and the little fellow's head is sent spinning.

I'm a short man; probably for that reason I'm shy until I get acquainted. Yet sometimes I find that my hand shoots out and does something decisive on its own. A lot of energy was racing through my blood that day on the plane, and as we disembarked, I stretched a stubby arm as far as it would reach across the giant curve of Rachel's back. If I'd reasoned the matter out, I might've expected a woman like this—bright, ambiguously sexual, obviously free—to toss me off as a presumptuous stranger and a comparative dwarf. But she was too open to new experiences to take offense. Or maybe my flood of questions flattered her. I probably tickled her funny bone too, since she kept tousling my hair once we reached the airport lobby, as if I was a cute, fuzzy little specimen she'd picked out of a zoo. As soon as the crowd pressing off the plane gave her a chance, she half-turned and smiled. "What shall we have for dinner?" she asked.

For Rachel, the question of what to eat is joyously complicated, since she prefers never to repeat herself at the table. These days, if we cook at home, she might tell me that we can fix her new recipe for Greek spinach pie or try this peculiar blue *fusilli* dressed in olive oil and capers. Then again, we might also go out to the new Tibetan restaurant one of her sociologist friends recommended. However, she'll try anything once, so when I offered, that first afternoon in the baggage claim area, to stir up some recipes from my Missouri childhood, her eyes widened. "Little farmboy," she said and bent to kiss my pate.

Looking back on that scene at the airport, I see myself pursuing her as if on a dare. For one thing, I didn't actually believe two people of such different sizes could fit together under a sheet. But I had her in my pocket as soon as she heard that long ago my grandmother devised a list of dishes that could be stirred up at the drop of a hat, because she cooked for so many folks who showed up unannounced at our farmhouse. "Five-minute succotash, three-minute chicken fried steak—all Grandma's recipes had the preparation time in their names. A modern freezer helps. I've cut half a minute off most of her items."

Rachel laughed obligingly—displaying healthy teeth—and in my apartment she devoured the greasy muck I served up. Then she asked for another beer. Soon we were lolling at the same height above our sticky plates, reminiscing about old-fashioned pie a la mode. Conversation died into leers, and we made our way to the kitchen floor at about the same instant.

With Rachel, I quickly found, the sport isn't erotic so much as it's good-humored exploration. She wants to peer into every crevice and find out what the other person can do with a pillow or a jar of Vaseline. By way of experiment, she's bedded most of the male assistant professors in Eugene, as well as a couple of undergraduates and a few tomboys as curious as herself.

Ordinarily I might be overawed by such a roll call of predecessors, but there's a laughing quality about her lovemaking that helps me forget the difference in our sexual polish. I never quite believe it when she grins, "You're the only one, Sam! The way you poke me there!" Still I nuzzle fiercely, thrusting the ball of my head into her armpit, clinging to her chest long after the animal appetite has been assuaged. "You're a leech!" she cries when I suckle so hard that it must hurt. "Don't you have a thumb?"

Remembering these semiamorous escapades on my weekends alone doesn't bring much pleasure, though. Before Sunday night when I meet her return flight, I pass a few dozen hours pouring one bourbon after another. At least the liquor keeps me from pacing around the apartment. The bedroom and bath are strewn with her discarded plumage, the kitchen is crammed with spice jars and cookbooks from all those competing cuisines. Only here in the living room, where I camp out, are my eyes safe from her leavings.

I sit in an armchair before three lowered window shades, a bottle perched on the table to my right. I wonder how long I can put off going to the toilet. I talk aloud once it gets dark, if there's no basketball on the tube. I address certain shadows cast by headlights passing in the street. Often the shapes are winged and flicker into the desk at the far end of the room. Bitterly I aim potshots at them from my blind, though as they pass I see them turn back and wink at me tauntingly, for my bullets miss them every time, every time.

For the past week I've been trying to persuade Rachel to buy a condo with me. I tell her that owning property could be a lot more satisfying than she thinks. It wouldn't be too big a commitment, either—nothing like running that farm where my grandparents lived when I was a boy. In a modern development, there are no crops to harvest, no livestock to tend. The lawns mow themselves, and you can sell whenever you need a change of air.

At first she reminded me that only a month before I'd wanted to move away from Oregon, not to buy real estate here. But on Thursday she noticed that I was brooding before supper, so she pulled on my earlobe teasingly and suggested that we inspect some models on our way to a restaurant.

We found the new development set inside a bowl of raw red earth whose lip was thrown up against the higher, tree-studded hills. Outside, the units were painted a dull steely blue, like nothing in nature. I am not here, I thought in sudden dismay as we parked the car. But inside, the shiny kitchens pleased Rachel at once. She joked about the mountain of pastry dough she could roll out on the vast countertops. Her face became so animated that I began to think of those places as homes, after all. In the end, though, I couldn't get her to focus on the down payment.

"With one of these dining rooms, you could take your good china out of the box and entertain our friends in style," I tried to tempt her.

"Sure," she agreed, working a paint chip loose from the wall with long fingernails. "We could have a regular old social life."

"Relationships are built out of doing things like that together," I argued. "Even funny old Grandma and Grandpa knew that."

An appeal to a past that's unknown to her, and therefore easy for her to dismiss.

"Actually, we already eat together five nights a week. That's a very domestic habit, and it doesn't require taking out a mortgage." She nudged my arm. "I'm feeling like *boeuf en croute* tonight. Or maybe pork lasagna. What do you think?"

Thank God we've agreed on one thing, at least. We will definitely vacation in southern Italy this summer. We're going to drive around the Boot, then ferry over to Sicily. We've decided this because Rachel has never seen these places, and she's been practically everywhere else, either attending a professional meeting or vacationing with one of her lovers. The destination isn't so important to me, although I'm glad to avoid cities in favor of a hard landscape, where crops are tended by swarthy farmers.

Yesterday, though, our plans became complicated by her fear that she'll die of boredom before our two weeks are up. Southern Italy's begun to look cramped on the map. This noon when I dropped her at the airport, she tossed some pamphlets about cruises from Palermo down to Africa on the car seat.

"But Sicily is huge!" I said. "A little continent, almost. Once we get there, we'll never want to leave."

"Ciao! I'm late for my plane!" She kissed the tip of my nose in that way I interpret as cheery goodwill. Driving back to the apartment, I couldn't shake the drizzle that keeps falling from these leaden Oregon skies. Then something clicked and I realized: I was brought up on exactly the feeling of desertion Rachel gave off when she pulled that bundle of pamphlets out of her bag and opened the car door in the same smooth motion. A feeling that, now that I think about it, I've been flying from ever since I left the farm.

On Sunday mornings it always hits me that if I don't sober up by nightfall, I'll miss my lover at the airport and a crisis will descend. Of course, I have every right to get blind drunk for two days and shout at the walls. It's my apartment, I'm not hurting anybody else. But if Rachel ever discovers my private sorrow, I'm afraid she may think it as amusing as our acts of love.

I pour mugs of thick coffee. I open the living room windows to clear out the stench. I dump empty bottles in the trash can by the garage. Finally I brush my teeth for a long time, until my gums bleed, like a rite.

In the evening she steps down the ramp from the jet, lifts her elegant, disproportioned arm and gives a merry wave. She never looks tired. Driving home, I'm careful to ask about the new ideas she's picked up on her latest junket. She rattles them off glibly: people to call, more meetings to arrange.

Tonight while she unpacks, I leaf through the stack of shiny brochures describing ferries across the Mediterranean. "Every photograph looks the same," I point out. "Cobalt sky with one puffy cloud and a forest of crumbling columns. Tin-faced native guide with mule. In fact, they look like the pictures of Sicily. What do we gain by gadding around?"

On the subject of our vacation Rachel's good humor has begun to fail. "You're not adventurous enough, Sam. If we didn't eat out, you'd never stir from your chair at night."

"I think getting away to southern Italy will be fabulous!" I exclaim, twitching my eyebrows to show enthusiasm. "It's just that right now while I'm teaching, I'm too drained to flit around. You don't give me credit for going into those grueling literature classes every day where I spill my guts. The summer will be different."

Privately, I think the signs of my slowing down are misleading. Granted, I've canceled half a dozen classes during the past month when I wasn't prepared. But the students never object; they can always use the time to catch up on their reading. Besides, lots of people feel doldrums in the spring. Can't we leave it to the ardent Sicilian sun to stir me out of my brooding in its own good time?

Meanwhile Rachel has left the living room. I find her sitting at the kitchen table, marking a stack of sociology exams. I lay a hand on her shoulder while I register her espresso maker by the sink, her battered spice rack which we've nailed above the stove. I remember how bland the food used to taste at Grandma's table on the farm, and suddenly I dig my fingers into my lover's shoulder, trying to push down another wave of nameless despair. "The problem can't be you, so it must be me. Just don't give up on me, that's all!"

I feel the astonished stare of her searching ice-blue eyes.

My belly goes icy and hot at once. Tuesday over dinner (sweet potato jambalaya with pickled coconut relish) Rachel says, "You don't talk much about your boyhood, Sam. Were you happy on that old farm where your granny cooked up succotash by the clock?"

"Oh, happy—" I rake a hand through my hair. Her intelligence, now that she's turned it on me, has led her to the dark heart of things almost at once. "Childhood isn't supposed to be happy, is it? The grown-ups are full of their secrets, and the kid is kept on the outside, powerless, isn't he? and wondering what he's there for."

"My parents didn't have so many secrets," she says in a tone that's probably meant to be instructive. "My mom let me pick out any summer camp I wanted. That was her style. The minute I was ready, she pushed me off to investigate."

She looks away, and the silence expands between us like a gigantic balloon, full of our private memories. At last we're separated by hundreds of miles, as Rachel, a tall, bony, pig-tailed girl, skips rope to the city park and scampers over the monkey bars, while I rattle around inside a lonely farmhouse. I find that all the outside doors are locked, and my family seems to have disappeared.

It's minutes later when we come together again amid the greasy plates and empty glasses from our meal. I find her grinning over me; my face must have sagged under the weight of old feelings flooding in. "You're not a traveler at heart, are you, Sam? You were forced into it and you got as far as Oregon on your own, but secretly you hate it. Am I right?" She walks around the table and lifts me to her chest indulgently, ready to play our laughing game again. But for once I hold back, since in her eyes there's no hint of the maternity I seek.

That evening spent remembering my Missouri boyhood has opened a vein. My mind drifts back to certain lumpy images even while I'm lecturing to my classes at the university. In the air above my students' heads, an axe-wielding old woman roams about the chicken yard, selecting for our dinner the bird that tries to flap away. My father plants me beside a cornfield and tells me to stay put until the tractor comes around again. Then he drives swiftly over a hill. In the farmhouse parlor a patriarch, my grandpa, lies on his sickbed, and when he calls for a glass of water, I hear the rooms creak with emptiness.

A dozen times I find myself working some family anecdote into my dinner conversations with Rachel. If the point of these stories is lost on my students, I think it should be clearer to her, since it always deals with my original reasons for flight.

When I was fifteen, I tell her, I actually tried to move off my grandparents' farm into town, to be closer to the high school and a few teachers there who had taken pity on me. I planned the move for weeks. I would rent a room in Lassos' Hotel, which served the railroad men. I'd work as a busboy on weekends to pay the rent. Finally at the supper table one night I cleared my throat and announced that I was ready to become self-supporting.

"But the town's a wicked place!" my grandparents cried. "Is there some girl at the hotel you're following?"

As I relive this episode, I can see creases deepening around the old couple's mouths. I'm drawn into the mystery of my isolation there as if it was fresh. In fact, I needn't have worried about getting free of the farm. Within two years Grandpa was dead and the land was sold. My father and I moved away to St. Joe to live with my mother. The next year I left for college and have seldom visited Missouri since.

Rachel seems oddly quiet these nights, listening to me. The peculiar food she searches out for us is less amusing now. She hasn't mentioned our trip to Italy in over a week. Meanwhile I'm talking nonstop. I hold her beside me on the sofa after dinner to prevent her from reading. She keeps her long face twisted, perhaps ironically. Possibly she thinks of me as an odd little manikin pressing his trouble on her in an awkward imitation of human suffering. "Why've you been keeping this stuff bottled up for so long?" she asks peevishly when I pause for breath. "Now everything's coming out in too much of a rush."

I try to break through the wall Rachel has thrown up by telling her my earliest memory of my mother. We're sitting on the lawn before the farmhouse. Mother is settled in a canvas chair, while I'm playing at her feet. The shade from the nut trees around us is deep. She's reading aloud to me—no words that I remember, but in a throaty voice, like cream. Then the sound breaks off, and I look up. Here's Grandma standing over us, wearing an intense frown. She says some quick words I don't catch. My mother makes no reply.

Suddenly I find myself jerked up and, though I'm old enough to walk, I'm being carried toward the house. I look over Grandma's shoulder at my pretty mama behind us in the yard. I scream out for her, but the front door opens and then I can see nothing more outside.

Such piercing scenes have driven away my spring doldrums; I never feel vertigo anymore. Monday I decide not to drive to the university, but to walk. The air is stirring and clouds race overhead. By the time I reach the classroom, my head is crammed with new stories, which I decide on the spur of the moment to deliver instead of the scheduled lecture about Henry James. I make no attempt to connect my remarks to any book assigned for the course; I'm offering my students a one-time-only chance for special enlightenment.

I grip the lectern and keep my eyes on the ceiling as I begin: Whenever I yawned as a boy, my grandparents would push me upstairs for a nap. They kept me in the dark room for hours, even after I woke up. From my place near the top of the stairs, I could sometimes hear voices below, doors closing, cars driving away— but I never knew what all those social noises were about.

Most Sundays a stranger would appear just as we sat down to Grandma's fancy dinner. He would be introduced as Cousin Fred or Bill or Ernie or Lloyd or Charles or a dozen more names. This stranger would sit morosely among us while the meal passed its slow course. Afterward he excused himself from the table as soon as he could. Then either Grandpa or my father would stroll out to the car with him, talking while the stranger listened with lowered head. Finally they shook hands, and the stranger drove away. But whose cousins were these men? Why did each of them come only once? On those walks to their cars what message did they receive that couldn't be delivered any other way?

The life in that old farmhouse was always churning, churning, while my father drew into his shell a bit more each year, until he looked gaunt at forty. Meanwhile my mother moved away to live by herself in St. Joe. I grew up isolated from my kin, allowed only to glimpse certain haunting shadows of their lives.

Still gazing at the classroom ceiling in order to avoid my students' bewildered eyes, I suddenly realize something else. Although I've been struggling for days to tell a heap of stories about my boyhood, I have no full-blown stories in me. I possess only these frozen pictures, obscure movements, gestures torn out of something's middle.

This deepening sense of mystery doesn't prevent me from speeding home Monday night to meet Rachel at the front door of our apartment, more eager than ever to draw her into my accounts. I cling to her almost as if she could tell me what everything means. Missouri, once my enemy, becomes my ally in this struggle to move her.

My lover and I adjourn to the kitchen, where she begins to fix dinner while I talk. Now I'm painting wonderful pictures for her, in which the unknown hangs so palpably that it brings goose bumps to my flesh. Were my grandparents hiding some crime or scandal that drove my mother off the farm as soon as she figured it out? I ask Rachel. For instance: Where did my grandpa get that wad of dollar bills he drew out of his overalls pocket and counted at the kitchen table late one night? Why did my father disappear from the farm for a month without even saying good-bye to his young son, or hello when he suddenly reappeared on the porch one morning, unshaven, wearing filthy clothes?

But maybe their secret wasn't criminal at all, I quickly add, since the air of the farmhouse was saturated with religion. Maybe Grandma was always pushing me upstairs for a nap in order to protect me from visitors she thought would imperil my Immortal Soul. Very likely those cousins who kept appearing for Sunday dinner were also Souls in need of saving. And my father's unexplained disappearance? He'd probably gotten his fill of my grandparents' piety at last and went off on a bender to purge himself of the Scripture and hymns, that's all.

The real point, I say excitedly, is that they let me see so little of themselves that for all I know, the truth might lie in either direction. Crime and religious obsession are equal possibilities. Or, for that matter, couldn't the two things be the same in a case like this? Religious crime, criminal religion—religion carried out in a criminal way—

My lover interrupts by nodding for me to uncork the wine. While I've been talking, she has silently mixed our cocktails, stir-fried a pile of vegetables, and for the past half hour her face has suggested no mockery. I believe that if nothing else, she understands my urgency at last.

When we sit down to the meal, I launch into a new fragment about how my grandpa once left me behind when he went on a fishing trip. On a bright summer morning one of those unknown cousins drove up with a fishing pole poking through his car window and pulled Grandpa out of the barn with a yell. "Let's go catch us some gar!" Both men laughed devilishly, and I watched the strange vehicle race away, carrying my grandfather off in search of a fish that never swam in northwest Missouri streams.

But as the memory breaks off, Rachel abruptly holds up a hand. "You've been talking nonstop for ten days, Sam. You've told me about that man with the fishing pole at least five times. I haven't had a chance to get a word in."

I start to apologize, to explain how all the pictures keep swirling before my eyes and I can't seem to stop them, but she interrupts again. "I have some news, so let's just eat until I can say it."

Now she's made me so nervous that after a second I burst out, "I still want to go to Italy with you. All this Missouri stuff makes no difference about that. I'll write a check for the plane ticket tonight."

She looks up from her Mongolian clams. I've never seen her eyes so far away. "You don't want to go to Italy, Sam."

It's always infuriating when somebody talks as if she knows your mind better than you do! It reminds me of the afternoon my grandmother caught me looking at a photograph of my mother, which I carried in my wallet—

"These days you and I have nothing in common," Rachel says. "That old farmhouse, those fields you keep describing—I wasn't there; I can't picture them. One thing I've learned by listening to you, though: buildings, landscapes don't move me. I must've lived in fifty apartments in my life, and I couldn't tell you the color of the living-room walls in any of them."

We both pause for breath, but she catches hers first. "You're on a journey where nobody else can follow, Sam. The best I can do is get out of your way. That's why I think we should try living apart this summer. Next fall we can touch base again and see what we feel like. Meanwhile Italy would definitely be a mistake."

I flash on how I felt when I was four years old and my mother called me into her bedroom to say that she was moving to St. Joe alone. I nearly weep again over that old desertion, but I catch myself in time and shout, "All I want is to travel with you! I dream about it night and day!"

Rachel shakes her head. "Why don't you go home, farmboy?"

I drop my fork, incredulous. "Nobody vacations in Missouri, for Chrissakes! The humidity is stupefying—it's even worse than here! Everybody talks in that impossible accent, and the food is god-awful! A person can't go back and turn over all those rocks!"

"Anyhow, I need to be around some other friends for a while. I've missed half the women's film series this spring, staying home to listen to you."

"Well then, I'm going to Sicily alone! You can't talk me out of that!"

"Take your time, Sam. Think what you're doing."

I'm thinking furiously, as a matter of fact, in hopes of coming up with the perfect retort. "What can you expect when the woman doesn't even believe in guilt?" I shout.

A smile brushes her lips as she rises from the table. She strides into the bedroom on tremendous stork legs and shuts the door.

"I'm sending you a postcard from Palermo," I cry after her. "Blue sky with one puffy cloud and a native guide in colorful costume. Watch for it!"

I hear the shuffling of luggage from the hall. Tonight I'll be left alone. I hope I fall into a satiric mood, because the alternative is too grim to imagine. The worst is, I don't know if, even for an instant, she took any of my stories to heart.

My legs feel as if they'll fly off from the churning. I run from the living room into the bedroom, gathering books for this morning's classes. Rachel's departure has turned everything in the apartment upside down. I tip over a chair, then find myself involved with some glass jars on a kitchen shelf. Suddenly I remember the main point of the day: my travel plans. Something is waiting for me in the brown scorpion hills south of Rome.

I leave the jars broken on the floor and dash to the telephone. I dial our—my—travel agent. My finger is bleeding, it leaves a crimson ring on the face of the machine. I tell the woman inside the receiver where I have to go, but she keeps asking me to repeat my destination.

"Sicily! I want to fly direct!"

The agent mentions layovers and advises that a train from Frankfurt might be cheaper; she'll check. Then I'm stranded on hold.

My whole body protests against this delay so violently that my grandmother cries, "Patience, Sammy! You can come downstairs in a minute. I'm just finishing my sweeping, and I don't want you tracking through the dust." Meanwhile I hear people at the front door, making sounds of leaving. From my bedroom window I've spotted their car—a green Nash that I've never seen before. I run back to the window to watch them drive away, since Grandma won't let me into the living room to meet them. Through the small square glass I can only see their backs as they walk between the rows of nut trees. It is a couple—young man and woman—carrying what appear to be cages with small animals in them. Rabbits? I think. Why wouldn't my grandmother let me see the bunnies? Was she afraid I'd make too much fuss?

Watching those cages disappear into the back seat of the car, I begin to blubber, but just as quickly I control myself, for fear of the disgrace if anyone downstairs heard me making such a sound.

Meanwhile the telephone receiver has dropped beside my knee while I inspect my finger. The cut has begun to clot. I put it to my lips just as the travel agent starts speaking again from beside my leg. I listen for a few seconds, until the sound becomes irritating. Then I reach down and hang up.

Where was I going?

Sometimes without planning it, I find that my hand has shot out to meddle with something decisively. Now I observe that it's reaching for the receiver again, and my finger dials the area code for northwest Missouri. It's my parents' number, and I wonder if anyone will be at home, and what they'll say.

My mother answers on the third ring and replies in that accent I perfectly remember. Was I expecting her to speak Italian, like some *mamma* in an ad for tomato sauce? But no. I'm so moved that I nearly weep again, only I don't want to alarm her, so instead I ask about Dad and the weather, just to make her talk.

She must be wondering why I've phoned in the middle of the day, when the rates are high and I should be at work. Finally she asks, "When are you leaving for Italy?" She doesn't add, "With that woman." We never mention Rachel, because something about my account of her has caused Mother not to approve.

"Oh, Italy. That's off. It's no fun traveling alone."

"Alone?" She would ask about Rachel now if she could.

"I was thinking I'd come and visit you instead."

My mother and I are equally surprised by this news. She sounds pleased, in a guarded way, but feels duty bound to point out that she and Dad live a quiet life. What will I do for fun?

Where do I get these answers? "I'm not coming in order to be amused, for gosh sakes! I'm coming to see what it's *like* there after all this time!"

She laughs shortly. "There aren't many country girls left here any more, if that's what you're looking for. I couldn't stay quiet on the farm myself, you remember. I moved to St. Joe and made you and your dad come visit me on weekends."

"But St. Joe was still in Missouri. And you still loved us. You just missed being a secretary like you'd been before you got married." I say all this by rote. It's the approved version of our past, although I have no idea what it may be covering up.

Meanwhile my father is sitting there in the den, but he doesn't pick up the telephone beside his chair to say hello.

"I'll be home in a week," I continue, my voice rising. "My work at the university's not important anymore. Some students complained that my lectures were getting weird, so I'm not sure if I'll be wanted back next year. I looked around for other jobs, but there aren't any. So I said, '*Basta!*' That means to hell with it all. I've been away long enough. I'm coming home to take care of you."

The telephone line hums a minute before she replies, choosing her first words carefully. "We're both healthy, if that's what you're wondering."

But then she relaxes, and in her quiet, easy drawl she tells me how it really is. "I moved off the farm years ago, Sammy, and then you moved away too, and you kept right on going. That was good; I really think it was. I would've gone farther myself if there'd been any way. Only for me at that time, given the money angle and the commitments that people make, St. Joe was as far as I could get. But I can tell you for darn sure, there wasn't any good reason to stay anywhere around here. Believe me, I've had years to think about this, so I know. It's only the old feelings we miss sometimes, and questions we wish we could answer when we wake up in the dead of night. But as for the place itself, there's less to it than you might suppose. You could drive out and look at the old farmhouse, which is still standing, by the way—I think a family named Sullivan lives in it now—but it's the same empty shell it always was. Anyhow, we'll be happy to see you for a visit. I'll bake something. 'Come for as long as you want,' your father says. Did you hear his voice just now? But the things you're remembering—they aren't here and probably never were. They're only inside you. That's what I wanted to say. You did exactly right to move on when you did."

Fishing for Ghosts

"My name is Yohn Yohnson,
I come from Visconsin,"

my grandfather sang roguishly as my young friend
Johnny Johnson and I slipped into our seats at the table. I blushed
for the sake of my schoolfellow, but it was sensitivity wasted, because he joined in exuberantly, losing the melody toward the end
but surpassing Grandpa in volume. I was shocked by this boister-
ousness and glanced over to see if Grandma disapproved, but she
stood with her back to us, stirring the oatmeal. When they finished
singing, Grandpa ruffled Johnny's Viking-red hair and Grandma,
ladling out our breakfasts, posed us a riddle.

"Your grandpa is going to take you boys somewhere, and it
begins with an *F*."

Johnny's eyes grew wide and he threw out guess after guess,
ignoring his steaming bowl. "Farming?" No. "To Farrel's for ice
cream?" No, we never drove into town for ice-cream cones. "To a
forest?" No, that was a silly try, because we had no forests around
the farm. As he racked his little brain for *F*-words, I tried to eat my
breakfast, but despair overwhelmed me. I guessed instantly that
Grandpa was going to take us fishing; and I felt sure that Johnny
would become so absorbed in this new pastime that I would lose
his private companionship for another day.

I was so bookish that I couldn't get anybody else in the Hickman school to like me, and my big opportunity to secure Johnny
as my one intimate friend was slipping through my fingers. He was
delighted at everything about the farm, but with all the family's at-

tention lavished on him, he barely had time to acknowledge that I was the one who had invited him to spend the week. Even Chester, our hired man, had caught us boys rambling off to the pond behind the chicken house one afternoon and took it upon himself to make whistles for us out of reeds. Since Chester tested the instruments first with his own lips, I had no taste for playing, but Johnny didn't mind the spittle on his mouthpiece and blew and blew as he danced happily beside the water. Afterward he told me he wished his dad—who ran the grocery store in town—had a job in the open air like Chester's. Wanting your father to resemble Chester struck me as ridiculous, but I was powerless to teach Johnny a proper attitude.

"No, and no, and no," Grandma said smugly to Johnny's last guess, firefly-catching. "I'll bet Sammy knows."

"Do you know, Sam?" Johnny turned to me urgently, for my grandmother's skill at baiting small boys was new to him, and she had succeeded in working him into a hard-breathing frenzy. Normally she would have resented Grandpa stealing me away from her for a whole day, but she was compensating for the loss by triumphing over a new victim with her *F*-game.

"Fishing," I muttered.

"Hooray!" Johnny shouted and dug into his oatmeal hungrily.

All this time my father had kept as quiet as I; but once the secret was out, he said to Grandpa, "Who's gonna help me fetch in that hay?"

"Chester'll help. Ain't enough bales to keep two men out there past lunch," said Grandpa between bites of toast and bacon. "I gotta take off a day now and then. I'm getting to be an old man."

My father held his peace at that, and after breakfast Johnny carried the shovel and I brought the pail to a spot behind the chicken house where Grandpa proposed to dig worms. As Chester passed us on his early-morning round of chores, Johnny shouted, "We're going fishing!" Chester grunted that he couldn't see any fish in the dirt where we stood and then glanced over at Grandpa, who was moving a large rock to find where the worms were juiciest. Perhaps some intelligence passed between the two men before Chester lurched off to water the hogs.

Johnny loved searching the warm mud after Grandpa turned the spade, and he loved watching the slimy mass of worms crawling over one another in the pail. He loved carrying his long cane pole and rummaging in Grandpa's tackle box for lead sinkers. Living in town, he rarely got to ride around the countryside in a pickup with poles stretching back from the right-hand window of the cab, so he also loved being the one who sat by the door and held them tight to keep them from blowing away. I hunkered in the middle, trying to avoid the gearshift, which jammed my stomach every time we stopped. Grandpa was tickled over how Johnny couldn't contain his joy and sang the song with his name in it as we sped down the dusty road toward the Little Platte River.

We left the truck on the shoulder before the bridge and clambered down the dirt path to the riverbank. For a hundred yards on either side beneath the bridge, the local fishermen had worn away the undergrowth so you could easily toss a line into the deep pockets of water around the concrete pilings. I preferred to stay here, because there were no branches to cut my chubby arms, and the shade from the bridge overhead was welcome on such a hot, muggy morning.

But while I was planning my comforts, Johnny and Grandpa made for the little trail at the edge of the clearing that led through rough thickets to catfish holes ever more remote. I had figured out long before that the fish themselves were only a minor part of fishing. Mainly, fishing meant driving around the county so you could inspect your neighbors' crops, while you searched out those hidden streams where you imagined the big yellow-bellied lazy ones were waiting to swallow a worm. It meant walking miles up and down a riverbank, not caring about the insects that crawled into your lunch sack, and fiddling patiently with your line according to some strategy involving the position of your cork and sinker. It meant lugging your string of slimy fish back to the truck at dusk, aching in your bones from the exercise and revolted by your own filth, if you were me, but pleased at the day well spent, if you were Grandpa or any other boy.

So I knew Johnny and Grandpa were only acting according to the laws of their natures when they pressed through the undergrowth and disappeared upstream. But Johnny, though a failure as my companion, was useful as a measuring rod. Seeing him hurry forward, I understood myself to be a different sort of creature, forced to live outside my true element like one of those catfish hung up with a stick running through its gills and mouth.

"I'll stay here and fish!" I called out.

The rustling up ahead stopped, and I ran in after them. Grandpa looked puzzled, but he didn't wish to deny my liberty, so I took a pole from him, along with a cup of worms, got my sandwich and pie out of the paper bag, and lied that I would probably be along later.

As I walked back to the shadow of the bridge, I was awestruck by my own deed: for a minute I could hear no bird or insect singing, and in the vast silence I realized that I had never been alone before so far from the farmhouse. In the beginning I could not savor this isolation as a release, because the obligation to start fishing presented itself imperiously. But when I had put my lunch down on a dry rock and unrolled my line and at last squatted to look for bait, I found that my cup had tipped over and the worms had crawled away. At first I was annoyed and began to search the ground for stragglers, but then it dawned on me that if I didn't find them, I couldn't fish. The moment I realized this, I felt glad even for the worms' poor sake.

Relief gradually wore off into boredom, however, and I began scouting over my little kingdom under the bridge for amusements. Away from the farmhouse, where I could leaf through my books or gossip with Grandma about my aunts, I was without resources. About nine-thirty I ate my pie, and a little later—because it was the only thing on my mind—I ate my sandwich. I expected that at noon I would regret my improvidence, and this miserable thought kept me from enjoying the food. But as it happened, there would have been no time later to eat, and the hunger I feared was swept away by the rush of feelings.

As I was idly poking about with a stick, I discovered next to the concrete base of the bridge an exotic variety of weed I had never seen before, and which, by its strangeness, has associated itself in my memory with that day on the Little Platte. It resembled miniature bamboo, composed of small links standing one on top of another like a column of sausages. When I pulled a link off the end, it made a popping noise.

There must have been dozens of these exquisite growths, but piece by piece I disassembled them all. Then I gathered up the hollow links scattered on the ground and began to create a miniature mortuary. I hunted ants and other insects to kill and stuff inside the links for burial; then I arranged my tube-shaped coffins in elaborate patterns to form a tiny city of the dead. I recall wondering if a scientific excavator from the *National Geographic* would stumble across my creation someday. I decided that the presence of a typical twentieth-century bridge immensely increased the attractiveness of the site for researchers, so my exotic memorial would quite possibly be found centuries hence, and admired.

Lost in my fantasy, I was startled when, about noon, I heard an ancient car engine rattle up to the bridge and die. A car door slammed, and in a few seconds footsteps shuffled down the path. I knew it was Chester before I saw him, because he owned the oldest car in the county and because he was identifiable by a distinctive sort of clumsy stealth. He crashed around, first against the bridge railing and then among the branches along the path, sloshing where his boots tumbled into puddles; but all these sounds had a silence in the middle of them, as if he froze guiltily after each misplaced step to cover up the clatter.

I crawled up among the spider webs in the bridge frame to avoid being seen, for I instinctively evaded Chester's eyes when I could. Away from the farmhouse, I felt like an idle and superfluous creature, and he was the keen-sighted grown-up who saw through me, but smoldered and said nothing. As I peeked around an iron thrust, he descended to the clearing, spied my unemployed fishing pole, picked it up, and trudged off down the path Grandpa and Johnny had taken three hours before.

I feared that when Grandpa saw Chester with my pole, he would conclude I had been shamming. I did not know the penalty for failure to fish on a fishing trip, but ignorance increased my dread. I longed to run after Chester and beg him to return the pole, but the idea of pleading with him was so loathsome that I couldn't bring myself to call out. I could only creep along behind, keeping a fix on his whereabouts by the sounds of his crashing and splashing about.

We went on this way for at least a mile over slippery terrain, sometimes forced to crawl around giant tree roots and rocks. I was scratched and exhausted; yet my gnawing fear drove me forward. Then the thrashing up ahead stopped, and I heard voices.

I shielded myself and waited for Grandpa to let out an indignant cry—something like, "Not fishing, is he? I'll wallop him!"—but the voices remained low so as not to scare the fish, and I could make out an occasional manly chuckle. Slowly I inched forward until I saw the three of them crouching in a row on the bank. I was ready to run down and implore Grandpa, when it flashed on me that Chester had baited my hook and was fishing. This act seemed so ambiguous that I stopped and then crept closer to overhear what conversation I could.

"Did my son see you drive away?" Grandpa was asking Chester.

"Nah. Soon as we got the hay in the barn he took the wagon out to pick up manure."

Johnny sat between them, holding his pole tightly. "Manoooer!" he said in a certain way.

Both men laughed softly. Chester said, "Manure's what makes a farm grow. That's all a boy like you eats, anyway, manure!"

Johnny denied this indignantly.

"Besides," Chester went on teasing him, "once you start working with it, you get to like it. You shovel it onto the wagon, you haul it back to the barn and let it ferment, then you load it on the manure spreader and throw it around. That's farming."

"Chester thinks everything has to ferment," chuckled Grandpa. Then he added, "My son loves farming more than fishing."

Chester saw where that remark might lead and took it up eagerly. "Sure, manure's got into his blood just like whiskey does in other folks. He could shovel it all day and never get tired."

Johnny found this description of my father's tastes so comical that he nearly dropped his pole, but he managed to say that he didn't believe anybody could be that fond of the stuff. Grandpa and Chester sensed a challenge and began to point out its physical and spiritual advantages. They became eloquent and ingenious, powerfully refuting the idea that any thinking person could find manure disgusting. They mentioned its warmth, texture, shapes, colors, aroma—here they branched into the possibility that its smell was inspirational, since my grandfather knew from his Sunday school preparations that the terms for *breath* and *spirit* are cognates in many languages. Chester built up to a sweeping description of the earth as a gigantic cowpie, exhaling its fragrant breath into the face of the heavens. Johnny egged them on with his incredulous, squeaky laughter, and Grandpa at last allowed himself a broad chuckle, not only at the list of manure's properties, I thought, but also at its connection with my father.

That day I had already rejoiced in an act of self-liberation and then, with the appearance of Chester, had been plunged back into my more usual state of powerless apprehension, but there was something about the laughter I overheard from those aliens on the riverbank that made me forget my fear of a whipping. Outraged, I stormed from my hiding place, rustling the bushes ferociously and frowning at Grandpa and Chester. Johnny I considered negligible for the moment. I suppose I planned to mop up with him later.

"Why doesn't my father get to fish?" I demanded, forgetting for the moment that I didn't think fishing was much fun. "Why does Chester get to come out here if my father doesn't?"

Hearing me descend, all three of them turned around, but Chester quickly looked back to the river and sat still on his haunches, concentrating on the tip of my pole, which he held lightly in one hand. Grandpa glanced around with a smile, as though preparing to welcome me with some pleasantry about my losing valuable property. But when he heard my words and noticed the expression on my puffy face, he turned back to the river too.

Johnny's giggles still shook him, but crouched between the men he managed to sputter out a schoolboy's taunt: "What took you so long, Sammy? You been helping your dad shovel manoooer?"

Grandpa touched his knee to shush him. I took this gesture as an admission of guilt and began kicking mercilessly at a rock. Then Chester caught a fish, and at about the same time Grandpa pulled in his line and indicated to Johnny to begin packing the gear.

In a show of delicacy I did not then appreciate, Chester took Johnny's arm and said, "I'll run this squirt along with me." Quickly the two of them disappeared up the trail together, Johnny carrying the string of catfish. My schoolmate looked back confusedly before diving into the brush; he could not have understood the mighty weight that lay on Grandpa's shoulders just then.

The old man called me over and told me to bring the battered tin box he called his tackle, and we started slowly up the path. I hung back for a ways, sulking to exploit my advantage. After a while he paused and made me go ahead. We toiled speechlessly over the obstacles. But in spite of my discomfort from the trail, I felt a tremendous angry power: without quite understanding how, I had broken up a fishing trip and plunged my grandfather into the only embarrassment I'd never known him to feel.

After several minutes he said, in no particular tone, "Whatcha got in your shirt pocket? Cigarettes?"

I sensed that he was trying to recover his power over me. I showed him the bundle of plant links I had brought along, hoping he wouldn't notice that I had stuffed each one with a bug for burial. He asked where I'd found them and showed me how they fitted together and why they made a popping sound when pulled apart. A small black ant rolled out of one into his hand, but describing the plant mechanisms had started his emotions flowing in another direction, so he spared my chagrin by blowing the crumpled insect away without comment. Then he began pointing out how other weeds along the trail were joined together. A grove of Queen Anne's lace stood close by, and he indicated the black dot in the middle of each plate of white blooms. "Always a devil in the purest field of snow," he said.

He was well trained in the fine tradition of allegorizing nature, and he told me how God's handiwork, visible in these plants, argued for a jeweler's intricate love of his own creation. I think that as we innocently examined the patterned leaves of a marijuana bush, which he called rope plant, we were both moved by a deep tenderness—somewhat inspired by God's craftsmanship, but far more by our unacknowledged rapprochement. Still, I felt Grandpa's mastery over me again, for I knew that all the others on that fishing trip were the normal ones, and I was that black dot.

We set off down the path again, this time close together and

conversing in a private way we adopted sometimes, far more deli-
cate than that rough, jocular style which I had observed between
Grandpa and Chester. I was deeply respectful, hoping he would
not call attention to my strangeness, which I was trying now to
hide. But evidently he was preoccupied with some guilt of his own.

"You know, Sammy," he began, "different folks like to do different things. Even you sometimes find other occupations on a fishing
trip, though I know you like to fish very well."

"Yes, Grandpa."

"Well, your father likes to farm more than any fella I ever saw.
Sometimes he comes fishing with me because he wants to pay me
that respect. But it's not a thing he enjoys."

"I know, Grandpa."

"But Sammy, fishing is my first love."

"It is?"

"Of course I love God more than fishing, and I love a few
other folks more, like you. But here's something I'd never tell the
preacher: I love fishing lots more than I like going to church."

"I see."

"Now, the only reason Chester wants to come fishing with me,
rather than go farming with your dad, is because he thinks fishing
isn't work. He's not a real fisherman—you can tell by the way he
holds his pole."

"Then why do you let him come along?"

"Chester recollects the same things I do around this county. He
was a man when your dad wasn't born. You'll know what that
means someday, once your friends start dying off."

"But Chester shouldn't laugh at my father."

"No, I take the blame for letting him. But if you think about
it again when you're older, you'll see why it don't mean a hill of
beans. Your dad's my son; Chester ain't."

Those appeals to my better judgment when I grew up were an
effective dodge, since they put off the day of reckoning until after
the pleader was dead. In my frustration, I asked why Johnny got to
ride home in Chester's car, when I had never been allowed inside it.

Grandpa said, "Keeping you away from Chester was your grandma's idea. She don't approve of any man that doesn't take a bath

three times a week. And I go along with her on it, because you're not like the rest of us, Sammy. I can sit with Chester because I've seen what's made him into the poor, reckless soul he is. With your friend Johnny, there's nothing particular to be hurt, because he's gonna grow up like Chester anyhow. He'll listen to any man that makes him laugh, and someday he'll go with any woman. But you're different, son. You're headed for the Methodist seminary. Your hands are clean."

I had just scrambled over a mossy tree trunk stretched across the path, and I self-consciously wiped my palms on my overalls, banging the tin box hard against my thigh. There was a lump building in my throat, because Grandpa thought so highly of me. He had saved me in my own estimation, by his tact and grace. How could I fail to respect him when, despite his age and strength and wisdom, he made no pretense to be as pure as I, the chosen white lamb?

I could have loved fishing for his sake after that, but soon all the trips came to an end, and within a couple of years we held the auction and let the farm go. I set up the folding chairs on the front lawn, row after row, and the whole neighborhood came the next day, a crowd by eight o'clock. First the men followed the auctioneer around the barnyards to bid on the machinery and tools, then about eleven o'clock everybody took out their sack lunches, and I poured dozens of paper cups full of iced tea at the front porch. Afterward people sat in the chairs to bid on the household goods. Nearly everything sold, including the cane poles and tackle box, and at the end of the afternoon the auctioneer said, "This farm's going on the market, boys! If we have a buyer in the audience, he can save us some trouble by making himself known." Harry Hopper from the far end of our road walked up and told my dad that if he could get a loan at the bank, he'd take it. I was sent into the house to tell Grandpa, who was lying half-conscious on the cot in the dining room where he spent his days, drugged so he wouldn't feel the pain in his bowels.

Grandma, bewildered that all her losses were coming at once, cried, "Listen, Jacob, isn't that good news!" and wept into her apron. I had no place to hide from that moment, because the buyers were swarming over the yard and a few families were traipsing into nearby fields to satisfy their curiosity before the place changed hands.

Those last two years were bitter ones, as we watched the old man's robust body slowly wither. We took him fishing for the last time, my dad and Grandma (who hated fishing) and I, not to a river like the Little Platte, but to the nearest small pond behind the chicken house. They walked on either side of him for balance—it took half an hour to make the trip—and I brought the tackle and a camp stool for him. No one had bothered to dig worms. I suppose we didn't expect he'd get so far, or that he'd actually want to hold a pole, but he did. I set about catching grasshoppers in the tall reeds and skewering them on his hook, while my dad fished beside him for company's sake. It was funny how eagerly the fish were biting that evening. Grandpa kept pulling them in, crappie, bluegill, whatever he had stocked the pond with, now he was getting them back, while I stumbled about for more bait.

Grandma, who stood by with her arms folded, tried to encourage him by saying that his luck had never been better. But she could not manipulate his moods as she could mine. He replied with shocking vehemence: "You don't know how it feels to be a baby again and have somebody else bait your hook." When he pulled in the next fish, I didn't know if he wanted me to help unfasten it or not, until he motioned me over. Then I realized he had given up on himself.

Yet he was one of the demigods of the earth in his time. After his surgery when I was twelve, just before he fell into his lingering decline, the doctor who had operated told us about wading through thick muscles to get at the intestine where the tumor grew. Strong and proud as a bull, full of stories from his youth when he had worked summers from sunup to past sundown, boastful of eating whole cherry or gooseberry pies at a sitting, and still a prodigious man in the early years when I knew him, while he retained his appetites and natural joy at being alive on his own land.

Down at the barn once I saw him raise up his rifle and blast the skull of a two-year-old heifer; then Grandma and I brought the clean pans and knives and watched or fanned the flies away while he and my dad butchered. Later—was it the same cow?—Grandpa praised the flavor of the dark steaks he had sliced off. He lifted up a bite with his fork and said, "You can taste the corn in it!" to show that he knew how to raise an animal for his own luxury.

And like the patriarchs, he dedicated the firstborn son of his son as an offering, a testament more of his bounty than his guilt. That, too, seems like such a noble passion—until I think that that son of his son, so consecrated, so lifted up, was only me.

⌒ End of the War

Grandma stands aside to let me pass through her condo door without a word of welcome. Instantly I know she's initiating the guilt ceremony. I don't call or write for six, eight years, not even Christmas cards, then I show up on the step unannounced, with no apology. Did I expect a maternal smooch?

"So how's life treating you?" I say to get her going.

"What would an old woman know?" she answers, not quite to the point and averting her face, in case I was going to offer a peck on the cheek.

Of course, I can appreciate why she wants to give me the full treatment. Imagine having such a juicy opportunity handed to you out of the blue one morning when you're eighty-two, when you thought all your great moments were history! Small wonder the sight of me's got her heart pounding. So shoot! I think, looking her up and down with a glee I can hardly conceal. Settle as many debts today as you feel like! That's why I'm here. Which of my crimes do you want to hit me with first?

She postpones the direct attack, however, and leads me into her white box of a parlor. Needs time to calculate a strategy, I imagine. Meanwhile, everything I see is reassuring. She's exactly the frail, bird-like woman I expected, tottering on stick legs beneath a shapeless midnight-blue dress. The room's jammed with familiars brought along from the farmhouse: whimsies, old khaki-colored photographs, the worn leather-bound Bible with Grandpa's name still visible in gold. I register each detail with a sniff of boredom, and relief.

Only, once she falls into her rocker with a soft plop and begins to speak, the tone strikes me as wrong. She pushes out a harsh crow-like sound from deep in the chest, but so low that I strain to hear. The first words I can decipher come when she stretches her fingers toward me like broken twigs. "Look, Sammy, every nail cracked in two. Seems like my hands'll split next."

Self-pity's an odd note. I don't know whether to laugh in her face or ignore the remark altogether. Give her time to warm up, though. She's not used to having me around anymore. I'll steer her in the right direction. "Eat Jello, Grandma. Three bowls a day. Heals 'em right up."

"Jello?" she asks tremulously, as if bewildered by my crudeness. She looks back at her nails.

Now I can hardly keep from snorting. Let's get with it, old woman! Your hands are eighty-two years old; what do you expect? It's me you want to ask about today—my untucked shirt, my three-days' beard, why I never wrote, where I got the shiny car parked out front. Concentrate: you probably think I stole it, huh? You think I flunked out of college and got divorced five or six times and I'm up to my ears in debt and I've just come off a roaring drunk, don't you? So let's hear it. Have you forgotten the rules of our game?

But maybe I missed a clue. Maybe she's shrewder than I thought. Does she want to trick me into some sappy words of sympathy, so she can smile wickedly and trip me up?

Now I'll get her going for sure. "What'll we do today? I came to take you for a ride just like old times. How about lunch downtown?"

She lifts her chin and bats her parchment eyelids. She's showing more spunk already. "I'm cooking at home today."

That's right, be perverse. "OK, you're cooking. At least I hope you don't mind if I eat here with you?" Now I'm almost laughing out loud. Next she'll accuse me of stopping by without an invitation!

"Stay if you like. It'll be hamburgs whether you're here or you're gone."

"I love your hamburgers," I say, grinning outright. She knows I always hated them. "What'll we do in the meantime?"

"Make some coffee if you want," she says, pretending indifference while she searches in her chair for a scrap of newspaper. Suddenly she can't bear to look at me straight, she's loving the old back-and-forth so much.

"Sure you don't want to brew it yourself? You never liked the way mine tasted."

"Just double the grounds and it'll turn out fine."

So there it is! I've tricked her into a touch of classic sarcasm already. She agrees; she never did like the way I made it!

I stroll out to the kitchen whistling. I fumble around for a spoon, and the cups make such a racket that she can't help but hear. In another minute there's shuffling from the hall, and before I can turn around she's slid up beside me, peering close around my elbow exactly like I want. She couldn't let me brew coffee alone after all!

She leans against the counter for support—that gesture may or may not be phony; I haven't figured out all her stratagems yet—and counts as I measure out the spoonfuls. "One more," she says, sharper than before. "Now one more." I smile down at her, feeling something inside click precisely into place. Only twenty minutes together and we're practically on our old footing again.

Although, as we wait for the percolator to start singing, I have to admit that some vibration still doesn't register right. She's sunken, of course, like any farmer's wife who's sold the land and moved into town. But that spark at the heart of her, that brilliant . . . Oh, now I see the difference. Well, that's not so much, after all. She's stopped going to the beauty parlor, so her hair's turned a dirty-blondish-white. She lets it hang straight down, not curled anymore to please her men.

Yet now that I'm studying her more closely, maybe that's not the only change. She's perched against a stool, staring at a point on the wall beside my face, and she seems really to have nothing more to say. Her chest rises and falls massively, as if merely breathing after the walk out to the kitchen required all her strength. The voice, when I ask about her neighbors in the development, seems unable to find its old edge. That's a disappointment, because condo living should be a terrific target for her satire! She must have lots more annoyances here than back on the farm. Alley cats must be creeping over the fences, scrounging garbage and howling beneath the windows at midnight. Teenage boys must honk in the parking lot and rage around corners. So why doesn't she rise to my bait? Except for that remark about my coffee, she's meek as milk.

The coffee itself turns out as strong as ever. That's good, at least. It's so bitter I have to add sugar before I can drink it. And she still takes hers black: another excellent sign.

"Your throat must be made of cast iron to swallow that!" I nudge her.

"Always was," she says mildly and shuffles back to the parlor holding her cup with both hands.

OK, I admit as we settle into our chairs again, so she's lost some of her fire. Eighty-two is a lot of years. Let's go at this slower, take a roundabout route. I've got the whole day, so I can afford to experiment. We'll see what she's still capable of.

"What've you been reading in the papers?" I ask, and maybe it's the coffee that rouses her to answer freely for the first time. She reaches for the newspaper stuffed in her chair and holds onto it like a talisman as she begins listing the farmers from our old neighborhood who've passed away. "Jesse Tate, and let's see, Horace Wallingham—did anybody tell you about him?" But I'm not listening carefully anymore. I don't expect so much from the conversation now. Instead I wonder: maybe her face across from me could be enough, along with the rasping of that voice and the taste of this bitter drink. If I half-close my eyes, I bet I can float back right now to the farmhouse kitchen where she used to preside. Aroma of fried mush and the peach pies she served us. Grandpa at the head of the table, furious with her as always, but gorging himself all the same on her desserts. I sink deeper into the armchair. . . .

But what's this? The ticking silence breaks my daydream. Her list of dead farmers has already trailed off, and the wrinkled face before me looks shocking compared with my robust memory of her bustling at the stove.

Panic rises in my heart, but I try to kill it by thinking, I'm just not used to seeing her in this white condo, where all the rooms are perfect cubes! I'm only confused because six, eight years ago, when I paid my last visit, her limbs moved more easily and her hair was tinted blue. But the panic squeezes tighter, and I wonder, Is she different to the core?

Of course Dad warned me over the phone that she's failing— that if I wanted to see her alive, I'd better come back to Missouri this summer for sure. Only, I thought failing meant that your reflexes slow and your cheeks go hollow where they were round before. Those changes don't eat out your insides too, do they, until you're transformed into somebody else? Because I wouldn't call that "failing" at all.

I'd call it a betrayal.

She's nearly whispering now, the sound pushed through dry lips. "This little building grows cracks in the walls overnight. I don't even bother to call in a carpenter. It's all coming down anyway." She waves a hand vaguely. "The whole development was thrown up on the cheap. It'll be dust in ten years."

I catch my breath. Is that her secret, then? Bones have bent, flesh has softened to the point that she sees ruin spreading out from her like a putrid river, corrupting everything in sight? Devastation so terrible that not even a visit by the grandson can block its headlong rush?

I turn my head away because suddenly it seems necessary to remember:

Last time I flew back to visit you (in only half an hour you made me so furious that I stormed off to the airport without driving out to look at the old farm, like I'd planned), you were already fascinated by the idea of dying, but you didn't think it was inevitable by a long shot. You saw it as a weakness, somewhat like drink, that you could conquer by fighting back. I can still hear how bitterly you spoke about Grandpa's surrender. "My brothers were glad when I married Jacob, because they said he was strong enough to support me all my life." Your version was that he'd failed you by growing a cancer. In fact he might have done it deliberately, according to the

way you saw things then. He'd spent most of his life preparing for
that last desertion, and sometimes he'd taken me along on practice
missions of faithlessness, like fishing trips.

But today what she recalls, when I ask, are the months Grandpa
lay in the big downstairs bed toward the end, not talking because
of the pain, the drugs. She wonders what he felt about his body
then—could he sense his spirit in a way healthy people can't? Did
he have an inkling of some veil that was about to be thrown off?

"He'd look up when the window turned red at sunset," she says,
holding her coffee cup still. "I'd ask him, 'What do you see, Jacob?'
His eyes were always shining then, but he'd never tell."

She forgets me completely for a moment, lost in the hope. So
remote now that I expect she wouldn't even remember how angry
she was when, my last year in high school, I told her I wasn't going
to enroll in mortician's school, like she'd begged me. When I was
a boy, she always said it was the highest profession, if you weren't
going to be a preacher. Black suits, gleaming hearses. In the little
towns she knew, there wasn't much greater dignity a man could
aspire to. The last time I visited, she was still full of praise for
the neat way the Cadman Brothers had taken Grandpa under. But
today the mortician's isn't the side of death she cares for. Not the
outside: how it can be tricked out with a white collar and a touch
of rouge. She only cares about the inside, how it feels and how she
can make it feel.

Well, she makes my blood boil! What a waste of precious days!
Even now her mind's clear enough; it's only more perverse than
ever! She refuses to be an old woman I could respect, with creak-
ing joints and flesh hanging in folds, but still bursting with scores
to settle, hatreds cherished to the last breath. No—she's willing
herself into a spectre, old Missus Life-in-Death, who's already on
the other side while she's still here. And she avoids playing those
momentous games we used to love, because she knows that if she
gave me half a chance, I could force the gleam back into her eye.

In fact I can barely hold in my fury! She's always been my great
antagonist, the one I completely understood. During these last
years while I kept away, while the pretty women were leaving me
one after another, hers was the only ghostly face suspended inside

my head every night. Not Dolores, Melissa, Francie, Yvonne, Jay-
cee. Lovely ladies all, of various sweet colors and shapes, yet not
one of them brought up within shouting distance of a farm. To
them it was a fatal mystery that I could dream only of her! (Neuro-
sis? moral lapse? tragic lesion on the brain?—they offered me their
diagnoses on the way out the door.) Waking, my mind was full of
words to call her. Dragon lady! Shrew! Crone! In sleep I punched
out the sounds with a laugh, and a fist shot into the pillow.

But what's this? While I silently rage, she's been holding out
another page from the morning paper. She wants me to notice a
gloomy prediction about cattle prices, as if that was my business
here! In fact the daily news still means something to her, I see. She
hunts out earthquakes, plagues, accidents, collapses, because the
fat black headlines stamp a seal on her belief in the personal disaster impending. "There's no dignity left in farming," she offers for
commentary on the livestock story. "It's all corporations plowing
the fields with hired help, or else it's young folk just sitting on their
family's land, waiting for the welfare checks to arrive."

Absurd! I nearly scream at her, roiling my legs in the chair.
Things have always gone from bad to worse, and at the same time
from worse to better! What does that stupid shuttling matter to
us? Why should *our* relationship have to change?

At least I can refuse to follow in her maddening new obsession!
Heart thundering, I think that for my own sake I must try harder
to create inside my brain the play she refuses! If I fix my eyes on her
great beaked nose, if I focus on the malign expression that used to
twist those narrow lips, and address her, not as a living person. . . .

Take the night you sneaked out after supper, while I was upstairs
greasing my hair for my one and only date with Louise Everhart,
sweet sweater queen of the junior class. You'd never admit where
you disappeared for twenty minutes, but when I went out to start
the old pickup, the rear tire was flattening before my eyes. You said
it was the Lord's will, because I was too young to leave you for
a silly girl like Louise. Then you volunteered to phone the Ever-
harts and tell them I wouldn't be coming by after all. My dad gave
you a few short words, and Grandpa called out from his sickbed
that this time you'd gone too far. But you only stood at the sink

with your back to us, humming a hymn, till Dad decided there was no way to patch the tire before morning, and my date was up in smoke. At that, like a miracle, you pulled a three-story layer cake with green frosting out of the pantry, thinking you could weasel your way back to respectability by appealing to my sweet tooth. I shouted that you always baked a cake in the afternoon if you were planning to pull some outrageous trick at night, and your green frostings reminded me of the rot that was spreading over my heart from never being allowed to date a sweater queen. But you went on humming, humming, because you thought a hymn in your mouth put you so close to God that none of us could touch you. Remember that, will you?

No, her wandering eyes tell me that she doesn't. If I mentioned the story today, she'd refuse even to give a scornful smile. Instead she pushes that accursed newspaper at me again. "Just read there," she says, pointing to another story about the local decline of something or other. "Or don't read, it makes no difference."

Meanwhile I'm whipping myself into a frenzy over crimes the ancient female sitting before me would be incapable of committing. Too bad she can't savor the irony. Years ago, she'd have cackled like a mother hen if she could have foreseen that just when her chick wanted smothering more than ever in his life, she killed him by refusing to stir.

The pity of it. (I am shaking my head dolefully. I am looking into the bottom of an empty coffee cup, into a very deep but dry hole.)

The pity of it all is this: you were such a *worthy* enemy. You had a good scream when you needed it, and your fingers were quick to pinch. Once I saw you kick Grandpa in the rump as he walked downstairs to get away from some preposterous thing you were saying. Kicked him so that he stumbled until he could catch himself on the banister, and you cried, "Don't fall, Jacob, because if you break a bone I won't wait on you!"

It was trench warfare every day then, wasn't it, old girl, with the big drops of sweat dripping off your long nose as you bustled about, gumming up as many of your menfolks' works as you could, and clutching me to your breast like an enforced ally or a prisoner of war! Like a good soldier you played by no rules, observed no truces, accepted no losses without swearing revenge.

You settled your debts in blood if you could. When I was nine or ten, a calico kitten wandered up to our back door one summer morning, scruffy and flea-bitten, with weeping eyes. She trotted over as soon as she saw me, rubbed my legs and licked my arms for salt. I called her Princess, spread a feed sack in the barn for her to sleep on, and got licked again every day beside the kitchen step.

Coming down that step, you always threw out an arm for balance because of your bowed legs. Then if my calico was waiting for me and you planted a foot on her tail, her screech unnerved you so that once or twice you fell. You showed me purple bruises and told me to keep the cat away. I moved her feed dish to the barn, but I couldn't tie her up like a dog, could I? So each morning she still reappeared where she'd first met me.

Once I saw you carrying her by the neck toward the chicken house. There stood your chopping block with the axe always at hand in case we decided on chicken for dinner. Quick as I could, I called out. You dropped the cat in the midst of the hens and shooed it away, scattering wings and tail and all with your whirling skirt. Afterward you said you'd found her stalking the birds and you were only chasing her out of the pen. The hens were twice the size of the kitten, but you were forced to take up the first story that came to mind.

Anyway, I couldn't spend the rest of my life watching, and maybe I didn't believe you'd really carry the game that far, so it happened. One morning there was no calico at the back step. I called, but she didn't come. I asked everyone on the farm if they'd seen her, but no one had, including you, and I might've thought the kitten had simply wandered off again, fickle as such creatures are, except that I noticed the chopping block had been freshly washed down. Even that would have proved nothing, except that the cleanup had been hasty; in one of the cracks I found a tuft of fine brown fur. Then there was no rival about the place to trip you up, was there, you heartless witch!

Ah ha ha ha! At last, success! I've worked myself into a passable fit of spleen without any help from the old woman! The artery in my forehead is throbbing as if the cat had been slaughtered this morning! Memory's a thousand times keener than my grandmother's voice, so I don't even mind when she puts aside her tiresome paper and withdraws to the kitchen to stir up some grease and starch for lunch. Watching her totter out of the room, I smile. I've just proved that I don't need to see her any longer in the flesh, or hear the grating voice. Strolling around these tiny rooms, straightening old photographs for the next half hour should do me fine. Even her retreat from combat today could play into my hands. She always did insist on making me struggle for every ounce of satisfaction. I could believe that since she isn't strong enough to battle me any longer in the old gory style, she's resorting to a new strategy: sly evasion, noncooperation when confronted. You see, I've found out your game now, old raven! Don't think you'll feast on these eyeballs before night!

Just at noon I join her at the dining table, where the familiar farmhouse crockery is laid out, and split the greaseburgers with her. The starch today comes in long strips, like apron strings. There, I'm back in fighting form! This should be easy, now that I've screwed myself to the necessary pitch. I was wrong to give up on her before. If she doesn't give me satisfaction outright, I can twist her words into the sounds I need.

I see my first chance in the meal spread before us. "These are great burgers," I tell her, chomping.

"Thank you," she says primly, cutting into one. "You never used to like them this way. Your grandpa was the only one who did. That's why I always used so much garlic salt. After he died, I quit."

"But you used garlic salt today," I say, grinning madly. Now let her admit she fixed them out of spite.

"That's right," she agrees so quietly I can barely hear. "You know today's the ninth of June."

Where's her mind gone this time? "The ninth of June?"

She nods so slowly I think she's falling asleep over her plate, but then from nowhere she drops the bomb I'd given up expecting. "He died on the ninth, fourteen years ago. I always cook one of his favorite meals for the anniversary. In the afternoon, I drive out to the cemetery with flowers. I was afraid I wouldn't get there today, because the car's been making a rattle. But the good Lord saw to it that you showed up."

I've never suffered such a total defeat at her hands. I have no stomach for her pink ice cream and dump it in the sink while she shuffles off to tie on a scarf for our outing. So stunned, my mind goes white for a minute, and when I come to, I find myself in the middle of the parlor floor, staring straight up at one of the ceiling cracks, which appears to separate before my eyes. My only function here, I have just been informed, is to drive her on an inspection trip to the grave.

At first she sits beside me in the warm car, not speaking, taking in the uneven rows of markers with a steady gaze. Old peeling limestone, topped with melted lambs or pasty angels, inscribed with snatches of hymns; in the farther rows polished pink or gray marble, tall and wide if the families had money, to lord it over their neighbors. Meanwhile birds warble, daisies spring up in the grass, sunlight dances off the white steepled church. But I think she does not notice these symbols of rejuvenation.

Instead nature's rhythm has prompted her to create symbols of her own. She has covered tin cans with aluminum foil and filled them with peonies and iris cut from the little bed in front of her condo. Carefully she hoists herself out of the car now, hangs onto the door to catch her breath, then pushes off for a tour of the enclosure. When I run around to offer my arm, she croaks, "Stay back! I know where I'm going. You were always too anxious for your own good."

My job is to carry the flowering cans. We leave one for each relative, saving Grandpa for last. For him she's brought a roomy three-pound Folger's can crammed with the tallest stalks. But when she kneels to place it over his head, she stumbles, and before I can grab her, she's taken what looks like a half-deliberate fall against the stone.

"Grandma, are you hurt?"

She only twitches her back, possibly to shrug me off. Her limbs are stretched in what may be the shape of prayer or else an embrace across the ground. I can barely hear as she starts to mumble confidences to some spirit that I don't believe in, but can't disprove.

The moment seems so private that I back away, an incredulous intruder. After all, this is the climax she has come for. Apparently those jackknifed legs are causing her no pain.

A little dazed, I wander off among the markers. As a distraction I force myself to read aloud the pious inscriptions that pop up on all sides. Near a grove of yews, I come upon four chunks of pink rock that look like giant candy drops. My mind is suddenly besieged by the ghosts of four great-aunts who died in the years after Grandpa. As I look, the women materialize one by one, hovering in the shade of the dark trees or calling to me from the long grass—four ele-phantine graces swathed in tiny-flowered dresses and holding the inevitable glasses of iced tea. Their voices sound sweet and girlish on the hot wind.

"Come and taste my shortbread, little Sammy."

"Are you going out with a nice girl these days?"

How they used to pet me, and they frowned whenever they over-heard Grandma quarreling. They were Grandpa's sisters, perfect ladies from Pennsylvania who wore real lace under their skirts and never helped their farmer-husbands outdoors. Behind their backs Grandma and I called them the sugarplums. I used to gag when Aunt Liza bent a powder-puff cheek close to my lips for a kiss, and once I nearly bit her. She and Aunt Sophie smell of talcum today—it swirls around me on the breeze until I cough. How eager the foolish ones are to live for me still!

"You look unhappy, Sammy boy," Aunt Vera tsks, dabbing her mouth with a handkerchief, ready to hear my complaints. They always loved stories about their sister-in-law, which they misinter-preted and spread among the cousins. Yet what comfort could I find today by accusing Grandma to them? Their only talent is to blink their doe eyes, hoping to tempt me into some wild confession.

Oh, away with you old hags! I've got nothing to tell that's fit for your pearly ears! Back under the ground with you! I wave my arms impatiently to dismiss them. You never knew me! I cry when Aunt Sophie stares back forlornly, reluctant to disappear.

I turn hastily to contemplate my grandmother through the thicket of markers. She is still thrust across the earth in a splay of limbs that tells how anxious she must be to dive below. Dive in and pull after her this undulating carpet of grass, the neighboring fence posts and fields, whole farmhouses and herds and ponds, all the secret shady places of the county where I grew up—anxious to clutch them to herself below and leave me standing alone on flat, denuded ground.

Finally she lets me pull her to her feet. Her knees are filthy from the fall, but she staggers off toward the car, ignoring my offer to brush her. Eyes, when I glance at them, nearly blank from fatigue after her exertions. On the drive back to the condo, we are silent as before. I will not go inside with her this time. The visit is over, and it has failed. Those ridiculous aunts offering sympathy were the final insult. As if I could be fobbed off with gossip; as if mere talk about something could be a substitute for the sacred thing itself!

As I escort her up the sidewalk, though, it crosses my mind that Grandma might fracture a leg sometime as she hoists herself up the step before her door, and an impulse sweeps over me. Without a word to prepare her, I reach out and hug her tightly to my chest in order to lift her weightless body up and set it down, a long instant later, eight inches above the walk on the little concrete platform. In my defense, she has always been unsteady on her feet.

Now she is at the perfect height from which to bestow a good-bye kiss. But she's so surprised by her sudden flight through the air—a second adventure coming on the heels of her great outing—that she gasps, drops back against the door, and doesn't even re-member to focus on me, the perpetrator who placed her where she is. Then, when I have given up my last scrap of hope, her eyes shift and she seems to look at me for the first time today with a flash of deep recognition. Still wheezing a little, she speaks. "Next year if I'm here, it'll be Spanish meatloaf whether you come by for lunch or not."

The next minute, everything's back to normal. She fishes in her pocketbook for the key and vanishes inside. I exhale deeply, a mixture of garlic salt and heart's weariness.

At the sound of the bolt thrusting shut, I wince and then legs are racing down the sidewalk toward the rented car. I sit inside now, torso twisted over the steering wheel to escape the intense sun. Im-mobile, because I can't bring myself to start the engine. Wondering, if I whiz down the interstate to the airport, where will I fly next?

And who will it be that's flying? Or, if a strange young woman in the seat next to me should speak, what words might break from my throat?

The sun is cruel, and a faintness covers me. To make a draft, I get the car in motion at last, keeping my head out the window, mouth gaping, chest heaving, eyes fixed on the nearly blinding reflection from the hood.

The car wanders about the back streets of the decayed farming town, limping from one stop sign to the next. Huge trees cast shadows that appear at every minute to block the way. In their dark irregular shapes I make out the gaunt, painful profiles of my true kinsmen, erratic fellow travelers about the earth and seas— flying Dutchmen, ancient mariners, wandering Jews, a host of displaced persons driven here and there by the shuttling wind. Their mouths are forever in motion on the pavement before my wheels. But though tradition holds them to be such a talkative group in their gloomy way, I wonder how, dispossessed of their homeland, these ancestors of mine ever managed to speak a word.

⌒ Bird Song

The truck stop rides like an ark on a sea of asphalt. Inside, the beasts clutch their drinks and hum to the jukebox, waiting out the night. My fast-talking new friend Seymour introduces me to some fine boys around the pool table and goes off alone to fetch us a couple of beers. Out of the smoke a shark-nosed fellow hands me a cue, despite my comical protests that I sprained my wrist just now opening the door of Seymour's car. For some reason the others laugh raucously at this story, but meanwhile they are pushing me forward into the circle of dim light.

Waiting for my first shot, I look over to the bar for my buddy, who is bending his arms hilariously around two blowsy females. He insisted that we stop here, and now I see why. Apparently he knows these women well and may be filling their ears with secrets about me, since they are both casting glances my way. One of them, noticing that I'm looking back, cups her hand around a breast.

Quickly I turn back to the pool table, anxious to begin the game. My gray-skinned opponent smilingly steps aside. I hit the white ball into a cluster of coloreds that toss it back and forth, then send it spinning into a nearby pocket that had escaped my notice. The other boys applaud good-naturedly, and I find Seymour offering me what must be my second beer, since I'm already holding an empty can in my injured hand. The sprain is nearly painless now, but I see that it has started to swell.

Seymour winks that he'll be back soon and disappears into the john with a couple of nasty-looking characters who've been lurking at the far end of the bar. I start to call after him, but the gleam from my opponent's tooth alerts me that it's my turn to shoot again. Several balls are already missing from the table, no doubt stolen by my enemy. As I concentrate on lining up my shot, the boys behind me begin stomping their boots in unison and join in a song the jukebox has been repeating ever since we arrived.

"Where's this rig headed?"
"I'm on my way north."
The man's face turns pale
As he lets out a shout:
"The sky's dark as hell;
The bridge is washed out!"
"This rig's headed north, friend;
You're welcome to ride.
No storm's ever stopped me;
If not, step aside."

Their swashbuckling voices ring in my ears as the white ball leaps wildly from the end of my stick. It lands far down the table in a complicated arrangement with its fellows that looks nothing like my intentions. That configuration proves to be the key to the game, though, when my opponent steps up in a sudden silence and taps the white ball so precisely that it darts straight from one colored to the next, klop-klop-klop, nudging each ball into a different pocket, the black one last. A few cheers break out, and then the boys crowd around me, jostling my sore limb. Everybody agrees that I owe this skillful player something, so I pull out a clump of bills and he helps himself, then disappears through a side door. Another partner hands me a fresh beer and proposes a second game, but this time I back off, outclassed, and head for the bar. I think I'll nurse my injury there and wait for my ride, who must be having quite some conversation with those buddies of his in the john.

At the bar there's less smoke, and the stool feels cool under my jeans. In the mirror I see a row of women suddenly alert to their chance. Meanwhile somebody new has taken control of the jukebox, for the brief quiet is now broken by a mournful plunking, and then a doleful female voice fills the air.

> Every time I look at you
> I smile like the angels do.

The melody is heart-wrenchingly sweet—nothing like the ominous
trucker's song that twisted my cue—and I begin to lose myself in
its yearning, when I notice that one of Seymour's lady friends is
standing close, gazing into my ear as she sings along.

> Love is sweeping through my soul
> Like a new broom sweeps clean.

Her high cheeks rise to a flame-like forehead over crystal eyes,
and her hair radiates a pale yellow halo. Her voice sounds piti-
fully sad. She smiles, however, perhaps noticing that I cannot take
my eyes off her gleaming skin. Then, as the bartender hands me
another beer, she turns back to face a tawny companion, and I
watch as they flip a coin. My angel appears pleased at the result,
while the other sport shrugs and moves away down the bar.

Now I am drawn swooning toward the sound that fills the place,
for the new jukebox jockey has punched another melancholy selec-
tion. My angel seems to approve of the tune as much as I, for she
sings along in tiny breaths, this time smiling into my eyes.

> Honky tonk hours
> Pickin' perty little flowers
> Drinkin' milk afore it sours
> Kissin' kiddies that are ours
> Thankin' God for His powers
> That've given us these
> Honky tonk hours.

When the song is finished she says, looking at my chest, that her
name is Blondie—"Like in the funny papers"—and asks with an
appealing shyness if I want to step outside for a fresh breath. I say
I'm only waiting for my new buddy who picked me up off the side
of the road this morning near Hastings, and besides, my head isn't
very clear. She laughs that Seymour may be busy in the john for
quite a while longer, so I might as well relax. Besides, the night air
will do me good.

As soon as I can get my balance, I accept another beer from the inpassive bartender in exchange for what appears to be my last bill, and Blondie takes my elbow and leads the way into the parking lot. She has the keys to a swept-wing pink and gray DeSoto, which I admire, though she seems to take no pride in it and points out a dent. Evidently the car really belongs to Blanche—or perhaps to Whitey; from what Blondie says, it's hard to tell what belongs to whom among those three, or who lives where.

We settle in the front seat facing the truck stop's blinking green sign. We can barely hear the jukebox now over the traffic on the interstate behind us and the crickets calling in the fields that stretch away on the other side. I admit that we're more comfortable out here, even though the upholstery is badly ripped where Palooka Joe once got mad at Blanche.

Blondie takes my good hand to keep it warm and asks if I'm ready yet. I say that I still have a few swigs of beer left, so she sighs and begins telling me about herself. The story is complicated, and I don't catch all the details. But as she winds up, I finally detect a theme. It seems her pappy once owned a farm just beyond the next off ramp, and they would have made it, except that when the chance came to get clear, the bank wouldn't lend him a penny more, so the land was lost. That's why, instead of living in a big farmhouse all her own, she shares a cheap place in town with some other girls. But at least she doesn't have to get up with the chickens now. Instead she can always come out here of an evening and meet the truckers, who often invite her on trips. She has traveled all over with them, to Ohio and Wyoming and even the Coast. Sometimes one of the fellows will treat her rough, but then she just gets out at the next stop and somebody else is sure to be going her way. The funny thing is, she's found that the truckers with tattoos are always the sweetest. Whitey believes the sweetest are the ones who keep an open drink in their cabs, but Blondie has observed that there are all kinds of drunks.

I reflect a little guiltily that I have no tattoo, and then I wonder how my puffy green and gray hand will feel in the morning when the beer wears off.

Blondie is saying that on several trips she didn't want to come

home. The happiest place she ever found was at a truck stop outside of Fort Wayne, where she crashed for a couple of weeks in a
storeroom over the bar. She thought she might eventually get on
there as a waitress, since all the girls liked her and lent her clothes,
but one day a burly fellow with a good smile asked if she wanted
to go for a ride, so thinking nothing about it, she said sure and
climbed into his cab, expecting to trick, but then fell asleep and
when she woke up there they were, forty miles east of St. Joe barreling down the interstate, so she thought, I might as well get out
now, because here's where I'm always gonna end up.

We listen to the great hum that fills the night, and after a minute
she asks if I've ever been hitched. I say not really. She says neither
has she. It's nice to think about sometimes, she adds, but it could
never work out, and she wonders if I know that lonesome song
they don't play too often, because it tells how the woman usually
gets the dirty end of the stick in these deals.

> You got choc'late on your lip, Mister Brown.
> That's why I took your hound dog to the pound.
> Told our little girl that you ain't comin' round.
> 'Cause you been eatin' choc'late all over town.

Her delicate high voice stabs my heart, and I choke when I say
that music seems to affect her deeply. She replies that it is her greatest comfort, since she can't ever drink enough liquor to get stinking
and weed gives her a bellyache and snow is scary no matter what
they say.

After I've emptied the last can of beer, she snuggles closer and
confesses with another sigh, "I'm perty cheap. Any good-looking
man can have his way." When I appear unable to straighten up in
the seat, she works my hand into her bosom and asks, "Or don't
you like women?"

"They terrify me," I hear myself say.

Now she looks at me curiously, and it must be the beer I've
drunk, or else those mournful lyrics, because without warning my
head rears back and I find myself breaking in deep sobs. She gathers
me to her breast at once and breathes with me awhile to make me
stop. My eyes are still streaming as she strokes my hair and says

gently, "Hush, hon, you'll get over it." When I'm quiet at last, she wipes my face with tissue, which quickly becomes a sodden mess, so that we have to pick the wet bits off my cheek and toss them out the window like snowflakes. Finally I'm resting my head in her lap and thinking about nothing but a huge woolly cloud. "Tell Blondie about it," she says professionally. I never thought I would, but the words start tumbling out and I can't stop them even when I want to.

I say that I used to be a slick lucky driver myself, roaring down the fast lane just like those guys inside the bar hustling pool. I got one job right after another, each one better than the last, and in between I took pleasure trips all over. Every place I stopped, I'd meet this certain kind of woman who was on her way somewhere just like me, so we'd decide to travel together for a while. Jane bought little girls' clothes for a department store, but she was hoping to get into management. That's why she went out to parties and bars every night, to keep up her contacts in the rag trade, and sometimes when I wanted a drink I'd go along. Marcia was a reporter chasing the city council in hopes a scandal would break, and she'd be there with her pencil ready to take notes. I couldn't help her with the writing, but at least I kept her refrigerator stocked, and she introduced me around city hall so that I could smoke with the other reporters on slow afternoons. Sabina modeled, which meant she had to be on call seven mornings a week, her makeup kit packed by the door. It was a dog's life, she said; she was always trying to decide if it was worth screwing somebody in order to get a part in a commercial. After the phone rang with another modeling assignment, I'd lie in bed while she showered, wondering who the somebody was who kept wanting to screw her, and if it was really him who'd just called.

The skin of these women felt rich, I tell Blondie, and it was a relief the way they got right down to the business of making love, because in those days neither of us had a minute to waste.

Blondie grows humorous, thinking about that fast-moving tribe I somehow got mixed up with. She suggests that they could be arranged like kewpie dolls or peanut butter jars on a shelf.

My mouth has gone dry from all the talking, but the beer cans are empty on the floor of the DeSoto. Meanwhile my date hums a tune sweetly to herself. She must be wondering how to dump me and get back inside the bar, where the action might be picking up.

After a minute, though, the melody breaks off and she takes up my story with a strange twist. "You talk about traveling: there's all kinds of birds in God's world. There's the big hawks that circle way up above the fields. Then there's the wrens and sparrows that just hop around in the brush. Or there's the flocks of geese that come through in V's every spring and don't stay more'n overnight. Yet every one of them's birds, ain't they?"

I look at her wonderingly. She speaks like her songs.

"Now all those birds are gonna run across one another sometimes, and when they do, naturally they'll nod howdy," she goes on. "But supposing one of the hawks that circles the fields every day meets up with a bunch of geese on their way south. He might say, 'Here, gals, let me be a goose too and come along.' 'Well, sure,' they'll say. 'Follow us if you can.' But his wings are made for floating and diving. He don't know about long distances and sticking together in a V. Finally he has to drop back, and then he finds himself lost far away from home. Which only means he was flying like he wasn't meant to, not that there's anything wrong with him.

"Now the kind of traveler I am, I just go round and round. And the fellas that give me lifts, like as not they're only circling too. There's nothing strange about the places we go: they're far apart, but it's like we seen 'em all before. In fact, you're about the only real stranger I ever ran into, and that's a hoot, because you talk like you was born right around here, the same as me!"

Her breast rises and falls softly beside my head: fragrant, lulling, a warm animal ready to share its living treasure. Yet something inside me still holds back. I ask, "What would make a silly hawk try to take up with a flock of geese, though?"

"Why, I never saw such a worrywart," she laughs exasperatedly. "Can't you let it alone?" But seeing that I continue to sulk, she offers, "It's always tough when a hound dog gets the blues."

"Huh?"

"Don't you know that one? That's a golden oldie. Maybe they didn't play it where you been listening, but you could catch it all the time on the radio back in Fort Wayne. It goes, 'Hum hum hum, de dum dum hum hum hum, When a hound dog gets the blues.' "

"That's nice."

"Yes, but real mournful though. I'm funny that way. I always think the sad ones are the pertiest, you know?"

"I know."

The hum of the modern prairie envelops us again, while my mind wanders in and out, chasing elusive forms. Suddenly Blondie shifts her hip.

"This whole thing wouldn't look so blamed tragic if you could see how ridiculous you act when somebody sings in your ear."

Suddenly she gets her wish: we both fall into a fit of giggles. Finally we are pawing at each other to make ourselves stop, and after a warm-hearted kiss she tells me, "What you need is to come out here to this truck stop more often. I swear, this place can always perk me up when I'm down. We play a few songs, and maybe one of the truckers wants to dance, or else I come out to the car with him, or Blanche does, and afterward we have a good laugh over it, and by the time we head for home, it's like the song says, 'We're tireder but gladder, older but not sadder, dum dum de da da.' "

Her finger moves above my forehead with the melody and, in a stroke of divine playfulness, it lands on my chin. Out of the richness of her life she repeats an offer that has become impossible for me to refuse.

Thought is suspended, and I realize in my hands the miracle of her flesh. We are unbuttoning clumsily in the cramped seat when the door of the truck stop opens without warning, sending an arc of yellow light over the parking lot. Seymour strolls out and spots the DeSoto. He approaches, grinning tolerantly. "Pull it out and let's go, sport. What I got in my pocket's hot cookies."

Blondie, waif of the highways, understands the importance of catching one's ride when it's offered, so she instantly draws away and closes my mouth with her fingers and helps fasten my shirt. Then she shoves me up out of the seat onto my feet. My swollen hand shoots with pain. I turn back to her, bewildered, still aching for her touch and not at all interested in Seymour's destination or whatever's bulging there underneath his vest. But Blondie's face is set as she slams the car door behind me. Emptier than I've ever felt, I turn from her, and after a minute I'm swimming across the asphalt toward the man.

"Don't take none of them funny cigarettes offa your buddy, Hound Dog," she calls after me through the car window. "You're drunk enough as it is."

∽ Melting with Ruth

White and red chickens in the street that I swerve to miss. Two seconds later comes the crash, with hounds yelping up the block and a drain spout tumbling onto my hood. A chorus of "Oh my lords!" from the old men sitting on the park bench opposite the hotel. I'm plunged into a black hole in the corner of the white building, my body numb as sparks from the engine fizzle away.

Now the black-suited cluster of old men hobbles up to pry me out of the cab, gasping, into the sun-drenched street. Then here come the Lassos that I haven't seen for years, Lucky and Lucy and their pug-ugly niece Ruth, down the stone steps from the hotel, crying about damages and the porch is sure to collapse and break the plate-glass window that spells their name in gold letters.

White-haired Lucky asks if I'm drunk or do I think because I'm a stranger I can bash his building without paying? My noggin's sprouting a lump and one arm hangs loose, so I can't fend for myself. The old men make matters worse by looking familiar. Their ruddy beaked noses say they're my uncles from long ago. The nearest one searches my eyes and decides to claim kin. "He's Sammy, come back to visit his grandma! Look how he behaves on his first day home, after he ran off to California and got too big for his britches."

"His grandma'll die when she hears about this."

"What was you dodging that made you swerve? Those chickens was plumb on the other side of the road."

I search my forehead for blood, but Uncle Alistair says, "Don't go pretending you're hurt. We got no sympathy for a queer boy like you."

Old Mrs. Lasso licks her pink lips. "He can't understand you anyhow. Bring him in the lobby out of this boiling sun."

As they shuffle me up the steps, Ruth, who went to school with me, pokes at the fractured boards and the pickup nosing into them. "Engine won't start, I bet. I'll get Ramon to come over with the tow."

"Leave that wifebeater alone!" Mrs. Lasso shouts down to her. "You get inside and look after this here no-good. Let somebody else call Ramon."

My mouth's working now and I say too loud, "I don't need looking after. I feel fine."

"Like hell," Mrs. Lasso says. "Where you going, Lucky?"

"Calling the highway patrol."

The uncles drop me onto a scratchy sofa and swarm around old Mr. Lasso, hollering and pointing. "He'll make the damages good," promises my Uncle Claude. They must figure I'm rolling in dough because I've just blown in from L.A., where folks are so crazy they pay me to take their pictures.

Mrs. Lasso butts in. "Where's Ruth? See if she slipped down to Ramon's by herself. He'll slap her silly if he sees her again."

Lucky's eyes widen and he scuttles to the door. "If that maniac touches Ruth," he calls back at me, "you'll have to pay medical bills on top of everything else!"

I'm starting to feel the pain in my arm, but nobody cares. I let out with, "How do you expect a man to drive straight in this town when there isn't enough traffic to keep him in his own lane? You've got no stop signs, no pedestrians, half the business district's boarded up. Grass is growing in the cracks. Any normal driver'd have an accident on these streets!"

The uncles circle over me in their shiny black suits, their sweat-stained fedoras. "That's the California talking in him. You go loco out there."

Ruth bangs the screen door again, having been found by Lucky and sent inside. Her aunt calls, "Bring a basin and a cloth. He's gone off his head." To the uncles she adds, "We'll put him upstairs for the night. His grandma'd have a fit if she saw him now."

The old men exchange looks. "Be sure to charge him double for the room."

"Put him on the third floor, where the spiders can take a bite."

When Ruth begins to cleanse my forehead, the water in her white basin turns red. Her hands feel callused, and her nose breathes warm straw-flavored air. At school she was earnest, prim; we called her the old maid in braids. But I'll die without attention, so I let her go on, turning my face so I can't smell the damp. Why are the Lassos afraid that my old buddy Ramon, who runs the garage, will beat her up? Meanwhile she catches sight of my limb hanging limp and tells her aunt that the Maysville doctor will have to drive out and set an arm.

Mrs. L. sniffs. "You got money to pay the doc, son? He won't come till five-thirty, so you gotta grin and bear it till then."

"Why in heaven won't somebody take me to Maysville? I can't lie here all day in this pain!"

The uncles only mock. "Who you think's gonna drive? You think we all got fancy pickups that can run off on any little errand?"

Ruth says into my ear, "It's already four. The doctor'll close up early if he can. Your uncles don't have their trucks anymore, since they retired to town, and ours needs a part that Ramon's ordered from St. Joe. So you'd just as well lie quiet."

"What I can't understand," clucks her aunt on the way to the phone, "is how somebody could run into an object as big as a three-story hotel, shining in the sunlight. Like it jumped into the road at him."

A swarthy head passes before the window and I recognize Ramon grown older, come to extract the pickup from the jaws that hold it. Ruth's eyes go strange, glimpsing him. "He'll knock down the porch if I don't go warn him."

"Ruthie!" cries her aunt. My uncles shuffle on creaky joints to stand between her and the door. Mrs. L. holds her fiercely and sneers at me, "See the damage you done? And you want us to hop up and drive you to Maysville to spare you a little pain!"

From the street comes a roar and a clatter of boards. One of the uncles snorts, "Squished like a June bug."

"Never get an insurance company to pay a dime for it, with the driver drunk and no cause for the crash."

I clench my teeth to keep from shouting: No cause! No cause! Why, every one of you's a cause! You're lucky the building stepped in the way of what I was aiming at! No cause, my broken arm!

A knock at the door. By the time I open, feet are clunking down the stairs out of sight. I'm left looking at a supper tray: a plate of brown gravy that covers suspicious lumps, a carton of chocolate milk, a wedge of pie. I bring in the pie with my good hand, but leave the tray where it lies. Afterward I doze, but bursting into my sleep comes a roar, then a moaning and groaning. When I shake myself awake, I find my mouth's open and those pitiful sounds are rising from me. The sling lies about my arm like dead weight, but the rest of me's twitching and sweat-drenched. What stupid dream brought me back to this malicious old town, I ask myself, where I've just been thrown out on my ear again by my skinflint granny, when I was nearly clear of *both* Doris and Cindy out in L.A., and who knows? if I'd stayed there, maybe I'd have stumbled onto a fat commission by now and would've been able to pay off the pair of them for good.

Through the early evening air comes another knock. The gravy's congealed into a fist and demands to be eaten. This time when I open—surprise—it's the uncles, still clad in black suits and fedoras, smelling of tobacco. Uncle Jethro's in front, sucking teeth. "Step aside, son, we come to talk."

They file past me like church deacons. Uncle Alistair carries a silver flask, and each has brought his own tumbler. Piles of cigar ash grow beside the chairs, and after an hour Uncle Claude reaches into his coat for the second bottle.

They toast me for carrying the family's beaked nose and pale Scots eyes. Once the inquisition starts up, I see they're not budging till the small hours, so I let my glass be refilled.

"Where's your wife, son?" Uncle Tony asks. He's pulled a third bottle out and is uncapping it. "Divorced!" he says when I tell him. "Why, that explains it all!"

"Let the boy alone," says Uncle Alistair. "They don't have such stable women out West. What Sam needs is a Missouri gal to set him up."

"You seen that Ruth downstairs?" asks Uncle Claude. "You knew her in school, didn't you? She and Ramon are untying the knot, in case you're interested."

"Thanks, but I only came on a one-day visit to Grandma," I say. "Now I'll be on my way home."

"On your way to California, son. Let's not confuse one thing with another."

"Oh, good morning, Mrs. Lasso! I didn't know the door was unlocked."

"Got an extra key. I was worried when you didn't come down for breakfast. Thought your injuries might of got worse."

"I was just tired. Four of the uncles left by two o'clock, but Uncle Jethro stayed for a private talk till dawn."

"Were they stinking?"

"I'm not sure. I don't know them very well."

"They should look after their health more. When they kick off, Lucky and me'll have to shut up the hotel. We been trying to decide how many of 'em have to belly up before we can't turn a profit. He says we can keep her open on three, but I think four."

"Be a pity when you have to close the place."

"Town isn't the same anyway, so don't cry over it. Question is, can we sell her when the time comes, or will we have to board her up and take a total loss? Ruth says we should put her on the market now, so we can divide the profit and enjoy it while we're still spry."

"Sounds like Ruth wants her cut."

"She's practically free and clear as it is. Got that bastard Ramon where she wants him. Gonna own half his garage if she gets him into court. He wants to settle now, but I say let a judge decide."

"That reminds me, Ramon's got my pickup. I better go check on the damage."

"Just sit tight and I'll send up breakfast. Lucky's already been to see your truck. He says it's fixable if you're not in a hurry."

"You mean stay here for days on end? I got to get back to my job in L.A.!"

"Hold your pistols. What good's a photographer with only one arm? While it heals, you can sit across the street on the bench and talk to your uncles of an afternoon."

"Besides, I wouldn't want to put you out."

Her laughter mixes with a smoker's cough. "We're in business, son! The breakfasts in bed are a dollar ninety-five. Only don't go tipping Ruth; she'd be insulted. She's bringing up the trays on her own initiative, because she don't like to see a man suffer."

"Sounds like she takes a different attitude toward Ramon."

Mrs. L.'s mouth draws together like a prune. "You gonna stick up for that deadbeat? I thought I recognized birds of a feather, but your uncles said to give you a chance. Now don't blow it. Pancakes and eggs'll be here in ten minutes, so I'd advise you to put on some clothes. In this hotel breakfast in bed's a figure of speech."

"That's fine."

"You're dern right it'll be fine. I'm whipping up the pancakes myself."

Ramon's corrugated garage sits among piles of smashed cars with their tongues out. Inside, in a clean circle amid the grease, Ramon is thumbing through a parts catalog. My pickup is parked to one side, awaiting surgery. One look tells me two thousand minimum, and I clutch.

He grips my hand for old times' sake. He tells me that he only needs my OK to call the warehouse in St. Joe. They send a parts truck through the county every Thursday.

How can I tell him those California women have bled me white, and Grandma won't lend me a dime? I sink into the worn chair opposite his desk, while his smile holds doubtfully. I know what he's going through. Ruth has him by the nose, and he needs more dough in the next six months than he's ever seen in his life. My pickup must've looked so promising last night when he drove up with the tow.

"Women," I start out sympathetically, "are the world's worst con."

His grin turns philosophical. Now he acts in no hurry to deal with the pickup, but reaches back and offers me a beer. My kind of garage. As we pop the cans, I abandon my vehicle to the forces of rust. Why should I expect to save anything from the general ruin? I only hope I have enough cash for bus fare to L.A. But my host's a poor sinner hitting bottom for the first time. Make him a gift of my compassion. I know it's rough, pal. "I saw Ruth at breakfast."

He comes back quicker than I expect. "They tell me you're divorced yourself. If you're looking for a good old gal on the rebound, she's your mark." He's already pulling another can from the cooler, enjoying himself like he's thought up some brilliant plan. Out of nowhere he springs a deal about the pickup. "Reconditioned parts are good enough. I'll throw in the labor free. Wouldn't want to make money off an old friend. If you can wait a week, she'll drive out of town good as new. Just hold tight at the hotel. Ruthie and her aunt'll put the fat on your bones. You always liked her in school, didn't you?"

I nod over my beer, which tastes bitter now.

"Well, there you are. Drop back anytime and tell me how you're getting along. Divorce doesn't take away from her. She's a bargain for a fellow like you."

"I definitely want to pay for all the parts," I say, feeling like a thief. This is an ugly way to take advantage of a man. "And I'll pay as much labor as I can. I'll mail you a check from L.A."

The alcohol's made his eyes bright, and he brushes this offer aside. "Just have yourself a blast. This is a friendly little town to vacation in."

"Yeah," I say over my shoulder. "It's people that make the place."

All the stifling afternoon shut up in this antique bedroom, I brood over the crime of letting Ramon fix my pickup under false pretenses. Why, even if Ruth didn't look like a mare biting flies, I can't *afford* another dose right now. Good thing she's still carrying the torch for Ramon, trying to get his attention with those threats about divorce court.

At last I talk myself half out of the fear of her and open my door, planning to sneak out for supper at a fly-blown café down Main Street. But surprise—here's Ruth herself, pretending to dust the hallway so she can perch outside my room. She feigns innocence and smiles hello. "I suppose the town must look all dreamy to you," she starts as if she's been practicing this line, "like when you lived here with your grandma as a little boy."

It's only kindness to set her straight, in case she thinks I'm about to invite her to L.A. once the pickup's fixed. "My childhood here looked like nails and broken glass. And this humidity is killing me."

She rubs the wall harder with her dust cloth, then tries again. "I hear you'll be stuck with us till next week."

"That's a lie!" I snap. "Grandma'll lend me cash for a plane ticket anytime I ask. Ramon can send the pickup out C.O.D."

Now her smile is trembling. "But you've decided to wait for it here anyhow."

"Not so much decided as still making up my mind."

Suddenly her good nature collapses like a load of bricks. "If you hate the town, why'd you come back to visit your grandma at all? You trying to shake money out of her before she drops off and leaves it to some other relation?"

I feel my neck flush. Coming back to try Granny was my last hope. You couldn't understand unless you'd seen how Doris cleaned me out with a moving van, and then Cindy swept the crumbs from my studio into her purse.

I tell this prying Ruth, "I only came back to see her because she raised me from a pup. In fact, I'm glad about the accident, because now I'll be able to visit her every day for a week. Only problem's the yokels you run into around here. Pretty disgusting tribe after you've lived in L.A."

"I see," she says, inspecting her dustrag for worms. "Well, you don't need to worry, because the yokels probably won't bother you anymore." Abruptly she trots past me down the steps, rapping her cloth against the banister wildly. "I just don't think we have to worry about you anymore at all."

I open the door suspiciously, expecting another amorous attack, but it's Mrs. Lasso, grinning like an old dragon. She's come on a social errand, she says, blowing smoke. She's planning a shindig and wonders if I'll still be in town Saturday night. Before I can deal with this threat, she says of course I will, since Ramon is known to be holding my pickup hostage for days to come.

Trapped, I ask what sort of shindig's in the works?

A Hawaiian dinner, followed by dancing to some old 45s, is the reply. The hotel's banquet hall is being swept, the autographed photo of Arthur Godfrey beside a palm tree will hang above the table, and Ruth's buying tropical fruit to fling together in a porcupiney centerpiece. All the hotel guests are invited, along with a few friends, including my granny, if she wants to walk over.

I don't think to ask why a party's being thrown at such a time. I'm caught up in the vision of these hayseeds wearing leis, singing to ukeleles over the hum of Missouri crickets. The vision is so absurd that I accept the invitation on the spot. I offer to bring some rum for the mai tais, and, shutting the door, I remark that the photo of Arthur Godfrey will be a real treat.

The next morning the whole crooked plot becomes clear. Down in the lobby I encounter Ruth struggling toward the banquet hall with a cardboard pineapple and a basket of coconuts. There can be only one reason why these hicks are stooping to such ridiculous party decorations. Nobody around here's given a Hawaiian theme party since Ruth and I were kids, and our families took us to the movie where Ma and Pa Kettle sailed to the islands on a slapstick steamer. They're reviving the idea because *Hawaii* means wedding song. Mrs. L. thinks my heart'll melt toward Ruth someplace between the papier-mâché volcano and the artificial waterfall. Ruth must be going along with the scheme because, though I made it plain how I felt about her last night, her hold on Ramon's weakening and she feels desperate.

I haven't got room to shed any tears for her, though. In fact I can hardly bring myself to help her through the banquet hall door, even when she glares at me over her armload of tropical junk. I get my revenge in sarcasm. "Looks like it's going to be a swell shindig for you islanders."

It takes her a minute to assume a sociable face. "Yeah, Aunt Lucy wants it to be as big as the night she and Lucky got married."

"Is it their anniversary, or is somebody else planning to get hitched?"

"Didn't Aunt Lucy explain? The party's a wake for fifty years in the hotel business. They've decided to sell out."

I feel my mouth drop. "Sell out?"

"And I'll tell you something else," she says, making one eyebrow into a dagger. "It was only polite of us to invite your uncles, who've been keeping the business afloat for years, and once we included them, we had to ask you, since you're related. In fact, we've been perfectly decent about the whole thing. Especially since you still haven't mended the damage you did to the front of the building, like you said you would. So if you don't want to come on Saturday, fine, because the party's for other folks anyway."

"But I do want to come."

"There'll be lots of childish people there who remember those stupid Hawaiian theme parties we had in the fifties. Actually, I don't think you'd like it much."

"I'd like it quite a bit. I remember those parties vividly. Besides, half my family'll be there."

"If you do come, don't sit close to my aunt and uncle. You'd probably insult them, and then they might pop you one."

"I'll be unusually well behaved. Now, can I help you set up the chairs in here or anything?'

"No thanks. Uncle Lucky wouldn't want a paying guest to un- fold chairs. Besides, I'm sure you've got more important things to do, like visit your beloved old grandma, who I don't think you've seen since your traffic accident."

"As a matter of fact, I was just going to call her."

"Well then, go ahead. And remember, the mai tais are at six, din- ner's at seven, and my aunt and uncle are always in bed by ten, so don't encourage your uncles to sit around drinking till all hours."

"Don't worry, I'll act so obnoxious everybody'll clear out right after the meal."

"Good. I'll leave it in your hands then."

Grandma phoned Mrs. L. to say that she's too old for parties. She seemed suspicious to hear I'm staying at the hotel, but refused to wait for Mrs. L. to call me to the receiver so I could explain myself. After delivering this message, Mrs. L. lingers in the hall, hoping I'll unload confidences, but Granny's indifference is too painful to discuss, so I bang the door shut.

I'm nervous, two hours later, poking my head into the banquet hall, but Lucky waves me inside. I find the party is in full swing, which means ten or twelve gray-hairs are sitting on the folding chairs, tapping their shoes to a scratchy 45 while Ruth hustles around with a basket of macadamias. At least the mai tais are strong, and after a few glasses I show the folks how to dress up a coconut so it looks like a wizened human head. Mrs. L. brings out some white paint and we all write our names below the little red hats. I paint *Grandma* on one, so she's here in spirit anyhow.

By this time I'm jittery again, because we're still on drinks at eight-thirty, and I know I have to bundle the uncles out by ten. I rub my hands and ask, "What's to eat?"

Ruth looks like she understands my worry, but she makes it OK by saying, "We put the ham in late, so everything's behind schedule. Take your time, Sam."

After dinner there's dancing, first Mrs. L. and Lucky alone, then a couple of uncles jig alongside a flock of old women they've known forever, who've come from down the street. After Lucky wears out, I take Mrs. L., until from somewhere Ruth is pushed onto the floor and her aunt disappears. My girl's let her bun down, so I don't mind two-stepping with her at all. The room spins around and the old men point and laugh. I'm flushed from the heat and my broken arm swings wide, but the old steps feel fun to do, and the applause from the crowd sounds sweet. Finally Ruth's panting so hard that we drift away to look for cooler air and end up sitting on the curb in front, just down from the gash in the hotel's corner.

We listen to music through the door, still wary of each other but both hoping for better.

"Pineapple moon," she ventures, and "Pineapple princess," I reply. She drops her head, but smiles because my tone is right for making up.

To get her started I ask, "So is the hotel sold, or just up for sale?"

Her eyebrow lifts as if I'd asked about her underwear. Wrong subject. "Just on the market. You buying?"

Still, this topic might work if I sound relaxed. "Just curious. I mean, what could a buyer do with it, after all?"

"You trying to doom me here?"

"Huh?"

"You telling me I'll never get out of town, no matter what I try?"

This is the gal who accused me of coming back to bleed Grandma. She's not getting away with that. "So the sale's mainly for you, to stake you someplace else?"

"Besides, there's lots of potential in this old building," she flings out. "Open a retirement home, maybe, or convert it to apartments. They opened a fancy restaurant in a hotel like this one down in Lexington. Now folks from Kansas City drive out there on a Sunday. All it takes is a few thousand to invest."

My sympathy retreats further under these wild imaginings. "But half the street's boarded up. Who'd live in the apartments if it was converted? And you're too far from St. Joe for people to drive out here for dinner. Besides—"

But what's this—tears? She was smiling while we danced, and her long hair looked fine. Hips smaller than I thought, the red mouth appealing. I'm searching for an apology, anything. Suddenly I hear a shuffle-stumble from the right, and a dark figure lurches into the light glimmering from the hotel windows. It's Ramon, drawn by party noises. He's been smoking weed, or else he's mixed his own jar of mai tais. Ruth gasps. He's gripping something metal that shines in the dimness. Monkey wrench. His face turns ugly when he sees her, and he growls.

The rum's made me stupid, because as she backs up the steps I'm unable to block him from following. The door bangs, then bangs again, as I stand dumbly. Over the music inside comes a chorus of shouts, then furniture crashes, and after a minute the crowd of gray-hairs bursts through the banquet hall door, spreads across the lobby and tumbles into the street. The uncles and Lucky follow, hoisting Ramon by his legs and arms. They heave him from the top step, and he arcs through the air before landing in the street beside me, where he lies groaning. Then comes the wrench, which hits him in the middle of the back, so hard I wonder if it's cracked a rib.

The old men shake their fists. "No wonder she left you, good-for-nothing!" "You smoke any more of that funny stuff and you'll end up dead!" Lucky gets off the killingest taunt: "That divorce court judge'll burn your hide for this!"

They pull inside while the gray-haired women back off up the street, satisfied. Ruth doesn't reappear, so I step over to see if my mechanic needs help.

Blood trickles from one nostril, but he's able to stand. He hobbles off toward the garage without a word, leaving the wrench behind. I stoop for it, then glimpse him halted under a streetlamp. "You can have her!" he bellows. At first I think he means the wrench. "Only get her out of town while she's still alive!"

Sunday morning—are the pious folk all at church? No: shufflings and creaks come from the banquet room as I pass. Ruth's sweeping up crumbs from the party, a hollow look about her. "Will you let me help this time?" She nods, and I want her permission to mean that, at least by local standards, I'm not the worst of men.

She points out where to stack the chairs, but acts indifferent when I begin to praise the party. For half an hour we avoid the big issue, but finally as we stand over the last heap of trash I catch her eye. "It's not his fault," she sighs.

I stare. "He brought along a wrench. He could've killed somebody."

"The wrench was bad, but what made him bring it's another story."

"You mean divorce court?"

"We're not fighting each other in court. That was just Aunt

Lucy's idea. We've signed a paper that says we're both free and clear." She muses. "He's a good man, really. Nobody can see the suffering but me."

"What suffering's that?"

"Remember Ramon's dad, that owned car dealerships over two counties?"

"That's right, the Ford Empire! What happened to it all? Ramon was the richest kid in our class."

"His daddy ran into the Edsel, which he overordered. Then these towns started drying up. By the time Ramon inherited, there was no money left. Closed down the dealerships one by one. Finally all he had was this last garage, so he said it was gonna be the best shop around. Kept on three mechanics till he got behind on their wages. Ten years ago he never put his own hands inside an engine, but he's had to learn." She twists a paper plate. "They say money can't buy happiness, but in a place like this you get a different view."

Her face looks weary under the fluorescent light. Come to Missouri for character. After a minute I bend to kiss the freckled cheek. But she continues to look beyond at the bare yellow wall, as if my fellow feeling was no tribute to speak of.

Tuesday afternoon, Hawaii still on my mind. At the bottom of the suitcase I find my long-neglected camera, with its black tower of lenses. Since the hotel may be sold, someone ought to preserve a record.

It takes a few minutes to learn how to poise the camera on my cast while I manipulate the light dial and click the shutter with my good hand. I begin snapping the architectural frills, delights of old-fashioned craftsmen that pop up everywhere I turn: tracery around my door, the long meandering wainscotted hall that leads to the stairwell, where I get a zoom shot of banisters curving down to the lobby. There Mrs. L. bends over her desk with a pencil, trying to make something balance. I snap her as a surprise, framing her head with that curve of polished oak that drops from the ceiling. She turns almost pretty with blushes to see the small black eye aimed at her, atop my long white plaster arm.

Over the next few days I capture them all, singly and in groups. Most memorable shots: the uncles stretched along their bench across the street, mugging shamelessly; Lucky smooching Ruth's cheek; the bittersweet panoramas of boarded-up Main Street, ending in its profitless bank.

Meanwhile Ramon's started work on the pickup. He says the reconditioned parts are no good, but if I'll give him an extra day he can modify them—and then he spies the camera. His explanation dries up and he grins uncertainly; but when I begin clicking, he climbs madly on top of the truck for a pose. "Push back your cap!" I say, and a sense of purpose comes into his limbs as he helps me get it right.

In fact everyone's flattered to be thought important enough for a shot. Folks realize they've lived precisely in order to be thus arranged. It's an apotheosis, though what we talk about, as I order them around, is how handsome everyone looks. Then we laugh outrageously.

We abandoned breakfasts in bed after that first awkward morning. For two weeks Mrs. L.'s been cooking my eggs while I wait in the lobby. But today Ruth invites me back to the huge kitchen—her aunt nowhere in sight. I'm served on a steel table amid the clutter of enormous blackened instruments that Mrs. L. once used to feed the railroad men.

Ruth stirs up waffles for us both, and we dip syrup out of a five-gallon restaurant jar. Sitting across from each other, growing stickier by the minute, we don't say much—talking's been our problem from the start—but we share silly grins at the old-fashioned feeling of a big breakfast, and the intimacy you get by bringing a customer behind the scenes.

Still, something inside me can't seem to rest. "Who was the man in the suit yesterday? Got a buyer for the hotel?"

"I knew you were a photographer, but not a spy."

"Natural curiosity. If it's sold, I'm afraid my uncles'll be thrown into the street. I should warn you, I'm looking for ways to jinx the sale."

She snorts. "You're not involved. You're leaving in a few days when your truck's fixed."

"I wouldn't be so sure. I'm beginning to feel attached."

"Attached to what?"

"Oh, hard-drinking uncles, funny pineapple moons."

Now I've embarrassed her. I should cut out my tongue. "Don't you want to joke about it?"

"I don't mind a joke. But you shouldn't make it harder on us, when we feel guilty about selling already. You were gone twenty years without a word, so it's hard to believe what happens here's gonna matter to you."

I can see now that I've been trying to work us to this point. I wanted her to concentrate on my next words. I wanted to close whatever gap still lies between me and Lassos' Hotel in one spectacular leap. Only: there she sits, sticky maple hand poised at attention—and it turns out I don't know what to say. How *could* the selling of a creaky old building in the middle of the prairie mean anything to me, after all?

I try to get my edge back. "So who was the fella in the suit?"

She grimaces. "That was the divorce lawyer Uncle Lucky bought me. He was dropping off a copy of the final decree."

You can feel the futility like butter sticking to your thumb. I've got to make a gesture. "You wanta ride out to L.A. when I go?"

Tosses back her head, recovers her poise at once. A very pretty smile. "I was hoping you'd ask. Sure."

Awkward pause, while I think over what I just said. "I didn't mean to live with me, you understand. Just to look for work."

"Right, I knew what you meant."

"Once you find a job, the Lassos won't have to sell and throw my uncles out."

"Are you back harping on that? I need my cut, whether I'm in California or I'm here! Besides, you know they're too old to run a business, and they're only making subsistence on this place anyway."

"And we already had the good-bye party."

She gives in and smiles. "That's right."

Now that everything's settled, I'm just making conversation so we can end on a better note. "So tell me, suppose somebody wanted to open a great country restaurant in this old barn. How would he remodel the kitchen?"

The question I should've asked in the first place. As we walk around inspecting the massive appliances, the closets stuffed with ancient cans of salted vegetables, I've never felt more at home. She's a sweet woman, really; it shows in her love for the place. We plan the new kitchen like five-year-olds playing house. We'll carve a door here, install the new range over there, and we'll need a second refrigerator for meats. She stands with her shoulder lightly touching my chest, looking over the prospects. Sure enough, you can still hear the clamor of old voices in the air: railroad men who used to live here calling for their dinners, laughing and stamping to the door, paying their bills, wishing you good-night.

If it wasn't for this cursed maple sticking to the fingers of my good hand, I'd take her shoulder and—

I step back. "So you'll be packed on Monday?"

"Oh—yes. I'll be ready."

Through the swinging door to the lobby I repeat to myself, Keep a grip, keep a grip. . . .

Saturday morning in the freshness I march down to Ramon's garage, full of ginger, and when he boasts that she runs like a dream, I challenge him to a test drive. We thump the doors, climbing in, and he revs the motor to show it off. We charge past the business district, and in another minute we're beyond the white clapboard houses, whizzing through corn rows. Then wheat fields and over the Little Platte bridge where Grandpa used to park when he took me fishing. Now the gravel road rises steeply up the hill that looks over Seven Corners, which I haven't seen since I was a kid. From here it's all undulating green carpets up to the far horizon where Iowa is. Two or three white houses, at intervals, and red barns. Tiny men gathering hay in a stubbly field. The dust, the humid fertile warmth, I sniff it in for heart's sake.

The pickup sounds good under Ramon's foot too. We grin mightily, sharing the wind swirling into the cab and the freedom of flying down the county roads. I stretch up and press my good fist against the ceiling to spend the energy.

But the drive back to town feels like the wrong direction, the end. How did Saturday get here so fast? At the garage again I look over the truck, the shiny white and red body, the black force of the tires. I ask Ramon what she needs. Something's been troubling him too—the repairs came too easy; he's not ready to let her go. After a conference I order the works: a searchlight mounted on top of the cab, mud flaps with ruby studs for the rear, a pair of chrome-plated horns alongside the hood for any time I feel like creating a racket.

When he admits, hesitating, that he'll have to order parts from St. Joe, I reassure him, "Good job's worth waiting for."

"Lucky said you was leaving with Ruth for L.A. on Monday."

"Just an idea," I shrug. "I could use an extra week—take more pictures, maybe work up some kind of an album, or a show. The scenery around here's got potential."

"I'd have to charge you labor for installing things like that."

"I'm expecting to pay."

He relaxes. "You want a beer?"

Wandering back to the hotel, I relive our ride—the memory of Grandpa driving over dusty roads when I was a boy, and the green grasshopper that jumped into the cab once when Ramon slowed. First the huge black eyes seemed dazed by the moving machine and the unearthly creatures inside it; but then the insect woke up to its mistake, dug its heels into my forearm, and sailed back through the window to where it belonged. I'm that grasshopper, only I escaped first and opened my eyes later.

Around the corner on Main Street, the broad hotel front comes into view. Now let's see: you'd need twenty grand for new furnishings, and let's face it, you'd have to hire a professional chef. You could do most of the carpentry yourself, and the advertising would be a snap, but you'd need a menu these Missouri folks could marvel over, and you'd have to promise them second helpings. Later you could refinish the upstairs, advertise "Bed & Breakfast," pull some cars in off the interstate. But the kitchen's where you'd live or die. You could put potted geraniums along these stone steps to soften them. Flags to dress up the porch, and a sign with red lettering, "Ruth's Country Dining."

I'll get to work on this hole in the corner. Lucky's got lumber stashed in back. Hell, everything's stashed somewhere in this ghost of a place. Got mummified sides of venison hung in the basement that we could dice into the soup. Impart a smokey flavor. Yes, isn't it delicious? The ingredients are secret—an old farmhouse recipe, you can be sure of that!

Only how do you buy a hotel on nothing down, and where's your start-up capital? Details! There's Ruth, finished with the breakfast dishes, looking ruefully at the damage my pickup made.

"Hey, help me find some nails! You'll have to hold the boards while I hammer!"

"I want you to come along when I visit Grandma this afternoon. I'm asking a huge favor of her, and you'll sweeten the air."

Looks at me slyly, trying to decide whose side she'll be on in the family tug-of-war. "Why would my being there matter?"

"You'll make my story sound genuine. I'm asking for twenty grand and a free hand. Granny's last chance to win me for capital-ism and Christianity."

Ruth chortles, till I say, "You'll be chipping in too."

"Am I putting up another twenty grand?"

"If only you could. But I'll settle for your consent."

Backs off. "Consent to what?"

"You've got to tell your aunt and uncle not to sell the hotel. Keep it in the family and lease the first floor to me for a dollar a year."

Sardonic smile. Thinks she knows me down to the ground by now. "How'll you earn back your dollar a year?"

I tell her.

A clicking in her throat—dumbfounded. "What do you know about starting a classy restaurant?"

"I don't need to know too much, because I've got a chef coming from L.A. He's a pal who's run a couple of swell moneymakers in Long Beach. He really knows how to dress up leftovers. Only problem will be taming his spices for these midwestern tongues."

"Does he want to move?"

"Everybody in California wants to move. But I can't call him till I know what his salary's going to be. That's why you've got to smile at Grandma."

"Ho ho. I'm leaving for L.A. in a pickup Monday morning. Why should I help you swindle an old lady? Why's my name on the restaurant?"

"Come sit on the steps. Next to the geranium pot."

"There's no geranium here."

"Where it will be." I love how the grin plays about her mouth— she knows what I'm coming to, but she's in no hurry to get there.

"You're gonna help me with Grandma because later you'll make a fortune as hostess of the restaurant that bears your name. Good evening, folks, a table by the window. Tonight's special is Missouri oysters sloshed in jam."

An exclamation point between her brows.

"That's why your family'll let me have the ground floor for a buck—the first year only. After that, we'll negotiate better terms. Because we're all gonna get rich off my hard work and my pal Larry's hot plates."

"Sam, you couldn't possibly make a go of it. We're hoping to sell to a sucker who doesn't realize how hopeless this place is. Not to somebody we know. And not so we can stay around and watch it sink."

"The most devious thing I ever heard a woman say. But it doesn't matter, because I've had a revelation. I love this building. I love my uncles living on the second floor. I love your Aunt Lucy and your Uncle Lucky. I even love Ramon, who beat on your pretty body. Taking photographs wasn't enough for me. I want to eat mouthfuls of this Missouri earth, stuff it inside me. And what's more, Ruthie, I love you. Nothing personal, I'm only taking you as a symbol of the place."

High-pitched strangulated laughter, but she doesn't draw away. Instead her mouth slowly settles into a straight line as she feels the joke against herself. "I'm going to marry little Sammy Calder and spend weeks fixing up the downstairs. Then I'm going to get tuckered up in my Sunday dress and wait for the first diners, and late that night I'm going to finally put down my stack of menus and I'm going to cry, because nobody came. You'll be out in the kitchen with your buddy from L.A., drinking the bottles of California wine you laid in. It'll be the old Ford Empire going belly up all over again."

Don't remember saying anything about us getting married.

What a sensation—melting with Ruth! As we lie entwined in one another's limbs, pore opened up to pore and mound sluggishly giving way to muscle here and there, passion spent, talking idly and taking our time under the sultry afternoon air, suddenly a thought stirs between us. We speak it more or less together, eyebrows saluting in unison. "People don't rush into things like this, do they?" she giggles. I roll over to pull my watch from the bedside table, careful not to hit her with my cast. Five-seventeen. Aunt Lucy must be downstairs in the vast kitchen, snapping beans for our supper. The uncles will be trudging up to their bathroom soon to wash, before stepping into the dining room in that black cluster they make.

But what time does Ramon shut up the garage: five? five-thirty? six? And supposing I don't get there before he slides the big panel door closed. Will he be around back in his apartment, reaching for a beer, so I can call him out to surrender the pickup for an hour?

In a panic of hilarity, we search for our scattered clothes. Mostly dressed and smoothing down her hair on the run, Ruth descends to the kitchen to tell Auntie that we're off to Maysville to the justice of the peace, but we'll want her best meal when we get back, and try to find some wine.

I tramp down the stairs a few seconds behind her, hoping to catch Ramon in time. And I do. He hands over the key suspiciously. I wonder if I should tell him—to help get her off his mind. Too complicated, I decide; save it for later.

I back the pickup out of the garage and snort around the corner to the hotel, where a small crowd of the old people I love has gathered in astonishment over such shouting and banging as

Ruth and her aunt have been engaged in for ten minutes to get my bride looking presentable. One of the uncles is asking another what everybody means about the hotel *not* being sold, since he didn't know it *was* being sold, while Lucky is warning us that Ramon might bull his way up the street and block us from getting out of town. Aunt Lucy wraps her nicotine-flavored lips around my cheekbone for a blessing, and Ruth says don't drive too fast because when you're excited is when accidents happen.

I remember she's never ridden with me before.

Backing up, I'm hit by the late afternoon sunlight on the hotel, with the dark figures grouped against its whiteness. I grope for the camera and lean out of the cab. Ruth looks over to see why we've stopped. They're positioned in a waving line that rises from the curb and links the hotel with the street, the light with the deepening shadows. Five men are wearing fedoras. The old lady's hair slants off at the same angle as the hat brims. There it is: I snap.

 Part Two

⁓ Storying You

"You remember how we used to plant the pifflebean when you was a boy, Sammy?"

"I'm not sure I do, Uncle Tony."

"Why, the pifflebean was the big cash crop in them days. Some folks call it the stipplebean too. Ain't that right, fellas?"

"Sure, Tony."

"What's it used for, Uncle Tony?"

"Why, to thicken molasses. They grind the beans into paste, then they mix the two together. At least they used to, before we quit growing it."

"Why'd you quit, Uncle Tony?"

"Yeah, why did we?"

"For two very good reasons. Number one, it was so darned hard to cultivate and harvest. The leaves on a piffle plant are like knives; they'll cut a man as he passes through the field. You can't drive a tractor through plants like that, because the tires get cut to ribbons. Consequently the only way to harvest your crop is with a piffle scythe."

"Another thing, son: all them piffle scythes is left-handed."

"That's right. It's hard for a normal fella to get a grip. And the number two reason we had to stop raising it was, and I hate to admit this, but the farmers around here got greedy. They found out a piffle bean'll absorb a lot of water. So they started to fill their wagons half full of beans and hosed down the load till it swelled up just like when you cook rice on a stove. Of course your grandpa wouldn't pull a trick like that, but there was lots of farmers, including my own brothers sitting in this room, who were getting paid twice what they shoulda been for their crops. Ain't that right, Claude?"

"Oh, some of us was awful wicked around our pifflebeans!"

"Finally the molasses people figured out what was going on, because they was turning out such watery molasses, so they quit buying from us."

"About how big is a pifflebean, Uncle Tony?"

"Some folks say they're as big as a coconut, don't they, Tony?"

"Some folks'll say anything, but the truth is, they're no bigger than an orange, or a coffee bean sometimes."

"What do they mix in with the molasses now, Uncle Tony?"

"Why, nothing! The pifflebean's the only thing that works. That's why molasses runs so fast these days. Don't your wife bring any home from the store?"

"I'm not married."

"Not married! Why'm I telling you about pifflebeans, then?"

"Another thing about them plants is, they grow waist-high unless you get a wet year, then they only grow knee-high!"

"Oh shut up, Chester, we don't wanta hear any more about pifflebeans!"

"You're the one that started it."

"Just shut up."

"By the way, Sammy, did you ever hear how your great-grandpappy tricked the gummint out of all our farmland in the first place?"

"Of course he ain't. His grandma never woulda told him that. She was ashamed of it."

"Well sir, back in those days there was a gummint agent hereabouts with a map of the county on his office wall for homesteading. The law was that anybody who walked in got a hundred and sixty acres, as long as he agreed to live on it. But nobody got more than a hundred and sixty, you see. Now your great-grandpappy arrived on the back of a horse from Pennsylvania, all spunky and conniving to beat the band. He always told us he couldn't abide

Pennsylvania because of those narrow valleys they got, where a man can't spread out. He come west because he wanted enough land that he couldn't see the end of it from any one place.

"So he walked into the gummint office and looked at that map on the wall, greedy-like, and he woulda taken every parcel on it if he'd been offered. But the agent said a hundred and sixty was the limit.

"Now this agent, he'd come from St. Louie, he wore a white shirt and all he knew about was maps. He didn't care about feeling the soil between your fingers; he was just gonna give his parcels away and go back to St. Louie and write out a report. So there was no use Pappy offering to figure out how the two of them could split eight or ten parcels between 'em, you see.

"Pappy always had a line of gab on him, so he kept working on the agent, probing for some weak spot. Finally it come out that the fella was a Baptist. Ever since he'd been dunked, he'd never danced or played cards. Pappy said, 'I bet you never took a drink, neither.' The fella said, 'Liquor is the devil's tool.' Pappy smiled. 'Nor took a bribe for a piece of land.' The fella said, 'I never took a bribe, and I never will.'

"Pappy said, 'You ain't doing nothing here, let's ride out and look over the county so I can decide which quarter I want.' The agent closed his office and they rode out. It was a bitter cold day, making up its mind to snow, so Pappy took a pint bottle out of his saddlebag and said, 'I think I'd better warm myself up.' He takes a drink; then he puts the cork back in the bottle and says, 'I won't offer you one, because I know you don't use the stuff.'

"They ride up one hill and down the next, it's starting to snow pretty heavy, so they stop under a tree and Pappy pulls out his bottle again and says, 'This stuff sure warms me up.' All the time the agent's pulling his collar tighter and wondering how Pappy ever cajoled him into leaving his chair beside the stove. Finally he says, 'I'd like a drink if you don't mind.' Pappy says, 'Sure, if you think it's all right.' The fella says, 'Oh, I don't think just one can hurt me.'

"Now all the time, Pappy's leading him farther away from his office. The agent doesn't know his way around the county without a map, and every time Pappy catches sight of something familiar, he heads away before the agent can make out where he is. By this time the agent's had four or five drinks, and the snow's getting too deep for the horses to walk, so Pappy says, 'There's a sheltered place. Let's put up for the night.' Of course Pappy's been camping all the way from Pennsylvania, so he's got his gear and his food. He just tells the agent to keep out of the way for a minute while he sets up camp, and everything'll be cozy. The agent is froze to the bone, and he says, 'I guess we drank up all that bottle.' Pappy says, 'Don't worry. I got another one in this saddlebag.'

"Well, next morning when Pappy slung that agent across his horse, the fella was so snookered he threw up for five miles on the snow. Pappy laid him out on his cot back in the office and watched over him for a day, while the agent went through the dry heaves. Pappy was scared he was gonna have a corpse on his hands. But finally the fella come around enough to sit up, and he thanked Pappy for saving his life with that whiskey. Pappy says, 'How you feel now?' The fella says, 'I feel awful. You ain't got another one of them pint bottles, have you?'

"After that, Pappy moved in with the agent for a few days at the land office. Which, by the way, I heard was out where the old McCabe farmhouse stood. You ever hear that, Alistair?"

"Why, no. I heard it was down at the courthouse in Plattsburg. I heard there was a dozen clerks in the office, not just one sitting alone in a shack on the prairie. And I heard this county was settled a whole generation earlier than in Pappy's days. Why, Hickman was laid out before the Civil War. Don't you recollect that centennial we had—"

"Some of the county was settled before the Civil War, but lots of it wasn't. There may've been a land office down at P-burg, but there was one over on the McCabe place too, a lean-to to take care of this neighborhood. Why, you heard all this from Pappy's own mouth, just like I did. So set quiet and don't make out like I'm storying you."

"I know you ain't storying me."

"You better believe it. Anyway, while Pappy was staying with him, the agent fell to drinking pretty hard, because every time he stopped, he got a headache. Finally he got sentimental and said to Pappy, 'You're looking after me just like the Good Samaritan in the Bible. What can I do to repay you?'

"This was the chance Pappy was waiting for, so he said, 'I'm gonna get married in about a week.' Now he hadn't even met your great-grandma yet, let alone proposed to her and been accepted, but that didn't stop him. The agent said, 'Well, I want to repay your kindness *and* I want to give you a wedding present too. What'll it be?' Pappy pointed to the map over the desk and said, 'You see these ten parcels? I want this first one in my name, which the gummint says I'm entitled to. I know you're a Baptist, so I won't ask for more than that for myself. But the woman I'm marrying is a real breeder.' "

"And that was true, too."

"Sure it was, even though he hadn't met her at the time. So Pappy went on, 'I want you to save me these other nine parcels. Don't put anybody else's name down by 'em. Every time I have a kid, you can sign him up for the next hundred and sixty acres. That way I won't be taking more than my fair share, but I'll help my children farm theirs till they're old enough to look after the land themselves.'

"The agent was still so groggy that he agreed. Later on, when he'd sobered up, he rode out and asked Pappy to let him off, but Pappy said, 'I know you won't go back on your word, because you're a Baptist.' The agent said, 'I should go back on it if I made a mistake to give it in the first place.' But Pappy said, 'A gummint agent can't give any promise that's impossible for him to keep.' Nobody could beat Pappy in an argument, you see."

"Fill your glass, Jethro."

"Don't mind if I do. Hmmm, that's stout stuff! You like that, Sammy?"

"Yes, Uncle Jethro."

"Good boy.

"Well, after that, Pappy needed to get married quick. He found a homesteader from New York, who was our Grandpappy Eleazer, who'd just put up a lean-to for the winter and had a daughter about sixteen, who was our ma. They had five kids so close together they was busting out like popcorn on a hot stove. There was some of us only eight months apart, and you can look that up in the family Bible!"

"Specially the first one, Claude here, he was only eight months after the wedding."

"I was not!"

"Yes you was, Claude, You was an early child. You can tell by the shape of the skull."

"Can't tell a thing by my skull."

"Here, Claude, fill your glass and set quiet."

"I am setting quiet. Get on with your story and don't say anything about when I was born."

"I won't. Well, so that agent give Pappy five extra parcels along our road in less than five years. He ended up owning nine hundred and sixty acres of prime Missouri land. He hired three of his neighbors part-time to help him work it, till we boys was old enough. Then he built that big farmhouse your Uncle Claude and Aunt Kate inherited, where they lived when you was a boy. By that time our family was setting pretty. Meanwhile, the agent give away all his other land and went back to St. Louie, but before he left, Pappy got him to believe that Ma was carrying a big litter, so the agent agreed to save the last four parcels; when the other kids came along, Pappy'd write a letter and the agent'd fill in their names on his final report. After that, them four parcels just sat vacant for a couple of years. Pappy didn't own them yet, but he looked at 'em like they was his. All he needed now was four more kids.

"That's what I remember about the early years: those two trying to have the next kid. Every morning Pappy'd ask Ma how she felt after last night, and she'd put him off by saying they'd just have to wait and see what came of it.

"Ma got awful skittish and didn't want anybody to touch her, especially Pappy. I think he wore her out, either in the head or else down below. Finally got to the point where Agnes, your grandma, she was the youngest of us, she'd get slapped every time she made a peep, because Ma couldn't stand the noise. That summer Pappy came in from the fields every afternoon, and they'd step into the bedroom and pull the blinds down. I suppose they was trying whether a different time of day'd work better. But in the end, five kids is what they got, and they couldn't get no more.

"Pappy was afraid the agent wouldn't hold the land forever, so he thought he'd make up a kid's name and send it to St. Louie. But Ma wouldn't let him. She didn't mind the bargain so long as there really was kids, but it went against her religion to invent any.

"Then in the spring Pappy come in for lunch one day and said, 'That agent sold me out.' Ma said, 'What you mean?' He said, 'He give my land to strangers. What kinda Baptist is he, anyhow, to go and do that?'

"But there was a new family pulled up on the nearest parcel, living out of their wagon and clearing a piece of land for their garden. It was custom for the family that was settled to help out the new neighbors, but Pappy wouldn't. He said the land had been promised him, and he'd never lift a finger to help a thief.

"Of course the end of the story's a good joke on Pappy, because the new family had four little girls who noticed there was four little boys among us, and they couldn't rest till they got us to the altar. Could they, boys?"

"You mean you couldn't rest till you was caught."

"I guess none of us rested much till that was settled. You ever hear that story, Sammy?"

"No, Uncle Jethro."

"What he means is, he never heard your story before, but he heard the true one someplace else."

"That's all right. Fill your glass, Sammy."

"Thanks, Uncle Jethro."

"Those days we had a plague of hoppers every year. Farming was lots tougher then, because the droughts lasted longer and the weeds was bigger, and we didn't have these fancy machines they're driving now. Come July, you'd get hoppers swarming over the fields, stealing half your wheat. Hoppers is nasty things because of those big eyes: they don't blink. If you try to swat one with your hand, he's got hind legs to gouge you when he kicks off.

"Then after the War, we got the DDT. The county agent said, 'Boys, we're gonna have the promised land. We're gonna raise eighty and a hundred bushels an acre, because the hoppers are gonna die.' So we sprayed like he told us, and that year the corn plants was green like an emerald. Like they didn't grow on this earth. The wheat was two, three inches taller than the year before. The weather turned better too. When you needed rain, you got it, and when you was ready to harvest, the sky was clear blue. All us Wilsons put money in the bank those years, and Jake, your grandpa, he put money in the bank too.

"Then the county agent come around and said, 'Boys, look at this gummint report. You're not gonna get any more DDT.' Finally they give us some new poisons, never quite as good. At the same time, the weather turned bad again. The fifties, there was some dry years toward the end, and we had the hoppers worse than ever.

"About ten years later, we started getting the cancers on our road. First your grandpa took sick. Finally he had his operation in St. Joe and died two years later. Then your Aunt Liza got it. She only lasted a year and a half.

"After a while it dawned on us what was happening. We called the agent and said, 'What about that DDT?' He said, 'The DDT was safe as sitting home a Saturday night.' We said, 'If it was so safe, why are our folks dying like the hoppers used to?' He said, 'They're not dying like hoppers. They're just dying like themselves.' So you see all the good that done us."

"If I recollect right, you was supposed to be a preacher when you grew up, Sammy."

"That's what Grandma wanted, Uncle Jethro."

"Of course your grandma is a funny old gal, pretty much like a prune. You don't need to mind that you didn't turn out like she intended, because nobody on this earth could please her for more than five minutes—"

"That woman was your grandpa's cross in life, son! Once he came wandering down to my cabin while I was sitting on the front step of an evening. 'Chester,' he says, 'Agnes has been laying into me about something for two solid hours, and I'm not gonna be able to sleep tonight. How about a drop of that stuff you got inside to relax me?' "

"Now I don't believe Jake ever asked you for a drink."

"He did, Tony, just this once! But I didn't give it to him. I knew there was too much danger. He had an alcoholic's wife. If he took one drink, he'd be a goner, just like that land agent you fellas was talking about before."

"Jake didn't drink because he was a Methodist. Don't go telling his grandson those old stories of yours that never was true."

"I'm not saying it happened every night, but it happened once, and that's no story."

"Chester, you're not even family—you're just a hired hand that wouldn't know how Jake or one of the rest of us thought about anything!"

"What I was getting at, when I asked Sammy about being a preacher, if you two'll let me get a word in, was that I thought he might be interested in a story about that preacher we had around here in the thirties. He was the biggest cusser you ever saw. You know in them days the Methodist churches all switched preachers every year, second Sunday in May. Naturally we got all different kinds, but this fella I'm talking about was a real dog-in-the-manger."

"Selkirk was his name."

"I believe you're right, Alistair. Well, this Selkirk was nasty in the pulpit. Every sermon went the same way. He'd pick out some sin and tell you why the Lord hated it, and how you could tell if you was doing it, and he'd wind up that if you kept on, you was goddamned. That's how he'd talk in front of our wives and children. And he'd talk about hell till you didn't care if you ate Sunday dinner or not. We had the brimstone and the sons of bitches with the pokers and you name it!

"For a full year of Sundays he never ran out of sins. If you tote up the ones the Bible talks about, it gets pretty curious how this guy reached fifty-two. There's the Ten Commandments which you could break, and the seven deadlies; that makes seventeen, and I imagine you could add a couple of others like not going to church, but a normal mind would never get over twenty. Which tells you about the nature of this fella, that he could think 'em up on his own.

"He was a pokey-looking guy, hairy as a bear, and when he walked along the street in town, you could see his lips move, like he was saying to himself, 'Goddamn this tree, goddamn that squirrel, goddamn goddamn.'

"Well sir, just like you'd expect with somebody that didn't have anything but sins on his mind, he took to visiting the women of the church in the afternoons, when their husbands was out in the fields. They'd get their washing and baking done, then they'd set and cool off for an hour before starting dinner. Soon as they'd hit the chair, one of 'em'd hear gravel in the driveway, and it'd be Selkirk stepping in to ask her to join him in a prayer.

"Of course you can't turn a preacher away, so in he comes, and he takes a bite of pie, and before you know it, they're on the floor next to one another praying, and it seems like this particular preacher always held hands with the person he was praying alongside, so long as it was a woman.

"Well, this story don't reflect so good on some of the family, but the truth is he started coming out to pray with a couple of your aunts pretty regular. He'd go to one house one day, and the other the next. Your Uncle Claude and your Uncle Alistair couldn't help but notice how the preacher's car was always in their driveways, so they started keeping an eye out.

"One afternoon they spotted his Model A pulling into Alistair's drive, so they waited ten minutes, then Alistair opens the screen door and walks in like he was coming back from the field for a drink of water. There wasn't a soul in the living room, but as soon as that door slammed, somebody in the front bedroom let out a 'Goddamn' that'd split your eardrums. Alistair headed in there and found the preacher crawling out the window. But your Uncle Claude was waiting outside with a pitchfork. Got the preacher with it too, more than once and right where it counts. That fella couldn't even get to his car because of Claude. He had to hightail it back to Hickman on foot. Next morning he had to ride a borrowed horse out and beg Alistair to let him have the car."

"Hee hee hee! Worst thing about it was, he had three more

months before his year in Hickman was up, and he couldn't just cook up some excuse and ask the bishop to relieve him, because the bishop'd ask the Hickman church about it, and the whole story would get out. So Selkirk had to climb into our pulpit every Sunday and look us in the eye and warn us against another of them sins he invented."

"Every sin except adultery. He never mentioned that one!"

"No sir, I don't think he ever did. Hee hee hee!"

"The collection plate'd go out and come back without a dime in it. I don't even know what he ate, those last months!"

"Of course now that we're onto the subject of wives, there's another wife that might be mentioned."

"Dad blast it! If you think I'm gonna sit through those lies—"

"Here, Claude, fill up your glass and leave Chester's wife alone for once."

"Now now, fair's fair. I let Jethro tell a tale on my Kate and Alistair's Sophie with the preacher, so that entitles me to tell a story too."

"The world's full of stories, but every time you start in, you always get around to my Wendy, and most of it ain't true, and the part that is you twist so it ends up a lie anyway."

"Fair's fair. I sat through a story and never blinked, and now I get to tell one."

"Well, I ain't gonna listen to it."

"Chester, you ain't leaving so early?"

"I can drink in my own room just as well as here. Smells better in my room anyway."

"Chester— Now look how you drove him away, Claude."

"Well, I didn't mean to, but he ain't family anyhow, and since he's gone, there's no harm telling the story, is there? Besides, young Sammy might find it entertaining, seeing as how he's not married and ain't got nothing to lose."

"Here, Sammy, you better drink up. No telling how long Claude's gonna spin this one out once he gets started. It's three in the morning, and I'll bet we don't get out of here till daybreak."

"Thanks, Uncle Tony."

"This story can be told short and sweet. The reason it always comes out so long is, Chester keeps interrupting, so it's just as well he left."

"Get on with the cotton-picker, then!"

"You know, Sammy, after Chester went to work for your grandpa, he dug up this gal Wendy and married her one weekend, and brought her back to live in his cabin. Musta been the first time he'd gone with a woman, and his brain went haywire. He picked her up on a Saturday night bender in town, her just passing through. If he was drunk she coulda easily got him into bed, and then if she drug him to a justice of the peace at five in the morning, he wouldn't of resisted—he woulda been so proud his pecker worked after all those dry years.

"You saw her when you was a youngster, so you remember the cauliflower ear and that big wen on her neck, and how one of her eyes opened too wide, but the other one hardly opened at all. When she walked down the road, dogs would crawl underneath a porch just to avoid the sight.

"Well, after a few months the fun wore off, and there was a couple black eyes and a couple dozen hard words between them. You'd see Chester dragging around at eight-thirty in the morning, like he hadn't got any sleep or any breakfast. You'd say howdy, and maybe he'd answer and maybe he wouldn't. He'd pick fights with folks then for nothing more'n sneezing out the wrong side of their nose. Even your grandpa was getting fed up with him.

"Of course it was lots worse for Wendy, I suppose, who was a city gal to start with, trapped in that cabin with no place to go unless she wanted to help with the farm chores, which was foreign to her. All she could do was wait for Chester to come in for meals and then listen to him complaining, like he always does.

"Finally she started going out nights. I suppose it began with walks up and down the road in the dark, just to let the wind blow her skirts. I don't know which was the first young spark to stop and trade a word with her."

"Mighta been one of your boys, Claude, or one of Tony's."

"My sons was clean livers in those days. I don't know about Tony's. Huh—looks like Tony's asleep, don't it?"

"We're all about asleep. Why don't you get on with it."

"I'm coming to the climax right now. Well sir, before you know it, she wasn't getting back from her walks till bedtime, and then after bedtime, and once or twice she stayed out all night. That was pretty hard on old Chester. I passed her myself a few times, driving back from town late. She'd either be hanging around your grandpa's mailbox, or sitting in the moonlight on that bank below the barn, showing her white legs up above the knees."

"She never charged for it, did she?"

"I heard old man Swenson paid for it."

"They woulda made quite a pair, with her ear and his red hair."

"I heard two bits was all."

"And overpriced at that."

"So anyway, word about her passed as far off as Lathrop, where there lived a bunch of triplets by the name of Dawson. The Dawson boys all looked alike, and they did everything together like triplets will: wore the same colored shirt on the same day, told the same jokes, rolled their cigarettes left-handed.

"One night they drove over and found her sitting by the ditch, and they said how about it? She was eager enough, but she said just one a night. She wanted her privacy. They joked with her and tried to work her up to it, but she stood on her principles.

"Well sir, at daybreak Chester found she hadn't come in that night. After he'd done his chores, he checked back at the cabin, but still no Wendy. By this time he was worried, so he started looking in places where he thought she might be. Finally your grandpa asked what's the matter, and they both started combing the farm for her. Then your grandpa runs into Jethro from down the road, calling for his cow that's escaped from the pasture overnight. When they exchanged news, they knew there'd been foul play. One thing missing on a country road may be an accident, but two things missing is foul play.

"Meanwhile, Chester'd gone his own way to the back fields by the railroad track looking for her. He didn't know a cow was gone too, or I suppose you could say he just knew about the first cow, but not the second. Anyway, by the time your grandpa and Jethro walked back to the tracks searching on their own, Chester'd already got there. First thing they heard was a big caterwauling.

There'd be a scream, then a cow bellow, then another scream, then another big moo. So they started running. They come over a little rise and saw Chester had sat down on the ground and was looking toward the tracks. Then they saw what the Dawson boys had done.

"They'd taken a rope and tied the cow between two trees beside the railroad tracks, and they'd used that same rope to tie Wendy onto the cow, like she was riding it backwards. Of course in those days there was about six, eight trains a day running on those tracks, including two fancy passenger trains into Chicago from St. Joe. Those Dawsons was planning to give the passengers a sight when they looked out their windows and saw this woman with the cauliflower ear kicking her heels into the sides of a cow, both of them bellowing to beat the band.

"Jethro and your grandpa went over to untie her, but Chester couldn't make up his mind if he wanted her untied or not. Seems like he wanted to see at least one train go by first. But they let her loose, and when she'd calmed down and the cow'd been milked, she tried to fire up the menfolk to fight the Dawson boys, or else she vowed to call the sheriff. Of course the Dawsons had more muscles between them than all us Wilsons put together, so we didn't go. And Chester didn't want the sheriff called, because then folks would ask how his wife got in that predicament. In the end, she had to drop it."

"I heard the Dawsons was twins."

"I heard that, and I also heard it was a mule."

"What you mean, you heard, Jethro? You was supposed to have been there!"

"That's your version. When I tell it, I say you was the one that found 'em."

"All this liquor ain't gonna make you sick, is it, Sammy?"

"I don't think so. I should be able to sleep it off."

"Why ain't you married, Sam?"

"Hard to say, Uncle Jethro. Suppose I just haven't met the right girl."

"You're not gonna turn out like Chester, are you?"

"Don't worry. I don't go for women with cauliflower ears."

"I notice you sorta drink like Chester too."

"It's just that the ladies I meet aren't like those four sisters you all married. Not many women'd be content to live in one place and work beside the same man for fifty years anymore."

"Where do you meet your women that don't wanta stay married?"

"Oh, everyplace. At my studio, in my apartment building—"

"There, you see. You're looking in the wrong spots. Take up farming and you'll find the right gal in no time."

"But I don't know how to farm."

"Of course you do. You spent every summer on your grandpa's place till you was eighteen."

"I mean, my mind isn't made for it."

"Your mind's full of prunes if you think you couldn't farm as well as the next fella."

"Besides, don't farmers usually go broke these days?"

"That's like we was telling you an hour ago. The young men don't go about it right anymore."

"It was all downhill after folks gave up raising pifflebeans, wasn't it, Uncle Jethro?"

"I believe you're right. Now look here, the sun's almost up. Time I got to bed."

⌒ Wise and Foolish Virgins

Minnie Hemplethwait was the only piano teacher in Hickman. On Sundays when she displayed her skills at the Methodist church, she performed the hymns rubato. The congregation stumbled after her like a clumsy giant, forever surprised when allegro slowed to largo in the space of a measure. Minnie ignored the blunderers, dipping and swooping above the keyboard as if enraptured. Afterward in the churchyard men humbly tipped their hats in tribute to her art and her manicured pink hands.

Methodists all over the state exchanged preachers once a year, in May. To Minnie these pompous, black-suited men looked identical—stoutly married, with brassy wives who directed the choir and offered advice about how she should accompany their solos. She ignored the advice and went her own way, though she made a point of smiling while the wives talked. At least none had dared to suggest that she drop her musical signature, a clever arpeggio she'd devised as a girl, with which she ended every number.

However, this year the bishop surprised the Hickman church by sending a new type of preacher, an unbecoming bachelor. The Reverend Selkirk wore dark greasy locks and a round belly which he scratched while waiting to deliver his sermons. Everyone saw at once that he was unmarriageable, and no matchmaker bothered to put forward a local daughter for his consideration. A single preacher was scandal, but the worst was, nobody knew who would direct the choir. In August the puzzled singers took a vacation. They understood that they could not return until they found a leader, because the music was suffering. They blamed the new preacher for their trouble. "The bishop should've known better than to send us such a lump!" "Have you noticed flies are buzzing the pulpit now?" "And where did he beg those shoes?"

Minnie felt less prejudice against the minister's person, since she kept her back toward him during the service. But she did realize an advantage from his arrival, since she felt quite able to carry on without the choir. She filled in with instrumentals—a Chopin waltz or a tarantella rendered at devotional speed. She was less pleased when the preacher slouched into the changing room one Sunday while she was powdering her nose and asked if he could drop by her apartment some night to discuss the musical crisis he had unintentionally created.

The shock of his reverberating pulpit voice in close quarters caused her to miss some of his words, but she feared he was going to ask her to turn the piano over to a pupil and lead the singers herself. Then she didn't know what she would do. It would be a thousand times harder to ignore a preacher than a preacher's wife.

The next evening Minnie heard bold footsteps outside on the staircase. When she opened her parlor door the swarthy, boulder-shaped man rolled in on sailor's legs. It was the first moment when she saw him clearly. Up close, his eyebrows twitched ferociously; his blue beard sprouted like a forest. He flashed yellow teeth and sat spread-legged on the divan. When he complimented her decor—a wilderness of antimacassars, African violets, and crooked furniture legs—his voice sounded like a river of cream.

"Will you do me the honor of this lovely settee?" he invited, better bred than she had expected. She didn't mind taking a corner of the divan in politeness.

"I always begin church business with a prayer," he murmured, as if the habit was a weakness. She nodded resignedly, seeing that he intended to broach the subject of the choir directly. But when she bowed her head, she found the preacher's hand stretched toward her across the swelling sofa cushion. After a second she took it, feeling thick hairs at the wrist. Then she closed her eyes.

"Oh Lord," began the bottomless voice. She could not attend his words because the sound filled her with such unexpected warmth. All her fears about the choir were forgotten. The preacher now struck her as an extraordinarily religious man. Before, she had sup-posed him ugly, a fat chimpanzee bundled in a rusty black suit. But the harmless brushing of his trouser leg against her knee brought the blood rushing, and she remembered how they said in church that the spirit was a flame; at other times they said it was a soft furry dove.

"Amen!" the preacher pronounced at last, and when her neck remained bent, her eyes clenched, Selkirk stretched his free hand across her bodice and lifted her chin. Her eyes opened into his.

"That was like music."

"I see you are devout," he said thoughtfully. "We should pray together often and often. Maybe we should pray again right now?"

"If you please," she breathed. Without knowing, she slid onto the Turkey carpet where he knelt already on padded knees. His huge paw steadied her, and when she closed her eyes again the resonant voice sounded nearer than before.

"My angel, my starlight, my golden cloud." Her eardrum trembled and her lobe pulsed, feeling prickles like the touch of whiskers. She enjoyed the most soaring feeling, even after the bari-tone ceased. She barely noticed the preacher's fingers, so lifted up was she, and it may be that in her mind she remained vir-ginal throughout that visitation, for her own eventual soprano cry was more like the arpeggio she played to end the hymns than an outburst of animal passion. She never opened her eyes until he was gone.

No gentleman had ever paid her such attentions before. Even after weeks of late-night prayer, she had trouble focusing on Sel-kirk's solid, darkly clad person, for she was used to love taking strictly imaginary forms. The preacher seemed not to mind that her glance habitually drifted past his head to the ceiling; the expres-sion only made her face appear more seraphic. Surely he was also glad that she preferred playing tender songs for him after supper, instead of idly chattering. He only needed to murmur, "How deli-cate, how like the dew!" as she opened her music. When the last chords died away, he led her back to the divan, where his practiced address quickly molded her into a convenient attitude. Afterward, when he had slipped down the outdoor staircase and crept along

Main Street to his parsonage, she still reclined on the Turkey carpet, rearranging her skirt, whispering dazedly to herself, "My time has come."

Indeed, she was in her glory. Though no one but Selkirk appeared to notice, her flyaway golden hair now spun like a rich crown. The Methodist choir never found a leader—the preacher explicitly discouraged it—but when the singers returned in September, they found in Minnie's playing all the direction they required. Her melody line had never rung out so firmly, and her tempos carried a surging logic that everyone could follow after all. As Selkirk sat by his pulpit watching her press deeply into the keys, he must have congratulated himself on his spectacular luck. After the service as he shook his parishioners' hands, his eyeteeth gleamed. "Didn't that anthem lift you right out of your pew?"

Such compliments were as close as he came to declaring himself for her in public. However, Minnie never heard them up in the choir loft, where she was still playing the people out. Nor did she glance at the preacher in church. After the service she walked home to Sunday dinner alone, while he made the round of the good cooks' tables from week to week on his own. She perfectly understood that his attentions were not for daylight hours. She welcomed him only when he glided up her stairs on tiptoe, panting at the exertion needed to protect their secret. She was equally glad for him to leave as soon as midnight devotions were over. She had no desire for an ordinary mate, with dirty socks and breakfast-table fuss about the household budget. On Selkirk's side, the fact that she never begged for more must have seemed the greatest miracle of all.

At Thanksgiving as usual Minnie was carted off by her cousins, the Collinses, to dine at their pig farm five miles from town. They were a loutish, roughhousing bunch who seemed to grow mud when everyone else had dry ground. They showed no respect for music and treated her like a comical rag doll. At their table she could barely take a bite. The patriarch, old bearded, foul-mouthed Timmy Collins, forked sausage and hocks onto her plate like insults. She'd have preferred a slice of turkey and a spoon of cranberries, but Timmy snorted, "Here, little lady, put some fat on your bones!" Up and down the table she heard snickers over the lapping of gravy.

The Collins women resembled Minnie no more closely than the men did. They cooked with fistfuls of lard, cleaned spots from dishes with their spit, and their talk was all about the pigs, for which they had pet names: Dipsy, Shoeshine, even Bloodwart! Minnie gasped, "Oh my!" when they told barnyard stories, trying to hide her repugnance behind a mask of shock. After the Thanksgiving meal Mother Collins and her five grown daughters pushed back their chairs and carried slops out to the pens. Even from the parlor Minnie could hear them bawling to their favorites, "Suey! Suey!" as they banged metal pans together.

On her way back to town that night in Billy-Boy Collins's truck cab, she thought how she had no connections in the world but these. Her piano playing was known throughout the county, yet the only conversation she got was in casual meetings on the Hickman streets. "Morning, Miss Hemplethwait!" or rarely, "That was a sweet piece you played before the sermon."

She had never thought about her impoverishment before. Suppose she needed to unburden herself sometime? Suppose she had a silent midnight joy that only a bosom friend could understand? Oh, she could take pleasure mooning over it privately, all right; she was plenty used to doing that. But what if she needed to speak about it too, to make the sensation complete? Bouncing in the filthy truck cab while lummoxy Billy-Boy picked a second dinner from his teeth, she saw how foreign everyone was, save the preacher. It couldn't have been worse if she was sojourning among a race that spoke Choctaw or Mandarin.

The week after the cousins' dinner, Minnie gazed down from her second-story window as the citizens of Hickman walked Main Street in daylight. At the shop directly opposite, she saw how the women lingered just inside the door to trade gibes with the butcher, Mike Scullion, or gossiped in twos on the sidewalk. She knew all those women by name, but even from a distance the working of their red faces told her they were sharing secrets she would never hear.

Her pride strangely cut, she turned from the window and fell to brooding. She dreamed not of the preacher—for she already had him—but of a friend who never traded intimacies with the mob below, one who saved herself for teatime confessions in Minnie's parlor. This friend had blue veins beneath her silver skin, a narrow queenly nose, and hair like the preacher said: a perfumed cloud of gold. "My dear, I've been waiting all week to see you!" the friend would breathe, pulling off her gloves. "Tell me your news!"

Minnie counted up the women in town, searching for a proper target. Not a married one, she decided quickly. They were too smug and cow-like, stalking the streets in their black tents or wallowing beside their drowsy husbands in the church pews. They would pretend shock at her confession, and Selkirk might even be threatened by their gossip. Minnie would never forgive herself if, recklessly, she unbent to one of those. A single woman, then—one who knew which commandments you didn't need to take so literally, but who kept her feelers out for the spiritual side of things, all the same. Wasn't there anyone like that?

For days Minnie's mind met a blank. In desperation she clung to the preacher's sleeve at midnight. Maybe he was all she would ever have, at that. The beauty would be treasured up inside, but never told.

Then after lunch one day she looked down from her window on Darla Murphy, shouldering her way out of a shop with a handful of cigars. Darla stood a head above the other women in the street, and her chest was packed as solid as Mike the butcher's. She was secretary to Bill Beagle, the lawyer whose brick office stood opposite the Methodist church. The cigars would be for him. Minnie watched with growing recognition as Darla ignored a clutch of loitering gossips, but threw her flat Irish nose into the wind and strode off on massive haunches.

If Minnie was like the bank of violets that grew atop her piano, Darla was a white and purple turnip. She had a way of dealing with legal clients over the phone that reminded everyone of her boss. "Beagle won't be back till Monday, so you'll have to cool your heels." Her blouses were adorned with a black tie at the throat, and her wool skirts shone on the seat just like the lawyer's trousers. The main difference between them was, Bill Beagle's fat head gleamed bald while Darla's chestnut hair wound into a careless bun.

Darla felt clumsy around china and lace. She preferred coffee and doughnuts over thin tea in eggshell cups. Besides, on weekends she shopped and cleaned house for herself and an aged mother. When Minnie telephoned her at the law office, Darla took a minute to think. Then she answered pointedly, "I can only spare you ten minutes on Saturday morning. Don't fix anything to eat."

She and Minnie hadn't exchanged two words since high school. Darla supposed the prissy miss was up against some legal question, maybe a loose end from a will. Either she lacked courage to ask Lawyer Beagle about it, or she couldn't afford a consultation off her piano playing, so she was hoping to wheedle free advice from the secretary. Darla knew all the tricks and would shrug her off in a second.

But when Saturday came, Darla found herself lured across Minnie's parlor floor inch by inch and persuaded to sit at the knock-kneed tea table to hear the strangest cockeyed story anybody'd ever told. The longer it went on the more Darla thought about the cracks her boss always made about German philosophy. "Why, that judge's opinion's no clearer than old Spinoza! It's like reading a fat volume of Swedenborg himself, to figure out what it means!" Darla had long since learned all of Lawyer Beagle's routines and knew how to mimic them. "There's a man on the phone who's making about as much sense as old Spinozy!" she'd call out, holding a hand over the receiver. "See if you can figure out what he wants."

Now at Minnie's tea table Darla thought, The little miss has been reading those German philosophers to pass the time! Why else would she blither on about her soul's great yearnings and perfumed clouds of gold?

Just as strangely, Minnie kept turning the conversation back to the Methodist preacher, Selkirk. Darla hadn't much use for men of that sort. She felt more comfortable with Lawyer Beagle, who could smoke in public whenever he wanted; he didn't need to go sneaking. Darla admired old Beagle because he scoffed at all the crack-brained folks who made a mess and then needed a lawyer to help them clean it up. Certainly she and her employer were above the ministers who passed through town year after year—men who spent their days listening to every John Doe bellyache about his troubles without getting paid for it by the hour.

Darla saw at once that Minnie and the Reverend Selkirk would be two of a kind. Inefficient, foggy-eyed. But what did that have to do with *her?* Minnie's moony, maundering speech was the danged-est, far worse than those pleading phone calls Darla handled at the office. Even after two pots of tea, the piano player still hadn't made her purpose clear—she hadn't *asked* for anything yet!

It was noon when Darla got away. She knew she would never go back. The morning was wasted, and her poor mother would be impatient for lunch. As the next week passed, Darla also grew annoyed because Minnie's goofy words kept circling in her head. "A musician is so susceptible to a melodic voice, you see!" What swill! Yet it had all sounded lyrical enough, the way Minnie raised herself forward on her elbows when she spoke. Darla finally admitted that much. In her legal career she'd seen plenty of other folks whose lips trembled as they talked, but she'd never detected such—what was it? Joy?

Maybe, Darla decided, Minnie hadn't invited her for tea in order to ask for help at all. She'd wanted to share some spinsterish kind of happiness—not like the harsh ricochet of Lawyer Beagle's laugh, but—how could she express it?—a mood almost spiritual. This was definitely the German philosophers running rampant. She'd never seen a purer case. Yet there was something almost enviable about the way the fit had taken Minnie over, the way she'd looked so lifted up.

Therefore when Minnie telephoned to propose another Saturday tea, Darla paused. "I'll be there at ten," she replied, giving nothing away.

From Minnie's side, their first conversation had gone well. Darla had not interrupted with jokes about pigs, the way a Collins woman would. She had listened with respect. Minnie had made a good start on her confession, always keeping to a lofty plane. The physical side of the affair was little more than a piece of cold steak to her anyway; she didn't care if Darla ever understood about that.

However, their second meeting did clarify the fleshly tie for Darla after all. For half an hour she observed Minnie's fervor in describing the Reverend Selkirk—the flame that burned beneath his skin, the doves that fluttered in his eyes. Finally Darla reared back, sloshing tea from her fragile cup. "Why girlie, you're in love!"

Put that way, Minnie's rhapsody made sense. Darla had heard of such feelings as the first step in various legal disasters. Besides, Minnie was just the type to succumb. But Minnie, taken aback by Darla's exclamation, thought soberly while she stirred in another sugar lump. She wasn't sure if being in love was the exact diagnosis. In Darla's voice the phrase sounded common, like those jazz lyrics on the radio. She began to describe the whole business again, hinting at pleasures finer than her guest had perhaps imagined. At last Darla, whose face had begun to itch, burst out, "Why, you don't mean he's had his way?"

Now the desperate truth was plain. Frail, dim-sighted Minnie had gone mad from the lecherous crime. There she sat, brushing back her yellow hair and protesting that Darla still didn't understand: Selkirk was the Lord's instrument, and a tool of the Great Thundering Human Heart! Suddenly the unstoppable soaring voice became too much, and Darla rose from her chair.

That second tea party broke up like a bundle of sticks, pointy ends shooting through the air. Bewildered, Minnie saw her new friend rush out the door and tromp down the staircase into the alley. Darla herself didn't know what she might do to assuage the tearing pain in her chest. That weekend she nearly phoned the sheriff, almost called Lawyer Beagle, came close to spilling the whole mess to her aged mother over the supper table. But she feared the sensation would only worsen if she started talking. Sunday morning she skipped church, pleading a headache. Back at work on Monday, she made obscene typing errors and failed to laugh at her boss's wisecracks. When Lawyer Beagle left for lunch, she looked after him like a wounded bird.

At quitting time on Thursday, she called Minnie to ask if she could drop by for tea next Saturday as usual. Minnie had a music pupil waiting so she couldn't tarry, but she replied, "Do come, my dear," with relief. This meant Darla must've kept the secret so far. Minnie had nearly phoned her friend a dozen times that week to plead for discretion, only she couldn't think how to phrase such a craven request.

The third Saturday Darla arrived hours early and plopped herself down at the kitchen table where Minnie was starting breakfast. "I've been thinking over all you said," she began, while Minnie, still in her bathrobe, blinked away sleep. "I'd like you to run it by again, so I can see if I got it right."

Minnie cleared her throat. "You mean about the soul's great hunger?"

"That's the one," Darla nodded, lowering her eyes.

It took some minutes for Minnie to find her true pitch and begin to build. But with tea to warm her stomach, she gradually reached the first climax and was able to move on to the next, her arms beginning to sweep above the toast crumbs. At last her uncombed hair threw off sparks and her voice soared like a loose balloon. In the midst of this performance, Darla raised her head and murmured something. Minnie's voice broke, and she shook herself as if coming down from a height. "What's that, dear?"

Darla repeated, "Lawyer Beagle's a single man too, you know."

Factually, this statement was true. Yet Minnie stared doubtfully at her new friend, this giant ear into which she had poured her confession, wondering if Bill Beagle could possibly be single in the same blessed sense as the Reverend Selkirk. Ball-bellied, florid from whiskey and all-night poker, reeking of tobacco, with his sharp eyes, his duck waddle, his sly good mornings to ladies on the street—he was earthy at every point where the preacher was divine. Still, there sat Darla on the opposite chair, eyes wide with fright over what she'd just exposed. Suddenly Minnie saw that bestowing confidences meant that you might have to receive them. She took a breath for courage and smiled as warmly as she could.

Darla, meanwhile, was awash in doubts. Bill Beagle had never made the slightest move in her direction. He merely banged into the office every morning, remarked sourly on some fool he'd just passed, lit a new cigar, and disappeared into his sanctum. Lots of days she only heard his raspy call when he wanted an errand run. He drove off twice a year to Kansas City for what he called his fishing trips, and then he stayed away a week. Once another legal gent had remarked, "So the old man's away swimming in the flesh-pots!" When Darla hadn't smiled, the legal gent had coughed and said, "Oh, excuse me!" In fact she had never thought about her boss's private life before. But today as she sat helplessly in Minnie's kitchen, an image arose on the opposite wall. Bill Beagle was carousing in a swank velvet chair with a bottle of high-priced liquor in his fist. Candlelight softened the shine on his naked head, while slender young things in low-cut dresses teased him with feather boas, swaying and singing to a radio. He puckered wet fish lips to blow them kisses, heighdy-heigh, heighdy-ho!

There it was, the stab in her chest again. In the silence while Minnie beamed at her encouragingly, Darla was working herself into an unusual state. Words failed to come, though her eyes whirled and her cheeks puffed. Minnie saw her friend rise and stumble toward the door without a good-bye. Outside, the staircase thumped and trembled. Once again the hostess found herself alone.

Darla's departures might have been taken as rudeness, but Minnie's imagination now helped her to forgive. She understood in a flash that her sister's soul must be crammed to bursting with its own climaxes, which hadn't yet found words. She ran to the window and hallooed into the street, "Be blest, my dear!"

Throughout the winter Darla kept up regular visits to Minnie's tea table. Though she never managed to apologize properly, she never ran off looking apoplectic again. Occasionally Minnie noticed, while she was talking about her own soul's loveliness, that the cords in Darla's neck had tensed, her nose was throbbing red. But soon Darla swallowed her passion down without uttering a word. Minnie was grateful for her friend's restraint. It was exactly this sort of tact, in Minnie's view, that distinguished her and Darla from the coarse small-town wives they saw on every side. She only spoke of higher things, while the other delicately held her peace.

As winter wore on, Minnie also observed that though her case was similar to Darla's, there remained one lasting difference be-

tween them. Selkirk would be leaving town next May when the
Methodist churches exchanged preachers again, while Darla had
hit on a man who would live in Hickman forever. In her tea
table monologues Minnie considered the different satisfactions
that were their fates. She granted her friend the pleasure of knowing that Beagle would always be at hand; proximity carried its
rewards. But personally, Minnie found that Selkirk's physical visits
had grown almost redundant. Already she was anticipating the
time when he would become only a pure, tender memory. He had
enriched her piano playing; he had shed his aura of manliness over
her parlor and kitchen. He had transformed her life, and now she
was ready to let him go.

Darla didn't hear much of this chatter. Sitting quietly while Minnie poured out pots of tea gave her time to fix her own thoughts.
One week she recalled the first time she'd seen young Mr. Beagle
on the street, when he still had his hair, and the morning soon after
when she'd gone to his office to show how well she could type. He'd
looked her up and down until he raised her color, and then he'd
grinned, "You'll do." Another Saturday she remembered when the
lawyer had first laughed himself purple at something she'd said, or
the time he'd come back from the courthouse shouting that he'd
won the Pappy Gibson case, and made her drink whiskey before
he'd let her go home. All these years she'd supposed those were
simply moments in her legal career. But now she understood that
there had been other vibrations, which Minnie had taught her to
call by their right name at last. The problem was, Bill Beagle *still*
didn't know what name to call them by—didn't know what he
and his secretary had finally become.

Once, leaving Minnie at noon, Darla went into a shop and
bought a tube of lipstick. The following week she rounded her
mouth every time Lawyer Beagle walked past her desk. Nothing
drew his notice, not even the Boston fern she put beside her typewriter to mellow it. Then she threw up her hands and took to
seething at his thick-headedness. Was there ever another man so
unable to recognize the blessing Heaven intended to bestow? When
Beagle finally saw that her work wasn't getting done, he advised,
"Stay home a day, if you're off your feed."

After that when she came to Minnie's for tea, she would gaze around the parlor more hopelessly than ever, wondering why the silly miss had been destined to enjoy such luck with the preacher, when she had none. Ignoring Minnie's happy nods and sighs, she said to herself spitefully, They probably go at it right here on the divan. Or on this Turkey carpet. Him lollygagging over her with his tongue out, both their bosoms panting in the dark. Sometimes Darla's head ached so badly that when Minnie offered her the sugar tongs, she nearly shrieked.

Then in the early spring as the two women sat together, Darla shocked her friend by starting out of a reverie to exclaim, "The law must say somewhere the preacher's got to marry you! You've been wronged, even if you don't know it!" This opinion was the fruit of long brooding. Of course Darla had no idea which statute might force Selkirk to the altar, since there were no broken promises or children in the case. She simply wanted to see what might happen if they screwed the preacher tight enough. To her mind Minnie's affair offered an important test.

Meanwhile Selkirk's final sermon was only three weeks away. "We don't have much time," Darla told her friend severely. She barely heard the astonished protests—"Why, my dear! A preacher's wife's nothing but a vagabond! You have to direct the choirs, with those horrid strange pianos!"—but set her face and began to think of what threat or cajolery they might use.

In the cool evenings she started taking drives, leaving her old mother at home. She parked in an alley off Main Street between the Methodist parsonage and the building where Minnie lived. She slouched behind the wheel waiting for the preacher to skulk past on his way to his mistress, so that she could study his profile for weak points. When she spied him dodging among the shadows, she could hardly keep from shouting, "You've debauched a woman with no lawful intent! How do you plead?" But she reminded herself that he was Minnie's property, after all. Darla could frame the strategy, but it would only work if the little miss sprang the trap herself. Unfortunately, so far Minnie had rejected all of Darla's suggestions: a tearful scene, a letter to the bishop, a public accusation delivered from the piano bench in the choir loft. Alone in her dark car, Darla could only stare up at Minnie's second floor window until the light went out. Then she gunned her engine viciously, repeating curses she'd learned from her boss.

On the last Friday before the preacher left town, when Darla's hopeless disgust had reached full tide, she got a surprise from the other direction. Bill Beagle stopped at her desk just as she was covering her typewriter for the night. "I'll be gone till Wednesday. Fishing trip down to K.C." He winked slyly, as he did whenever he announced an excursion. Her role was to chortle knowingly. "Right, chief! I'll keep the poachers at bay till you get back." To which he would reply, "If old Spinoza calls, tell him to cool his heels."

This time Darla gazed at the round sagging face, the protruding cigar butt, the dancing pig's eyes, and she didn't answer. Instead she turned her back and began sharpening pencils. Lawyer Beagle stared in surprise, then walked thoughtfully out of the office. Probably she was suffering indigestion or a female complaint.

Darla destroyed every pencil down to the nub, thinking furiously. Both men were deserters, all right; they used you and threw you aside. She had known that truth already, but this time as she muttered to herself in the twilit office, a hideous thing occurred. The two men's heads, the dark and the pale, appeared before her, dancing side by side. She watched while they settled just above her desk and slowly merged to form a single oily, smirking globe. The masculine shape pulsed and glowed, now hairy, now bald. It leered and winked and sprouted a gigantic cigar which spoke in tongues. "Your honor and gentlefolks of the jury," it wheezed through a ring of smoke, "let us pray!"

It brayed at its own joke and burst insultingly like a rotten pumpkin, staining the walls with yellow ooze.

Suddenly Darla's heart stopped, because she understood: Selkirk, Beagle, every John Doe was really the same. Rough and wild on the outside, but filled with nothing but fetid air. That night and the next she didn't sleep. She paced the bedroom at home, and by Sunday morning she'd pieced out the implications of her vision. It was as if chains had burst. Darla saw that if Minnie wasn't prepared to act in her own behalf, any other woman might do it for her. There was nothing to honor about men. Darla no longer minded that her campaign had taken so long, since she was certain now to win. First she would nail the preacher for her friend; then she might consider exactly what she wanted from Beagle at her leisure.

That Sunday as she waited for Selkirk's last sermon to be finished, Darla eyed the pulpit almost calmly. She'd walked past the parsonage before the service and had seen his luggage crammed into the old Model A. He was planning to leave town right after the hand shaking, without even a public good-bye to Minnie. Just like him to fly away as quick as he could, Darla thought; he was probably expecting to take up with the next piano player he found in the new town where the bishop was sending him!

At length the sermon was delivered, the final hymn was sung. Minnie played the preacher up the aisle with a stupendous march fit for a host of trampling cherubim. As the church doors opened she modulated into a rhapsody, half Chopin and half her own dreamy benediction.

Darla hid herself in a niche by the vestibule and waited for the building to empty. Good-bye, good-bye, she heard them saying, oh good-bye!

In the empty room Minnie's notes resounded for another minute. At last she ceased and gently sighed.

Darla felt breathless, imagining the regret that must be racking the pretty miss up on the piano bench. Crushing loneliness and the longing for another chance. Oh, if only I'd begged him, he would've taken me along—

Darla stepped forward and coughed. When Minnie did not look up, Darla hissed, "I've come to help! But we've got to hurry!"

When Minnie still did not answer, she was grabbed and yanked into the changing room. Her arms were shoved down coat sleeves and she was pushed out into the bright noon air. She squinted as if she didn't recognize the friend who was forcing her inside an old Chevrolet.

The car roared up, swung into Main Street, and hit the highway doing forty. As they passed the last house there was still no

Model A in sight, so Darla floored it. Wind blasted in on Minnie's side and drove tears back from her eyes.

After ten minutes Darla pointed to the horizon. "Up ahead! We're gaining on him."

Minnie kept darting her nose at the windshield like a young robin. However, she did understand that it was Selkirk's car in front of them. She stared at the black glob that was belching exhaust and suddenly cried, "Go bravely, my love! Go on, heavenly creature!"

Darla threw her a contemptuous glance and turned her eyes back to the road.

They drove for an hour, two hulking beetles at full throttle. Selkirk lagged going uphill, but he glided faster on the downslopes, so the women were always drawing near only to fall behind. Finally the preacher must have noticed that he was being followed. At the gravel road to Lexington he hung a left, leaving a trail of yellow dust. Then the women lost sight of him for a minute. But when they rounded a sharp bend, Darla saw the Model A parked beneath a tree. Selkirk had already gotten out and was walking onto a wooden bridge that crossed the Little Platte River.

Darla drove onto the bridge itself before she braked. By now Selkirk was peering into the lazy water, showing them his back. Minnie sat humming to herself, oblivious. Perhaps she didn't understand that the man they had been pursuing stood only twenty feet ahead. But Darla realized it was now or never. She thumped her door and ran to where the preacher was whistling quietly.

"I brought her to you!" Darla cried. "I packed a suitcase! I bought everything new for a trousseau!" After a second, while the whistling continued against the gurgle of water, she added, "You can't leave her ruined! You know you've got a duty, now that I've brought her this far!" Her large arms waved and her skirt flapped against her hams as she waited for a sign that Selkirk had heard. But all she could discern was that the whistling had stopped.

Then behind her, Darla heard a car door creak. Minnie's shoes sounded on the bridge timbers. Darla whirled, frantic over the preacher's silence. "Don't be scared of the silly coward," she shouted to her friend, trying to sound disgusted. "I packed you a suitcase. Nice frilly things. Go on, he's stopped for you."

Still Selkirk did not turn, but gazed into the creek as if it was a window of dreams. Minnie's eyes seemed to focus and her mouth fell open. "Oh no," she gasped softly. "How could you ever think— Oh, why did we *stop?*" As Darla looked, the piano player's face blazed with shame. Suddenly she backed off and began running toward the highway. Her voice faded as she disappeared around the bend. "Just to see him out of town, like a final blessing, that was beautiful. I thought you *understood.*"

Only when Minnie was gone did Selkirk shove away from the bridge rail and look at Darla. No expression crossed his heavy face, but there was something veiled behind his eyes as he tipped his fedora, walking back to the Model A. He climbed in and pulled onto the road, squeezed past the Chevy and sailed over the bridge his former mistress had refused. Darla was forced to step out of his way and coughed as the yellow dust rose. She watched until there was nothing left but the rugged trail of gravel winding up the far hill.

When Bill Beagle got back from Kansas City the next week, he was surprised to find his office locked. He phoned his secretary's house at once. Old Mrs. Murphy answered and reported that her daughter was ill. The lawyer offered condolences and hung up quickly. He had a splitting headache himself and wanted to get home for a nap.

He was fit as a fiddle by the next Sunday, though, when he encountered Darla's mother going up the aisle in church, stoutly leaning on her cane. The sermon had been delivered by the new preacher, the Reverend Moffit, who had showed a welcome wit in contrast to the hellfire spouted by last year's fellow. Moreover, during the offering Mrs. Moffit had performed a pretty soprano solo with unusual trills. The congregation looked pleased at the way their luck had improved, and Lawyer Beagle bestowed some of his good spirits on Mrs. Murphy.

"How's my best girl?"

The old woman laughed, but then realizing the reference was to her daughter, she sniffed. "Acting like a child. She used to could kill a horse with a fist between the eyes, but this week it's been migraines and fainting spells."

Bill Beagle held up a hand in sympathy, but the mother went on, "Staying home's fuddled her brain. This morning she skipped breakfast, only drank some weak tea. She told me she's quitting you and running off to the city to work in a saloon!" Mrs. Murphy's dewlaps shook. "Excuse me, I shouldn't have told that part. But don't worry, she won't do it. I'll have her there at eight tomorrow morning, dizzy spells or no."

"I don't know how I'd replace her," Bill Beagle said, alarmed. "There's not another woman in the county who could handle those pushy ones over the phone. She'd make you laugh to hear her! Besides, who else would work for an old coot like me?"

"Old coot, ha!" the mother chuckled. "You were always a head-turner, Lawyer Beagle. If I'd been younger when the mister passed on, I'd have chased you myself."

They reached the door where the new preacher stood shaking hands. "I never would've refused you," Bill Beagle winked. "Only now I expect our Darla'd be jealous if we took up together."

He introduced the old lady to the preacher, while at their backs the piano sounded gorgeously in slow waltz time. Soon came the tinkling arpeggio everyone recognized, and outside past the door the sky was piled with golden clouds.

⌒ Bootlegger's Daughter

The bootlegger's name was Harrison Grimshaw, but his customers called him Shuffle-Two-Foot after the accident with the plow. Somehow he married a Pearse, you'd almost say by mistake.

The farmers drank on his porch every day of Prohibition. Folks drove out from Hickman at all times of the night and pounded on the kitchen door, pleading for him to tap a keg. The quality of his brew was what set him apart. It smelled like corn on the cob. It tasted like grain slathered with butter.

Nobody knew how he made it. He winked, "Blackberries is the secret." Another time he claimed, "I only light the fire when the moon's full." People repeated these stories, laughing but not believing.

The liquor made him richer every year. Though he still wore the same overalls, his wife began to order dresses out of catalogs; she didn't need to sew her own. She drove to Hickman for oranges and lemons, and made bank deposits once a month. The daughter, Cecile, showed up at the one-room school with bright ribbons in her hair when half the kids didn't know to wipe their noses.

Still, it was a business with a certain risk. Neighbors complained about the rowdies who drove past shooting hunting rifles at the stars, and once a cow got killed in the Perwinkles' field across from the bootlegger's barn. That happened even though Shuffle-Two-Foot was careful who he sold to. For protection he gave the sheriff a jug at Christmas, with a bow tied around the handle like pigs' ears.

Mrs. Grimshaw didn't let the trade discourage her. She marched into church on Sunday morning and left the congregation gaping, the way her smile glittered and her earrings danced. After the benediction she glanced around the churchyard, while little Cecile hid in her skirts, until she got a nod from everyone there. Then she yanked the child into the car and drove home. If she hadn't dared to show her face, or if she'd been more familiar, either way she'd have gotten no respect. But as it was, the other women couldn't bring themselves to stare her down.

Cecile had it worse on the school playground. She curled against the fence with her double chin buried in her belly, muttering curses while the other kids shouted, "Liquor Lips!" Her mother told her to sit up straight at her desk and pronounce her words like the actors did on the radio, but nothing helped. The girl dragged her body down the road toward home every afternoon, with shoulders sagging and neck bent as if to show the world how her father's reputation had shamed her.

Then came Repeal. Shuffle-Two-Foot had scoffed at the idea for years. "The politicians'll never let it through! They're getting too fat off things the way they are!" After the newspapers confirmed it, he told his customers bravely, "Sure, I'm still in business. I'm a habit folks aren't likely to break."

Taverns didn't open in the county for months. Even then, Shuffle-Two-Foot was more convenient for the farmers. However, people started asking, "How you doing?" as if he looked in poor health. One day a fellow honked at the gate and inquired, "You got any bargains for old friends?" That was a death blow, because it meant that soon he'd be expected to give it away.

His stock began to pile up in kegs. Men who used to swear by him said, "I never drink that rotgut! It'd poison a horse!" Folks in town remembered him as a small-time crook and never drove out anymore to buy.

He made things worse by bellyaching. "Mankind's a nest of vipers. They're ungrateful for the chances I took." His old cronies found it hard to sit on the porch and listen, even though he'd started pouring free samples to hold them.

When the wife stopped going to church with Cecile, the neighbors thought it was because of the fall in business. At the same time she quit coming to Hickman for fancy groceries. By now Cecile was old enough to drive into town for supplies, and any woman who saw her swaying along the sidewalk would run over to ask how Mrs. Grimshaw was keeping. By instinct the girl lowered her round head and blushed. "Still under the weather. Doc doesn't know what to think."

Then out of the blue the wife died. Word spread like duck wings, and a crowd turned out for the funeral. Old Shuffle-Two-Foot stood beside the grave, putty-faced, supporting himself against Cecile's haunch. He snuffled loudly during the prayer, but the daughter held steady as a boulder, her stark eyes fixed on the casket.

Afterward people jammed into the house, where Cecile had laid out a spread. She carved ham in the kitchen, her face pouring sweat and her broad back turned against the curious. Meanwhile, neighbor women opened closets to feel the linen. They were disappointed to see oilcloth on the dining table and linoleum tacked over all the floors. But their husbands knew where the kegs were stacked and rolled one up from the barn, not concealing their glee. Though they had stopped buying, they didn't mind saluting the dead. Some of them vomited on the grass before their wives could pull them away.

Everyone said Shuffle-Two-Foot looked finished that day. He wept into his cup and swore he'd lost his protection from the Temperance League. He'd never been much of a farmer, but now it was plain that he'd have to live off his crops and herd. Once he and Cecile had spent the money left in the bank, they'd be around asking neighbors for handouts.

The only person who stayed that night to help Cecile clean up was a cousin named Martha Pearse, a Temperance Leaguer who wore her hair in sausage rolls and fastened her collar with a steel brooch. Martha clicked her tongue as if the bootlegger's daughter deserved any misery that fell from the sky. "You got to start coming to church again," she declared while Cecile swept up mud tracked in from the cemetery. "With your mama gone, you're sure to fall. Anybody alive would, with that one for a daddy and oceans of liquor down at the barn." Cecile never looked up, but dragged her broom across the floor like a scythe.

In the following days Martha's conscience pricked her. After she'd told the other Leaguers about her prediction for Cecile's soul, she realized that she was duty bound to rescue her cousin if she could. She put off the visit, complaining that Cecile had turned into a sullen stay-at-home since high school, until she wore the subject out. Finally there was nothing to do but hike up the road to the bootlegger's house, a Bible packed against her hip.

When Martha stepped into the kitchen, she found broken dishes and chairs upended. Sitting in the parlor with her bare feet on a table was Cecile, looking like a mound of dirty laundry. She didn't answer her cousin's halloo, but let herself be found. Martha pulled up a seat, ready to declare how shocked she was at the ruin of a clean house, when Shuffle-Two-Foot tramped in with his dogs. "Hey, girl, the stove's cold!" he shouted. "Where's dinner?"

At that Cecile, who'd kept quiet as a stone, came roaring out of her chair. "Get back with the other pigs!" she cried, swatting him with her fat fists. "Don't you see someone's come to comfort me, with my mama fresh in the grave?" He glared darkly into the parlor, then ran outdoors with the dogs yelping after.

The uproar filled Martha with fright, but when Cecile hulked back to her place and silently collapsed, Martha took courage, seeing how badly her cousin needed help. She began describing the church altar decked with wild roses, but mercifully avoided the dangers of living around liquor. Cecile sat unmoving and let the sounds blow over her.

Martha came every morning after that. Cecile's face was always dotted with toast crumbs. She had nothing but foul words for her father, and her hair was a greasy thatch. Once Martha took pity and asked where the comb was kept. Before she was half-finished unratting the mess, Martha noticed tears rolling down her cousin's cheeks. Cecile muttered, "The last one to touch it was my ma."

Little by little the girl opened up. She waited for Martha on the porch, and the comb would be lying on a table nearby. As the braids were wound about her crown, Cecile confided, "My daddy drinks from a flask while he plows the fields. Every week he loses something else—a hammer or a tractor tire."

Another day she sighed, "Mama's plan was, I'd go off to a college where nobody'd know the money came from bootleg. I'd meet a young man who never touched a drop, and we'd live in some fine town. Now that's all up in smoke."

One morning as Martha came through the gate, Cecile tottered across the yard with only a shift stretched across her belly. Her face was raw from weeping. "Daddy came in my room last night, blubbering over Mama. But what can I do except roll him in a blanket when he's soused?"

Martha hugged her cousin's shoulder, frightened by the tears.

"I been so miserable, last night I asked myself, 'Why don't I just drink my troubles away like the old man?'" Cecile went on. "So I wrapped myself in Mama's shawl and traipsed down to the barn to look at the kegs. He keeps a speckled cup there on a barrelhead, and I drew some bootleg and drank it straight. Back in my room I threw up twice. The world's still spinning so I can hardly stand."

Face to face with sin, Martha uttered a proverb through dry lips. A spark of temper stirred Cecile's heavy bones. "What do you know about it, preaching at me and never even smelled the stuff! Here, I got to show you where he makes it, so you'll understand."

Martha gasped at the idea of looking at the still and broke away, her feet slipping across the grass. But a single backward glance caused her to halt before the gate. Her heart swelled with pity at the sight of Cecile's white shift whipping at the knees, and her eyes red as rockets.

Martha had no strength to resist when her cousin lurched over and clasped her hand. Cecile led the way past the barn, and the two stumbled up the hill to a thicket where the bootlegger's tumble-down shack was hidden. A hardness had come into Cecile's jaw. She screwed her mouth as if to conquer her disgust and flung open the door so that Martha could see the pipes and jars, gray with ashes from a fire. She waved her free hand to emphasize the horror. "Look how those tubes coil just like water snakes! Feel how this greasy dust sticks to your arms so you can never wash it off! And that's only the start!"

Martha's eyes rolled and she let out a tiny hiss, but no words came. Meanwhile the sight of the still had brought Cecile's color back. She gripped her cousin's hand tighter and jerked her down the hill, promising, "Now I'll show you the kegs."

Martha's feet followed helplessly. Behind a haymow in the barn they found the row of barrels, with one upright barrel supporting a speckled cup. Martha panted as if choked by the dung-flavored air. Cecile nodded. "Don't you feel how close it is here? And those cursed kegs like living hearts to share your sorrow, that they want to help you forget?"

Martha was close to tears. "Oh, what could it taste like, that it hooks people so bad?"

"You'd have to try it to know."

The darkness covered them like a blanket. No one would ever learn what they did here.

"You were in the devil's clutches," Martha wailed, sausage rolls trembling beside her ears.

"Not exactly the devil," Cecile replied evenly. "It's worse, but it's different." She bent to unscrew a tap. Martha heard a soft gurgle, then the cup reappeared and she smelled a sweetish reek. She shook her head to signify that she wouldn't take the handle, but found that her fingers were already grasping it. She peered into the bottom and saw a glint of gold.

"It'll make me drunk," she murmured. She had calmed the minute the liquor came close enough to taste.

"The men put away cups and cups before they're weaving," said Cecile. Martha stuck her tongue onto the drop at the bottom and held it there. Cecile advised, "Drink it straight. That's the only way."

Martha reeled in her tongue. "It's a sin," she pronounced clearly. Then she threw back the cup and took it down.

As the pain flashed across her face, a car honked in the driveway. "It's my pa!" Martha choked, dropping the cup. But when the two wild geese ran into the sunlight, they found that it was a rare customer for Shuffle-Two-Foot, so Cecile heaved off to find him. Martha lit out for the road, still swallowing to push the burning down her throat.

She collected herself for a week. Then on a cool morning she stepped into the bootlegger's kitchen and found Cecile moping over a heap of stringbeans. Martha's face was pink from her walk, and she began brightly. "I been thinking you should see more people for your health. You should throw a party and meet my friends from the League. We can stir up some summer recipes I cut from a magazine."

The four cars that pulled in the bootlegger's drive the next Tuesday brought twelve miserable narrow-chested rabbits Martha had bulldozed into visiting Cecile. They offered child-sized hands for her to shake and repeated, "I'm sorry you lost your mama," in dry, spinsterish voices. Inside, they spread pastel skirts over the dining chairs and passed Martha's marshmallowy salads. Their neat lips sucked tea from weeping glasses, while Martha kept the conversation on safe topics and away from the fact that they were sitting in a bootlegger's house. Cecile took the far side of the table where she could reach a plate of damp raisin cakes. Her hair shone from washing, and she looked so unusually decent that Martha could imagine her giving way soon on the point of churchgoing. Evidently a visit from the League was enough to bring even a bootlegger's daughter into line.

Cecile wiped crumbs from her chin and surprised everybody by speaking. "I want to show you young ladies what I showed Martha last week."

Without waiting for an answer she seized the hand of the nearest girl, Verna Perwinkle, and led her stumbling out the door. The others glanced at one another uncertainly. But they had been brought up never to decline a polite offer, so they gathered their purses and followed in twos. Martha's face crimsoned and she bustled to the head of the line. "Just what do you think you're doing, missy?" she whispered.

Cecile pushed stolidly past her. She led the procession up the hillside to the tumbledown shack. Alone, Martha raged back and forth across the field, crying, "Hide your eyes, girls! Don't even think of looking!" But the Leaguers had thrown off their shyness and pressed forward, because just then Cecile kicked open the door. They were expecting to see baby chicks or bunnies. As the dust settled someone cried, "Goodness, it's the still!"

When they had set out to pity Cecile that afternoon, they hadn't bargained on such rudeness. They turned their eyes away as if they could banish the contraption by wishing. A smile brushed Cecile's lips. Now that she was sober, the still no longer depressed her. When she was satisfied that her visitors looked sick enough, she swung the door closed. "I'll show you one thing more, and you'll know me to the bottom."

She tugged Verna Perwinkle's rigid fingers and the others followed raggedly down the hill, no longer able to imagine where duty was taking them. Martha ran after, urging, "Loose yourselves from her spell, girls! Loose yourselves!" In their terror they were unable to hear. They stepped into the barn and gathered around Cecile, who stood before the upright barrel that supported the speckled cup. The shadows were so deep that they might have been in the belly of a whale—except that Martha was charging through the door behind them, commanding them to fly.

"This is a rotten thing to do to us," Verna Perwinkle muttered to Cecile. "Our mothers'd kill us if they knew we were here."

"You think life's a tea party, but it's lorn misery and tears," Cecile replied.

Another of the girls, Pearl Jasper, peered over Verna's shoulder. "But are the kegs full?"

Cecile nodded solemnly.

"Then I'm getting out," declared Verna, tugging her hand free. Peering around the haymow, Martha gloated to see one lamb breaking toward her.

"You got to hear my story first!" Cecile cried. "Then anybody can leave that wants."

Verna hesitated, and curiosity overcame her. She edged back to the circle before Martha could run her out the door. Sighing, Martha gave in and crept to where Cecile was posing herself to begin. The bootlegger's daughter lowered her head and recited her miseries in a cracked voice. She told about her daddy drinking in the fields and her mother's dying wish that she go away to college and find a teetotaling man, until she ended by vomiting on the bedcovers. Everyone exclaimed, "Heavens!" their faces drawn with sympathy and disgust.

Cecile lifted her eyes and saw how they had hung on her words. She inhaled the rich air and declared, "I know my drinking was a sin, even though I couldn't help it."

Martha, flummoxed a second time by the story, nodded weakly. Cecile went on, "Martha drank some herself ten days ago."

The others turned to stare. Martha's glowing ears confessed her shame. Cecile said firmly, "That was a sin too." Everybody breathed together. "I won't take any more myself," she concluded, "but I'll draw some in this cup."

They were shocked by the gurgle when the tap was turned and retreated as Cecile came toward them, holding the speckled cup before her breast. First she offered it to Martha, who closed her eyes and shook her head no. Then she offered it to each of the Leaguers in turn. Everyone shook her head, eyes fixed on the cup.

Cecile paused at the end of the line and bowed her face again as if she was repeating a prayer. The cup was still visible before her. Suddenly Verna Perwinkle cried out, "I can't stand it anymore, give it here this instant!" She grabbed the cup from Cecile and took a gulp before anyone could stop her. She fell to choking at once. The others pounded her back while she flailed her arms. It was minutes before she could talk, propped against a keg.

One of the girls, wiping Verna's forehead with a snowy handkerchief, said, "See, liquor's not good for you."

Pearl Jasper whispered to Cecile, "I'll take it." Quickly she raised the cup to her lips. The others looked just in time to see her cough. However, there was only a drop left, so she didn't fall into a fit. "It only burns a little," she reported.

Cecile drew another draught. Now the girls passed it eagerly, all except Martha. One of them, giggling, tried to force it on her.

"It'll hook you forever, surer than shoot!" Martha declared, twisting her tongue with spite.

The carousers pretended to slur their words to shock one another and laughed madly whenever someone said the name of a boy they knew. Cecile kept her face like a mask. At last she pounded the barrelhead and announced, "If you don't want your mamas to find out, you'll need coffee before you go." Chastened, they followed her to the kitchen. But as she handed mugs around, she unexpectedly grinned. "Now we know a secret on both sides, don't we?" They fell back before her shining eyes and slunk away as soon as they could. Only Martha stayed after.

"That was wrong and wrong and wrong," she proclaimed when she couldn't get Cecile to look at her. "I never saw a more deliberate sin."

"You don't need to come here anymore," Cecile answered sharply. "You were never invited in the first place."

Martha's cheeks ballooned and she flung out the door. That night Shuffle-Two-Foot, who had passed the day in a cornfield, asked how the party had gone. "We'll find out soon enough," said Cecile.

Three days later Verna Perwinkle stepped across the road to knock on the kitchen door. Cecile sat resting her forehead on the table. Verna thanked her for the entertainment, then flushed. "I was wondering if, you know, your daddy has more."

Cecile looked up. "The whole wall of kegs. Why?" When Verna stumbled over the next words, Cecile nodded. "I'll draw some into a quart jar for you."

Verna pulled two quarters from her pocket. So she was expecting to pay. "Don't tell Martha!" she pleaded. "I promise I'll drink it slow!"

At suppertime Cecile laid the coins beside her father's plate. "That's from my tea party. More might be coming soon."

Shuffle-Two-Foot snatched up the silver and inspected it. He'd only made a dollar that week himself, so he was glad to see that his daughter had turned enterprising. But he knew the danger of selling to the wrong people. He didn't fancy starting a quarrel with her over nothing, yet maybe this wasn't nothing. He leaned back in his chair, vacillating, while the coins rubbed together in his hands. However, Cecile didn't bother to notice him and went to bed early.

Over the next week all the Leaguers except Martha made an excuse to visit Cecile alone. They wore frightened faces and hemmed around the point, until she led each one to the barn and drew a quart jar. They refused to look her in the eye again, for fear of seeing themselves reflected. At night she stacked the coins next to her father's plate. "That's over five dollars," she said finally. "I guess you can call the party a success."

"If it ends now," he replied gloomily, "before somebody's mama calls the law."

"If it ends now, it wasn't much," Cecile laughed abruptly. "But I expect they're the kind who'll want it steady, once they've started."

The bootlegger crumbled his bread without eating, wondering what spell his daughter had cast. He thought young girls drinking alone in their rooms was a sorry pass. He remembered the farmers who'd sat laughing on his porch during the long summer evenings, or had taken his moonshine on fishing trips. They were the ones liquor was meant for. What would any shy, sneaking girl know about its pleasures?

One night it wasn't quarters he found by his plate, but dollar bills. "A couple of them are buying extra," Cecile gloated. "Their friends are putting in orders."

Shuffle-Two-Foot barked an oath, but his daughter cut him short. "I been through nothing but suffering and I'll die an old maid, so I deserve whatever pleasure I can find! You're taking your profit, so keep your trap shut. You don't know anything about it."

The next time she drove to Hickman for supplies, she heard her name called as she stepped from the car. She wondered: wasn't this Blondine and Gemma Grossfogle, daughters of the dentist, running up to her?

"We heard about your tea parties! What a wicked girl you must be!"

They had never spoken to Cecile before. When she'd come to church with her mother in the old days, all the well-heeled town kids had stood apart in a pack, smirking as if she was only a side-show in the bootleg circus. She was struck to the heart now by the sisters' gleaming skin, their bloodred nails and yellow hair. Which of the Leaguers had told them about the party? Cecile couldn't answer them for a minute, wondering if the feeling in her gut was fear at being found out. She decided it must be rejoicing. Blondine and Gemma were prodding her elbows, making jokes as if she was somebody like them. They acted as if they wanted to buy bootleg, but didn't know how.

She took a breath for courage and said, "I'll tell you a story about how I been since Mama died." Blondine and Gemma listened politely while she started in on her despairs. They shook their heads sympathetically when she told how she would never go off to college and find a teetotaling husband, but when she came to swallowing liquor in the barn, they broke into musical laughs. Blondine said, "Don't drink it if it doesn't agree with you, goose! Give it to those that like it."

"Why don't you bring a couple of jugs along when you drive into town?" Gemma suggested. "Make the trip worth your while. I heard your daddy's moonshine's easier to digest than what they sell in stores. Nobody's family has to know."

Cecile was startled by their boldness. Their winks and grins made them lots more interesting than Martha's dopey friends. "I'll think about it," she muttered. The sisters left her with promises and sweet good-byes.

Next morning she packed a hamper and parked on the same street in the shade. After an hour Blondine and Gemma appeared carrying gunnysacks. They climbed in the back, talking as if they were glad to see her, but all the time they were shoving jars into the sacks. They handed over two dollar bills and walked off smiling like calendar beauties.

Cecile began parking there every noon, waiting to see who would call her name. Gradually business picked up. Trim young ladies sauntered by, people she didn't recognize. They knew her, though. They came up to the car window and remarked on the heat. "Time for iced tea!" they said and showed her the bag they'd brought to carry the liquor away in.

She no longer gave all the earnings to her father. She kept the dollar bills rolled in rubber bands and only threw the old man some coins to keep his curiosity under control. He'd become a nuisance, ranting about the law. "The trade's lifting me up just like it lifted you," she boasted. "Besides, the sheriff's a friend of yours."

"You see how high it lifted me!" he cried pathetically. "And the sheriff don't admire me like he used to, either."

Once Martha Pearse caught sight of her cousin parked in town and stepped over to the car. "I heard what you're up to, missy," she huffed. "You're a laughingstock, in case you didn't know. The young folks point when you drive by."

Cecile felt excitement in her belly, like she felt every time she made a sale. She didn't think the feeling was fear this time, either. She believed it was pride or even joy.

"It's only a matter of time till somebody calls the law," Martha warned. "Even if you stopped selling today, there's too many quart jars spread over town."

Cecile gave a cackling laugh that drove her cousin back from the window. "You and my old man are made of the same stuff! Don't you know keeping secrets doesn't matter in bootlegging? All you need is respect. If my customers are laughing, well, that's what liquor's for."

Blondine and Gemma came along minutes later. Cecile was glad to see them, for in spite of her triumph she felt oddly alone after Martha left. She tried counting up all the money she'd made, but this time the calculating didn't help. She watched as the sisters climbed in behind her, making the usual jokes about iced tea. They didn't appear to pay Cecile any special attention. She turned to face the windshield again, then became aware of a hand offering dollar bills over the seat. A longing rose inside her and she said, "You can take those jars for nothing. You sent me lots of business, so it's fair return."

One of the sisters cleared her throat. "Why, honey, that's Christian of you. We never expected favors."

The other sister sounded almost embarrassed. "You know, you might come to a party if you wanted. To see where it's drunk."

Cecile's mind was circling. She'd made them take notice, all right, but what sort of party did they mean?

Gemma explained, "On Sundays everybody gathers under the Little Platte bridge. A fella brings his banjo and a couple of us dance, or we lie in the shade and pass a jug of tea."

Cecile was surprised to hear that their crowd drank in open air. They were even bolder than she'd thought. The idea of seeing it done excited her, only she wasn't used to boys.

"Is there necking?"

"Sometimes a guy drives a girl the long way home, is all," Blondine assured her. "You don't need to be afraid."

"I wouldn't dance," she said. "And I couldn't go alone."

"We'll pick you up, of course."

After the sisters left, Cecile drove straight home. That night she raked through her mother's closet, searching for a dress she could let out for the occasion.

Shuffle-Two-Foot's eyes bugged when he saw his daughter at Sunday breakfast. "You going to church?" he asked suspiciously.

She shrugged, as if she wore a lavender skirt and black heels every day of the week. "Some friends are taking me to a shindig." She told him nothing else, though he drummed his fingers to attract attention.

She sat watching the road until two o'clock, wondering if the sisters might forget. Martha could have been right—the town crowd only laughed at her and wouldn't want her at their party. At last the Packard roared through the gate in a billow of dust. When Blondine and Gemma hopped out, she saw that two young men were sitting in the car. Shuffle-Two-Foot was hiding upstairs, so Cecile answered the knock. The sisters exclaimed over her outfit until she wondered if she might be overdressed. But when the young men smilingly shook her hand, confidence warmed her heart. On the way to the bridge she listened as the couples traded jokes about people she didn't know. They rattled on so long that she thought they must be trying to amuse her, though no one addressed her directly. She was almost certain now that Martha had been wrong.

They parked behind a line of cars along the side of the gravel road and hiked down the dusty trail toward the bridge. One young man strode ahead to scout for snakes while the other one came behind, warning Cecile to watch the nettles. Blondine and Gemma brought up the rear, toting gunnysacks. Conversation died and Cecile saw out of the corner of her eye that the fellow behind her was following closely. It made her stomach feel peculiar to know that he must be watching her moony hips ride up and down. Then one of her pointy heels stuck in the dirt and she tottered. The young man reached out a hand to steady her waist, and she saw a flash of blond hair near her shoulder. Anything might happen next. But they heard the sisters coming up, so she pushed ahead and the young man fell back. She wished she could have seen his expression while they stood together.

The plucky sound of a banjo up ahead brought a new thrill. She rounded the concrete abutment and looked down on the crowd spread in the shade beneath the span. Some were dancing, others lay on blankets—boys and girls in light-colored summer clothes. The surprise of so many couples, looking so rich and free, drove the heart into her throat. Everyone was a stranger; she didn't see a Temperance Leaguer among them. No one had noticed her yet, but she felt how great her power had grown. Open jars sat on every blanket. She knew they couldn't have had a party without her.

One girl pointed as she inched down the slope, staggering because of her shoes. Other heads turned to stare. "It's the bootlegger's daughter, all rigged up!" cried a voice. She had not expected to hear her father named. Next came a hoot and a whistle. "Who brought her?" somebody laughed. As she reached the flat bank, a snub-nosed boy ran up to demand, "Did you come to sell?"

Blondine and Gemma hurried down the trail to put themselves between her and the rude boy. "She came to see who drinks her famous liquor and what happens when they do!" Gemma winked to some friends.

Cecile couldn't interpret the grins that encircled her. But she remembered how her mama had stood up to crowds, with her diamond-bright stare and saucy earrings. She stiffened her spine and prepared to step forward. She would sit on a blanket, and maybe the young man who'd followed on the trail would surprise everyone by sitting down beside her.

In fact he was standing nearby, wearing an odd conspiratorial smile. When Cecile moved, he crossed his legs without warning and threw a lanky arm across her shoulder as if to keep himself from falling. Possibly he meant to distract the scoffers with a harmless joke. Yet Cecile was embarrassed for him to touch her now that everyone was staring. The next moment she noticed his hip was nudging her through the crowd. She felt too faint to break free. Waves of slender bodies parted for them, and Cecile could only duck her head to avoid the leering eyes. Finally she found herself brought to a stop, and when she glanced up, she saw a swarthy, square-jawed fellow whose chest was barely covered by his white shirt. He was standing alone, without a girlfriend in sight, like a rogue of nature. She forgot the hot feel of her cheeks, she was so taken by the strong yellow teeth and dark brow that blocked her way. The youth who had shoved her forward said, "Here, Billy-Boy, dance with her!"

Suddenly she was on her own, while the smiling muscleman looked her up and down. He smelled of drink and his nostrils twitched when the banjo started again. None of the couples who had been dancing before moved. Cecile realized that they were waiting for her and this Billy-Boy to perform. Hands began to clap around them, and she saw her new partner brace his thick legs and toss his shining hair. Abruptly he reached to grasp her wrists. "Oh!" she said, wondering if she could dance after all. But in the middle of the thought she found herself nearly twirled off her feet. She was whirled completely around, and before she could catch her breath it happened again. Billy-Boy stepped along to grip her flying hands and spin her across the dirt like a top. Her head felt incredibly giddy, and the sensation in her gut might be panic or joy, she had no idea which, because Billy-Boy pumped and pumped until the lavender skirt flew above her knees. Her calves knocked together and her feet nearly tripped a dozen times before a heel caught in a crack and Billy-Boy's hand reached out but missed, and she felt herself falling away.

She screamed as she hit the ground. She rolled back over front through the powdery dust toward the river, with no one to stop her until she struck hard against a weathered log. For a second everything was sickening blackness, but then she could see again and the bridge settled into place overhead. Billy-Boy was nowhere, but the legs of the crowd were running up to surround her. Voices shouted, and the liquory breaths of two boys fell on her face as they reached to prop her against the log. In her ear a mouth laughed, "Too bad, Liquor Lips, here, up and dance some more!"

Her bosom panted painfully, and she couldn't tell if she cared where the drunken dancer had gone. Then someone new bent down, and the face was Blondine's. The features tilted sideways and the breath reeked. Cecile saw that she had taken her jar from its sack. Blondine lifted it forward, coaxing, "Here, hon, steady yourself with this."

Cecile's mouth opened to protest—"I never touch it anymore," she would have said—but Blondine's hand was quicker. Cecile coughed at once, a heaving spasm that scattered the liquor from her throat everywhere. Blondine scooted back, exclaiming, "Oh, honey!" Cecile's body writhed helplessly as chokes pushed up from deep inside. After a minute it was clear she was going to die. No one in the crowd seemed to know what to do. She no longer looked human, lying against the bleached log with her eyes bugging and her face blue.

A lean, freckle-faced young man dressed in a beige linen suit had just descended the slope unnoticed. He saw the crowd gathered near the river and ran on stork legs to see what they were gaping at. He forced his way through to Cecile at once and bent down, his carroty hair falling in a shock above piercing green eyes. The others backed off, muttering, as he gripped her shoulders with his long white fingers and jerked her neck to straighten the windpipe. "Ahoogh!" she went, dribbling liquor down her front, and the rattle stopped. She gasped air and tears streamed from her eyes.

The freckled young man wiped her face, then got her sitting up against his bony chest. He made no haste to pull away, though she nearly crushed him. Now the crowd tittered at the sight of them, Jack Sprat and wife, both powdered all over with dust. A voice cried, "Give her a smooch!" Gradually her heaving subsided, and she turned to see who had saved her. When their eyes met his orange lips parted, as if he suddenly understood what a spectacle they made. In a minute he had her standing on unsteady legs. As the banjo started up once more, she grasped her rescuer's arm and sought the path that led to the cars.

Sitting inside his sweltering Buick, the gallant young man contemplated her round, dirt-streaked face. "You're Harrison Grimshaw's daughter, aren't you?" he murmured at last. "How'd you get in a jam like that?"

She had forgotten the soreness in her belly. She stared back at his dotted skin, his cavernous cheeks and flaring ears, thinking frantically, I don't know who you are. Did you go to high school with me, or did you ever buy from my dad?

When she didn't answer, he abruptly turned the key. "I'll drive you home if you like," he offered. "You must want a bath and a rest."

I waited so long to be pulled back from death's door, she cried to herself. If you'd come even three months ago, I'd be happy today.

"That's a rough crowd to get mixed up with," he observed once he'd turned the car around. "I'd be a little careful if I was you."

She gazed at the tender bones that lifted his collar apart. Facing the road ahead, he smiled confidentially. "I don't go to that bridge often myself. Drinking gives me a headache, and I feel more alone around those folks than if I'm by my own self. Isn't that funny?"

"I know exactly what you mean!" she blurted out. "I've seen enough of their boozing to last my whole life." Then she bit her lip; her confession brought back the memory of her disgrace. What must he think of me, she raged to herself, flat on the ground and spitting liquor?

As they drove through the bootlegger's gate he asked gently, "So you weren't there to sell?"

"Agack!" she cried deep in her throat. She felt as if the choking might start again. But the young man appeared not to notice her anguish. He had already jumped out and was walking around to open her door.

Shuffle-Two-Foot had been sitting on the porch pulling at a glass of brew, wondering where the trade was taking his daughter now that it had left him behind. When he saw her step from a strange car supported by a gawky youth, shoeless, her dress grimy and torn, he shot from the chair and ran to heap curses on her.

"Are you soused, Cecile?" he shouted. Then he recognized the boy. "Why, Tim Hay, did you do this?" Before either of them could answer, the old man cried, "If you been tumbling her in the bushes, I'll take a strap to you both!"

Cecile's hands were clutching at her neck to relieve the strangling. But when she saw her father rear back to throw a punch, rage flooded her chest and the power of speech returned.

"You old fool, get up to your room!" she yelled and would have kicked the bootlegger's shin, only she remembered in time that the young man was looking on.

Her father saw no reason for restraint, though. As he flung his fist at her he screamed, "You're not your mother's daughter! We found you in a ditch!"

Tim Hay tried to step in between. "She needs a bath and a nap, Mr. Grimshaw—" he began. The old man heard nothing, but elbowed the youth in his eagerness to get at his daughter. With a gasp of surprise Tim cradled his belly and went down at their feet. Cecile gasped, seeing her rescuer hurt. She grabbed the bootlegger's ear and leaned close to bite his chicken neck. The old man howled, backing away, and fell against the Buick.

Cecile wiped sweat from her forehead and stooped to comfort the youth, who lay moaning with his knees drawn up to his chin. "See what you did, you pig!" she cried at her father. "To the first one that treated me decent, even though I'd never laid eyes on him before!"

Her father pulled himself up against the fender and stared. "Don't you recognize that lizard skin? He's the Baptist preacher's boy. You must've seen him a hundred Sundays in church."

She appeared not to hear, she was straining so hard to pull Tim Hay to his feet. Wheezing, the youth asked if she was hurt, but she only shushed him. She draped one of his long arms across her shoulder and began easing him up the walk toward the kitchen door. "I'll brew a pot of tea," she murmured, not looking back. "We'll have the whole house to ourselves."

"He's nothing but a teetotaling holier-than-thou!" the bootlegger called after them, the cords rising on his throat. "You'd be better off peddling jars to your girlfriends—you'd only end up in jail and could still call your soul your own!"

Tim Hay's orange head bobbed weakly as he pulled one leg after another over the threshold. Then the door slammed. The old man, left alone, turned his burning eyes from the house toward the barn, where his last comfort lay stashed. "The preacher'll never marry them. They'll have to stand before a justice of the peace, and even so there'll be nothing but lemonade at the wedding party. Well, they'll get no dowry out of me! I've got one secret that nearly any man would give his eyeteeth to learn. But I'll take it along to the next world and ply God's angels with it before I'll turn it over to a noodle like him, that could get no joy from it!"

 Part Three

The Devil You Don't Know

The trains passed so close to Molly Greek's boarding-house that plates rattled in the cupboard a dozen times a day. The men who repaired the track rented rooms on the second floor; Molly and her daughter, Zena, slept in the attic. When Johnny Acorn showed up one boiling summer afternoon and said he'd just gotten a job at the Hickman *Sun* and could pay cash, Molly scratched her head and decided to put him on the enclosed back porch.

Zena, who was twelve, helped the gangly young man push the washing machine into the kitchen to make room for himself. She inspected his pale, narrow face, his ice-blue eyes enlarged by spectacles. She noticed the intelligent way his hands moved as he unpacked the battered suitcase crammed with books and maps.

"I was on my way to California," Johnny said agreeably, "when this water tower caught my eye. I thought, here's a place just the right size to be worked over by a fellow like me. So out I hopped, and here I am!" He laughed, spreading his arms as if he was a giant puppet who had come to play.

Zena decided to bring rugs and curtains from the second floor so the porch would look homier for him. "The railroad men won't miss this stuff," she said, trying to sound older than she was. "They can't appreciate what a braided rug does for a floor."

He thanked her, grinning. " 'From each according to his ability, to each according to his need.' Ever hear that one before?"

"Is it Old Testament or New?" she asked unwillingly. It would be disappointing if he proved to be devout.

"Neither!" He laughed again, his spectacles glinting. "I see I'll have to teach you folks everything!"

That night when Johnny took his place at Molly Greek's dining table, the railroad men winked at one another about the stranger's bow tie, red suspenders, and specs. They saw to it that the platters reaching him were always empty. No meatloaf, no potato, no cole slaw. Johnny drank his iced tea and flashed a smile at Zena, who was serving, as if he didn't notice anything queer. The girl was embarrassed for him to see the men's crudeness. She slipped over to him with half a peach cobbler while the others were still cleaning their plates.

"Hey!" roared Stan Posen, observing the girl's betrayal. The beefy fellow snatched at the dessert, but Johnny raised it in time. Stan only knocked a tea glass over on his own pants, and his chair fell back against the sideboard.

Hearing the clatter, Molly Greek flew out of the kitchen. "That's ten cents onto next week's rent for broken glass," she declared, legs apart and hands on hips.

Stan pulled himself upright and glowered at Johnny. "You owe me a dime, friend."

"Gladly, gladly," Johnny nodded, his mouth full of cobbler. He pulled a coin from his pocket and flipped it over the men's heads to Molly, who recovered in time to snatch it from the air. Then, while Zena watched, Johnny turned to Stan Posen. The lines of his smile had altered. "But in exchange, I'll ask a favor of you. Can you tell me what Comrade Vladimir Lenin has written about money?"

Stan's frown gave way to a pop-eyed stare. The other men's laughter died, and Molly Greek pursed her lips.

When no one answered, Johnny exclaimed, "Surely you're not ignorant of the greatest thinker in modern times! You don't suppose that dime's just a piece of silver, do you? Can't you see the tyranny of it, that makes your lives such a burning hell?"

His face had taken on a gleam that none of them was prepared to meet. The railroad men lowered their heads, while Molly Greek wrapped her apron tighter and slipped away through the swinging kitchen door. Only Zena could not take her eyes off him: he was more mysterious than she had dared to hope.

In the silence Johnny turned to polish off the cobbler and poured himself another glass of tea. "I love the laboring class," he declared at last, laying down his fork. "It's the only class that matters in the long run. But it's a dull class sometimes, because it doesn't realize its destiny." His immense eyes now searched his hearers like a revival preacher's, while the men bent over their plates as if to ward off blows. "I'll give you some advice, friends," he rapped out suddenly. "Treat every man as your brother and you'll have no regrets."

He stretched out a bony hand and gripped Stan Posen's unwilling paw. "To all here I say, unite!" He turned to Zena, who stood riveted near his chair, and shook her sticky hand. Then, white teeth ablaze, he strode out the parlor door.

In succeeding nights the railroad men ate quickly, not daring to look at the foot of the table where Johnny sat waiting for another chance to speak. He nodded to each of them as they ducked out after the meal. "Evening, Matt, Chauncy, Archibald." They stared straight ahead until they reached the front stairs and could bolt up to their rooms. Afterward he would wink at Zena, who was loading up the dessert plates on her tray. She didn't know whether to smile back or weep for him, for wasting his time on such thick-witted clods.

She brought him oranges at breakfast, and when he lay on his narrow bed with a book from the Carnegie library, she would knock and ask if the cat was with him. "Come look for yourself," he would call. Instead she perched in the chair across from the bed to watch him read. He turned the pages quickly, moving his lips while sweat poured down his forehead. Zena wondered what could be going on in his mind. The books were merely old histories of Europe, yet he seemed to inhale them.

Once, when he passed her on the front porch, he whispered, "Shall we bomb the post office, or take the sheriff hostage?" She laughed in bewilderment. She treasured those startling remarks, taking them as proof that he had come just for her, after all.

She began reading the Hickman *Sun* in hopes of finding clues about the strange game he was playing. However, none of the articles revealed Johnny's personal touch. The *Sun* only printed auction announcements, club news, births, marriages, deaths. The editor, Old Man Stewart, had hired Johnny simply to take down whatever items people phoned in. He wrote letters while Stewart dictated, and on Tuesdays he canvassed the Main Street businessmen for ads.

Out of courtesy, Johnny also insisted on fetching his boss's hot lunch from Lassos' Hotel every noon, and he delighted in learning how to set up type, even though it was not part of his job. "There's dignity in every form of labor," he said. "I want to know how to do as many things as I can."

Johnny's energy amazed the editor, who sagged under the weight of years and the pull of a great belly. Old Man Stewart had forgotten that journalism was a high calling, until Johnny flattered him one day by asking why he never wrote editorials. When the young man bent over his desk to compose a news item, his long black hair tumbling onto his forehead, Stewart thought he looked like a son somebody might have wanted but had been denied. The editor never smiled back and often barked out his orders, but after a month he awarded Johnny an unannounced raise.

"That's fifty cents too much," Johnny said at once.

"No mistake," Stewart answered gruffly. "Just don't let it go to your head."

"Well then, thanks," Johnny grinned. "Money is a necessary evil, at least till the new day dawns."

Stewart's eyes hardened. He hadn't realized his employee might be religious. That was an unfortunate soft spot. Afterward he began to notice an argumentativeness in Johnny's remarks that contradicted the smile. The editor pursed his mouth. He decided he'd been foolish to sit alone in the evenings since Johnny came to town, pining for his own youth when he might have fathered noble children.

The clubwomen who called in news to the paper were curious about the pleasant voice that answered the phone now. "Where did he come from?" asked Mrs. Deanna Pope. "You never see him in church."

"He's far better spoken than Mr. Stewart! Courtesy costs nothing, and a smile costs nothing. That's a lesson we can all learn from the young," said Mrs. Julia Moreno.

"Could he have picked up his manners abroad?" asked Mrs. Madge Terhorst. "He sounds like some foreign accent, the way he puts *r*'s in funny places."

"My husband says it's East Coast, the same as the bow ties."

"Maybe his family were refugees. Pearl Jasper heard him in the library, going on about the Russians. He knew about the czars, and the saints, and the author Tolstoy. Pearl said he got quite excited."

"He might've been injured when he fled. He has that little limp."

"That's from bending down all the time while he talks to Molly Greek's daughter. You see the pair of them walking all over town together, holding hands."

"The girl could use a new father, if Molly was to be so lucky."

"Why, Mr. Acorn's not half Molly's age! He'd be better matched with the daughter, if it came to that. Anyhow, Molly told me she's not interested. I said to her, 'Yes, and Christmas comes in July!'"

Ben Perrera, who doubled as city and county clerk, phoned the *Sun* to report the filing deadlines for local elections. "It's the same every two years," Ben told Johnny confidentially. "You could look up the story in your file and reset it without writing out everything new."

"I suppose in three months we could reset the old story about the results too," Johnny laughed.

"I reckon you could. There isn't much turnover in the offices, that's for sure."

"Why's that, do you suppose? Don't other folks want to serve?"

"I expect it's just a case of better the devil you know," Ben chuckled. "Moss Thayer's been justice of the peace since I was in high school. Hiram Husch has been mayor for fourteen years."

"What's the mayor's platform, Ben? Is he progressive at all?"

"Platform? I never heard him say. He's president of the bank, is the main thing."

"I see." Johnny's end of the line fell silent for a second. "How much does it cost to file?"

"Two dollars, if you want to put that in the article. But don't worry, nobody's going to run except incumbents."

"I'll be right over," Johnny said and slammed down the receiver.

At the mayor's Saturday night poker game, the story won some good-natured chuckles. "Ben Perrera comes running into the bank with his tongue out. He stands over my desk and yells, 'Mister Mayor, you got competition!'"

"Why, the young puppy!" said Old Man Stewart. "This is the first I've heard. I'll tan his young behind. To think I just gave him a raise!"

"Now leave the boy be," Hiram Husch said grandly, reaching for the pot in the middle of the table. "It'll be good experience for him to run against me."

"That'll be my pot," interrupted Bill Beagle, the lawyer who sat on the mayor's left. "You want to watch that the womenfolk don't get wind of him, that's all. So long as the men do most of the voting, you're safe enough."

Hiram Husch looked startled, not so much at Lawyer Beagle's warning about the election, but at the pair of queens spread on the table against him. He withdrew his fat hands and settled back to draw on his cigar. "Why does the boy want to run, though? He wouldn't know what to do with the job if he got it. He hasn't lived in town long enough to understand about road contracts. He must think being mayor's only worth the dollar a year salary it pays."

"That's what galls me," Old Man Stewart shook his head. "He's just grandstanding. He's full of fancy ideas about the power of the press and the beauty of labor. He should forget politics and start figuring a way to get ahead."

"The kid'll have to get beat up once or twice before he knows what we know," remarked Lawyer Beagle as he shuffled the deck. "Then if he wants to run for mayor, there'll be room. Old Hiram'll be pushing daisies by that time."

"Pushing daisies is a long way off," said Hiram Husch, sulking. "I got several thousand to make off that job yet, and I aim to keep it till I'm done."

Zena was the first one at the boardinghouse to read in the *Sun* that there would be two candidates for mayor. She showed the article to Molly Greek, who only shrugged. "He's a bigger fool than I thought. I don't want you studying algebra with him anymore. He'll poison your brain."

"I think it's interesting," said Zena, practicing her discernment. She often felt older than her mother. "He'll lose, of course, but the point is, he's willing to try."

"He'll get exactly one vote, no more. Your father had a lot of cockeyed ideas like that, though at least he never ran for office."

"Mayor Husch deserves to get beat anyway." Zena poked her finger into the batter her mother was stirring. "Stuck-up old toad. And his wife, with those emerald-green dresses and that spit curl, ugh! Doesn't she know spit curls went out when she was little?"

"That's what Johnny's been teaching you on those long rambles of yours, isn't it—to have no respect for your betters!" Molly pushed her mixing bowl away and glared at her daughter. "He needs a girlfriend his own age. That'd straighten him out in half a shake."

Zena flushed. "He's not interested in any girlfriends. He's thinking way too big for that."

The newspaper with Johnny's front-page story made a quick circle of Molly Greek's dining table that night. But the railroad men swallowed their laughter the minute Johnny stepped through the parlor door. Parker Volo hid the paper under his chair and all the men turned red faces toward Zena, who was bringing in the first platter of fried chicken. Her eyes were bright as she said to Johnny, "I saw your name in the *Sun*."

He thanked her cheerfully and paused to see if someone else might mention the election. When no one did, he pushed aside his plate and addressed the dozen voters he saw before him.

"It's true, friends, I've filed for mayor. A manifesto is forthcoming. There'll be copies on your dinner plates next weekend. Meantime, I'm ready to answer every question."

Silently the men tore flesh from chicken bones and lifted it to their mouths. They forked up mounds of snowy potatoes and chased peas into their gravy. At last, his smile fading, Johnny turned to his own supper. Then another thought crossed his mind and he looked up. "I trust you're all registered?"

Stan Posner's mouth went hard, as if some invisible line had been crossed. He reared up from his plate and faced Johnny head on. "Hell, railroad men don't vote! That's for plutocrats with time on their hands!"

Someone else at the table snorted. But before Johnny could answer, the big-shouldered fellow commanded Zena, "Clear away now, we want dessert." Then even Johnny understood the subject was closed for that night.

At the newspaper office Old Man Stewart put off his confrontation with Johnny from day to day. The trouble was, the press and free elections sounded like a natural combination, yet the editor was planning to order his employee to drop out of the race. Stewart was capable of doing that. But first he required a formula that would leave him a patch of high ground to stand on when he had finished.

The old man's trouble was aggravated by his soft spot for the innocence of youth. Sheepishly, he had watched Johnny write up the first big news story and headline it CONTEST FOR MAYOR! FIRST TIME IN FOURTEEN YEARS! He had seen Johnny compose biographies of himself and Mayor Husch (one "a child of starving immigrants," the other "born with a silver spoon") and place them in boxes next to the main article. Stewart had reread the front page after Johnny left the office and had bitten his lip. The next weekend he wasn't able to face Hiram Husch over the poker table. He felt humiliated at losing control of his own business. One part of him might enjoy firing Johnny, if it came to that.

When Johnny asked to use the press to print his election pamphlet, Stewart saw his opening at last. "Don't you have any scruples at all?" he cried, struggling out of his chair.

"I'll pay if you want," Johnny said mildly, gazing down at the white head bobbing before his chest.

"Pay has nothing to do with it! You wrote a news story about yourself! You turned my front page into an advertisement! You made it look like I'm supporting you!"

"Well, aren't you?" Johnny asked, his eyes expanding with moral purpose. "You're the voice of the people in this town. If you're not in favor of change, why then, I despair of anything good ever happening here."

"I'm voting for Hiram Husch like always!" Stewart roared. "What'd you want to be mayor for anyhow? It wouldn't suit you. Now just pull out. You broke a law of journalism, and you've got to take your punishment."

Johnny helped the old man back to his chair. "If you didn't want me to write that news story, you should've stopped me," he said quietly. "But that has nothing to do with me staying in the race. And like I said, I'll need to use the press this weekend."

"The front door'll be locked to you," Stewart replied, shoving the other's hands away. "And you'll be out of a job on Monday if you don't withdraw. What's more, I may catwhip you."

Johnny's customary smile turned into a curve of surprise. He grabbed up his hat and slipped out the door without another word. He paced the streets as dusk gathered, his eyes sweeping over the little town. He took in all its marks of peasant life and the shadow of the enormous steppe that lay beyond the last houses. Surely everything here looked exactly the same as in Russia or Spain, he thought. But could he force this particular place to open to him like a ripe melon, when he had no rifles, no allies, not even a secure hold over the local organ of communication?

Finally he heard a lonesome dog bark. He passed downtown again to look over the *Sun* building by moonlight. He discovered that the windows facing the back alley were unfastened. Then he walked swiftly back to his room, whistling, and lay across his bed to compose the election pamphlet.

"Whatcha doing?" Zena asked through the kitchen door. "We had Irish stew for supper. Didn't you want any?"

"Got some dessert left?" he grinned.

"Apple buckle. I'll bring you a dish."

"Then I'll read this to you, Citizen Zena. You can be my first critic."

Early Saturday morning Johnny stood on a garbage can and hoisted himself into the *Sun* building. He had never set so much type before and his fingers were clumsy. He soon gave up on fancy effects and crammed the words together without paragraphs. By late afternoon he had run off two hundred copies. Ink smeared his forehead and he had torn a thumbnail, but the bundle of newsprint looked clean and beautiful. At the bottom of each sheet was the sentence, "A new day is dawning workers of the world unite you have nothing but fear itself don't tread on me."

When he climbed out the window, he was planning to slip off to the boardinghouse unseen. But a cry of animals and a hubbub of voices in the air surprised him. Then he remembered: it was the second Saturday of the month. Livestock fair day. When he peeked around a corner, he saw men and cattle crowding the town square. He had been so intent on his printing that he hadn't heard the clatter until now.

The livestock fair was bigger than church on Sunday. People came from farther away for it. Though the hour was late, Johnny might still pass out some of his pamphlets, so his ideas could begin circulating.

He made his way toward a group of farmers who were talking about the stock they had traded. One of them was passing around a flask. Johnny greeted them and pressed a paper into a fat old man's hand.

"Here, what's this, young fella?"

"I'm running for mayor. This explains it all."

"Mayor?" The old man laughed and pushed the paper aside so that it fell onto a cowpie. "Hiram Husch was mayor the last time I heard."

The group moved away toward the trucks. Johnny snatched up the pamphlet and ran over to another couple, who looked at it up-side down. One man folded the sheets carefully and hid them in a coat pocket.

Now men were driving the last animals onto the backs of wagons. It looked as if Johnny had missed his moment. Still, he ran around the square, searching out stragglers. He gave away two more copies to farmers hurrying past. At last, breathless, he wheeled to a stop under the flagpole. He raked his long black hair and cried out, "Hey, everybody! I'm running for mayor! These are my ideas!"

An old woman was hastening along the sidewalk. She gave him a once-over and burst out laughing. "Good luck to you, sonny!" she called. At that moment another truck engine started up. Exhaust spewed from the direction of Hiram Husch's bank.

"Farmers don't vote for mayor," a far-off voice shouted. "We live in the country, young man!"

Johnny, who had been looking around wildly for some last chance before darkness swept the square, suddenly relaxed. "They don't vote for mayor," he muttered. He gazed down at the muck he was standing in.

Zena was swinging on the front porch when he got back to the boardinghouse. "Where you been? You smell like cattle to my nose. What you got on your shoulder? Are those next week's *Sun?*"

Trudging up the steps, Johnny raised his eyes. The questions roused him from a daze, and he smiled faintly. "My election manifesto. Want to see?"

The girl began reading his points aloud in the light from the parlor window. She had heard them the night before in Johnny's room, but in print they appeared even grander.

"Could you really do all these things?" she asked. "Start a college and build a hospital and put the hobos from the trains to work sweeping streets?"

A glint of playfulness returned to his eyes. "Why not, comrade? It's either that or shoot myself."

"But how?"

"Oh, I'd give speeches to fire people up, then I'd raise taxes to pay for everything. The construction would bring more business to the town to support the taxes. That's really all it takes, if you can just get folks to listen."

"Have you given any speeches yet?"

"A few here and there. Not too many so far."

"What'd you do today?"

"Printed these things. Then I gave some away at the livestock fair. Of course you can't expect folks to go along with new ideas right at first. A couple of farmers got mad when they saw what I was proposing." He stared into the pleasant darkness of the street.

"What'd they do when they got mad?"

He turned quickly, as if she had caught him off guard. But her innocent look brought his smile back. "Oh, the usual stuff. They started yelling that I was a communist, and one of them threw a rock. About busted the newspaper window—came that close." He showed her with his hands. "When they heckled me, naturally I had to answer. So I read out from these pages, just like Lenin's speech at the Finland Station. Then another bunch of farmers came up and started clapping, facing down the ones that were mad."

"What happened after that?"

"You should've seen it! Big fellas in overalls lifted me on their shoulders and carried me around the square. 'Johnny A. for mayor!' they shouted. Somebody even fired off a rifle!" He crowed and spread his arms, inviting her to laugh.

"Johnny A. for mayor!" the girl repeated, clapping her hands. Then she fell silent, studying his face in the window's light. "That was brave," she murmured. "You deserve to win so you can do everything you want."

Zena told her mother the story of Johnny at the fair while they were washing dishes later. Molly Greek had to admit that it took guts to face down a pack of insolent farmers. When she carried out her garbage—the last thing she did at night before going up to bed—Molly happened to see her neighbor, Mrs. Sally Coopersmith, sitting on the next porch. Mrs. Coopersmith, a widow, had watched Johnny loping off to work every morning and had been struck by his dauntless air. She found Molly's story about the livestock fair so revealing that she repeated it to her Sunday school class the next morning.

By Sunday evening Johnny's heroism was known in every Methodist house in Hickman. "Apparently a most visionary young man," ladies told their husbands. The Reverend Toppit was indignant that farmers would treat any political candidate so rudely. He wanted to have a look at the famous campaign pamphlet. Perhaps Johnny could be invited to address the men's club, if his ideas were sound.

Hiram Husch found a copy of Johnny's pamphlet stuffed among the cushions of his wife's chair later the same week.

"I don't know how that got there," said Mrs. Husch. "The cat must've brought it in."

"The most outrageous bullytripe I ever saw," pronounced the mayor. "We got a communist among us, the first one I ever saw. That's why I didn't recognize him sooner. We'll run him out of town on a rail. Tar and feathers would be too good."

"He's not such a bad boy," Mrs. Husch said carefully. "Some of those words sound almost pretty. Not that he knows what he's talking about, I'm sure," she added, seeing her husband rise on his toes. "It'd be a disaster if he was elected."

"Disaster is right," the mayor replied. "Disaster to your pin money, for one thing."

At the next poker game Old Man Stewart dealt to the mayor. "I fired the boy twice this week. I especially fired him for using my printing press. Then I fired him for campaigning over my telephone. When the women call in with club news, I can tell he must be talking to them about his danged pamphlet, the way he looks like a tomcat licking its whiskers. 'Why, how nice of you, Missus Blandings!' he says so smooth it'd turn your stomach."

"Pass the whiskey," said the mayor.

"You got a month till the election," observed Lawyer Beagle, "if you want to hold onto the job."

"The women wouldn't really vote for him," said the mayor finally. "The men'll vote for me, and they'll carry their wives along like always."

Bill Beagle cleared his throat. "Half the men in town are too busy to register, is one problem. But their wives have got plenty of time to slip down to the courthouse while the kids are in school and the old man's at work."

"Registration just closed," observed Stewart.

"Been lots of foot traffic past my law office all week," said Bill Beagle. "Ladies on their way to the courthouse every time I looked."

The mayor downed a tumblerful of whiskey and poured another.

"I fold," he said and slid his cards onto the table. "Boys, we got to do something or those road contracts will be lost to me."

"And the new water contract," Stewart threw in anxiously. Deep in his bones the editor felt certain that his friend had a right to profit by those public works projects. It was a natural tribute to his position at the bank. It was not corrupt at all.

Johnny was the corrupt one, Old Man Stewart thought bitterly, with his dang-fool ideas that a million dollars couldn't accomplish. How could a town like Hickman afford a hospital or a college? Who would pay those hobos that Johnny wanted to put to work? You could mislead the public badly if you promised things like that.

"You got any more whiskey?" Stewart asked. "We're awful dry tonight."

The game didn't break up until two in the morning. Even then the night didn't feel finished to the players. "Let's run the young devil out of town on a rail," said Hiram Husch, stumbling up from his chair.

"Damn right," said Bill Beagle, a pool of saliva sliding down his chin. "Send the communist back to Russia."

"I'll go along and report the story," said the editor, grabbing up the last bottle.

Johnny awoke to a rattling on the back door of his porch. As he rose from bed, he heard a high-pitched man's voice singing. He pulled on his pants and, seeing who it was, invited the old men inside. He put a hand on Bill Beagle's shoulder to quiet him. Then the three patriarchs took places on the bed, while Johnny faced them from his only chair.

"You got any liquor, son?" the lawyer asked. A cigar moved in his mouth, dribbling ash down his vest.

Johnny shook his head soberly.

Suddenly Old Man Stewart emitted a surprising wail. "How could you break into my shop like that? I would've turned the business over to you in a couple of years, if you'd only played by the rules."

Johnny's eyes widened as the editor folded in on his stomach like a cat surrounding a ball. Lawyer Beagle was asleep at the foot of the bed, his shoulder rounded against the wall. "Repose," murmured the mayor, "before battle."

Johnny waited, but no more words came. He stood up and helped his opponent stretch out on the bed. He pulled Old Man Stewart into the chair, where his wrinkled head fell back on the antimacassar. Then he maneuvered the lawyer's body across the mattress behind the mayor. Finally, Johnny lifted the men's shoes off, all six, and spread blankets up to their chins. Mouths opened in painful snores as he slipped into Molly Greek's parlor, where he plumped his jacket into a pillow and lay down on the sofa to try to sleep.

November third dawned white with hoarfrost. Only a few men wearing overalls stood quietly in line on the courthouse steps when the polls opened at seven. After they voted, there was a lull. At eight-thirty the first trickle of women appeared, widows and well-to-do spinsters who had no families to get off to work or school. Some of them lingered after their business was done and traded a few remarks with the poll watchers before wandering away. Late in the morning a circle of young mothers stopped by and briefly filled the polling room with their chatter. They minded one another's babies while the voting took place in a corner, and went out into the street together. Then the businessmen from Main Street came to vote on their lunch hour. Now there was loud confident laughter and the trading of weather forecasts for the winter. No women appeared then at all; most of them were back at home getting ready to serve a hot meal. But other housewives did hurry into the courthouse alone between one and four. These were middle-aged women who had been too busy to leave their houses in the morning. On their way to buy last-minute groceries or meet their children after school, they darted in and ran out a minute later without two words to anybody, brushing their hands against their coats. Finally half a dozen tired, silent husbands cast ballots when they got off work between four-thirty and six. By that time all the women were back in their kitchens again, peeling potatoes or heating up the oven. As the poll watchers closed the big oaken doors after the last voter had left, they remarked to one another, "Never seen so many ladies before, did you?"

Four of the poll watchers were men, two were women. They had all performed this job for years. They only wanted to see that the counting went smoothly now. As soon as they'd finished the plate of sandwiches brought over from Lassos' Hotel, they unlocked the ballot boxes and got out their pencils.

"I'll mark down for the mayor's race," said Mrs. Cora MacInnes.

"I'll read out the votes to you," said Mrs. Edna Kvasnika.

"No need for you ladies to mark anything down at all. We men can count by ourselves for a change. We don't mind staying up late. You run on home to your husbands."

Mrs. Edna Kvasnika did not look up. "One for Johnny Acorn." Mrs. Cora MacInnes adjusted her spectacles and made the first black line on her pad.

The tabulation went slowly. The man who had unlocked the ballot boxes doled out the papers in little handfuls. Not until nine o'clock were all the votes tallied. Then Mrs. Cora MacInnes announced the results. In the mayor's race the total for the first precinct was 73 to 32. For the second it was 65 to 38. For the third it was 60 to 41.

"Looks like we got a new mayor," she said, drawing a square around the figures.

The man who had been doling out the ballots looked blankly at the man beside him. "What do you think, Harry?"

"I think we need a recount, is what."

The second tally required another hour, because this time the man who passed the ballots to Mrs. Edna Kvasnika fingered each one as if testing for counterfeit paper. Finally the numbers were confirmed. "What's next?" asked one of the men.

"Why, we type up the numbers and you read them out on the courthouse steps like always," said Mrs. Cora MacInnes.

"I think I'll phone the mayor first," said a man.

"Lock up the ballots, then call whoever you want," she answered, ripping off her tally sheet.

Ten minutes later Hiram Husch stormed into the courthouse.

"Go home now, Cora, Edna," he commanded. "We got to check this again."

"You're not mayor anymore, Mr. Husch," said Mrs. Edna Kvasnika. "We don't have to take orders from anybody, you know."

When the results were read to the crowd outside, a thin cheer arose among many boos. Folks craned to see if Johnny would step forward and make another speech like the one he'd given at the livestock fair, which none of the townspeople had heard. But though an encouraging silence fell, no Johnny appeared. His absence was curious. Hadn't he stood among them on the steps just minutes ago, grinning down at the ladies, saluting the gents? It seemed out of character for such a bold young man to be scared off by a few catcalls. Disappointed that there would be no show, folks drifted off home. The women said nothing, walking beside their husbands. The men shoved their hands deep in their pockets, wondering how such an upset could have happened.

The next morning when Johnny showed up for work, Old Man Stewart fired him for good. "The mayor's salary is a dollar a year," the editor said savagely. "Live on that if you can."

That afternoon Johnny walked up to the front porch and collapsed beside Zena in the swing. "I'll never budge 'em," he muttered, kicking at the floor. "The ones who voted for me don't count."

"Budge who?" the girl asked. Instead of answering, he told her about being fired.

Zena took in this news, studying his thin, unreachable smile. "You could work on the railroad, I bet," she offered. "Your muscles would get big as Stan Posen's."

"I could," he nodded. "Taste the sweat, pitch in beside my fellow man. Only it's not mental work," he added, staring off where the tracks hit the Hickman station and disappeared beyond. "It's not fighting work either. My brain would get like the others' if I did what they do."

"When're you going to start all those projects you promised?" the girl asked sternly. She wanted him to sound more hopeful. She wasn't used to the way he looked with no plans.

He gazed away at the two gleaming tracks that vanished in trees a long way off. "The first city council meeting's not till December. I'll have to see how far the members will go. They'll have all the votes. Besides, I haven't researched how to build a college or a hospital yet."

"You got two years in your term."

"True." He glanced at her, and his face nearly took on the old spark for a second. "You can build a whole world in two years, can't you? The Great War only took four."

"Mama'll let you stay on without work if you ask," the girl said confidentially. "She's let others before now."

The first clubwoman who phoned the *Sun* the morning after the election got Old Man Stewart to take down her news item. When she asked where Johnny was, the editor exploded, "Gone to blazes like the rest of his kind!" The clubwoman pulled her ear back from the receiver in shock.

It didn't take a week for Stewart to drop around to Molly Greek's boardinghouse in search of his former employee. His news sources had dried up overnight, forcing him to put out an edition that was ninety percent ads and no society items whatsoever.

Zena was swinging on the porch again, wrapped in her heavy coat, when the editor came haltingly up the front steps. "Where is he?" Stewart asked with no introduction, though he had never spoken to the child before.

"Out walking, I expect."

"Did he find another job?"

"No."

"Tell him to come see me in the morning. Or shall I leave a note?"

"I'll tell him." But as the old man turned to ease himself down again, she added pitilessly, "I doubt he'll come. Mama says he's cut his ties."

"He needs to eat like everybody else, don't he? Can't live off being mayor," Stewart snorted. "He wouldn't know how to make it pay."

Meanwhile Johnny was walking about the town in everwidening circles. He told Zena he was searching out the secrets of his new domain. He had counted pine trees and dormer windows and tabby cats and picket fences and lightning rods. In the alleys behind Main Street he had also kicked stones in the mud wallows where truck tires got stuck.

Then he found a stout stick and strode along faster with it to pace out the blocks. He used it like a rifle, taking aim at ducks passing overhead or returning the fire of little boys. He left the boardinghouse each morning as if he was going off to work. He didn't trouble Molly Greek about lunch; instead he stopped by the Carnegie library for an hour to read the out-of-town papers that arrived by mail. Their news seemed to leave him inflamed. He only nodded briefly to the librarian before bursting red-faced into the street. He gazed right and left ferociously for a minute, until he recognized where he was. Then he set off in some direction, cursing all plutocrats and fascists to perdition. But half an hour later he was whistling again. When he wore out the town with his rambles, he followed the train track as far as Five Mile Bridge.

At Molly Greek's dinner table the railroad men no longer feared him. They joked about their work or somebody's girlfriend as they had in the old days, ignoring him. Zena still stood beside the kitchen door facing Johnny, watching to see if he would look up from his food. But when he did, the faraway expression never left his face. At night he sat alone beside the big walnut radio in the parlor listening to the comedians, waiting for the bulletins from overseas.

"I'll never get any more money out of him," Molly Greek sighed one morning after he banged out the front door to begin his walk. It was a drizzly winter Saturday when a normal fellow might have found some reason to stay inside. "He'll never turn a hand in this town again."

Zena explained to her mother patiently. "He's made his promises, and now he's keeping to himself while he figures how to carry them out, that's all."

Molly looked at her daughter in surprise. "Putting tramps to work, and building a college and a hospital? Why, child, nobody could do those things. My taxes would go sky-high if he tried! The folks who voted for him didn't want any of that! It was mainly just his face they liked." She shook herself and picked up a mop. "Here, take this and get started."

As Zena began her weekend chores, she added matter-of-factly, "When he walks around town, folks call him Mister Mayor. If he went anywhere else, he couldn't have that."

The next morning fell sunny but bitterly cold. After breakfast mother and daughter wrapped themselves in wool and walked to church as usual. The railroad men were mostly visiting their own people, if they lived within driving distance of town. One fellow was sleeping off a bad head upstairs, and another was washing his clothes in the kitchen. This was the atheist, Matt Opey. Fortunately, Molly thought atheism was a joke and didn't mind him.

When Molly and Zena got home at noon, Matt Opey met them in the parlor. "He caught the ten-forty to Chicago. He said there's a war going on, so he's joining up to save Spain. He said he'll have a better chance over there than against the city council. He left you most of his things to sell, to pay what he owes."

Matt Opey shook his head, as if Johnny's escape was bad business. Zena gave a cry and rushed to the back porch to see if the news could be true.

Old Man Stewart had less reason to doubt the story, when he heard it at the Husches' house on Sunday evening. "I knew when he wouldn't come back to work that his brain had gone peculiar."

Hiram Husch laughed at the editor's doleful face. "I got Lawyer Beagle researching the case right now. I think we're going to declare him deceased. We got to call another election, and it might take forever if we waited to make sure he's not coming back."

Molly Greek stepped onto the porch and glanced around at Johnny's unmade bed and scattered papers. "The plutocrats have driven him out!" Zena sobbed. "They couldn't stand that he was better than they are."

"That's the first thing you got to learn about men: give them what they want and they hit the road every time," said the girl's mother. To herself she added, Especially when they're still wet behind the ears.

"I expect I'm finished with vote counting," said Mrs. Cora Mac-Innes to her husband that night over cold pot roast. "The men can do the job by themselves if there's another election this winter."

"We can't declare him legally dead for seven years." Lawyer Beagle shook his jowls, accepting a late-night cup of punch from Hiram Husch. "What's more, the town charter says if the mayor can't perform his duties, the council picks a successor from among themselves to fill in till the next regular election."

"They'll choose Jesse Leach!" cried the banker, pounding a fist on the arm of his chair. "He's always wanted to sneak into my place. Now why'd that young Acorn run off? I could've whipped him next election without half trying. Leach'll be a danged sight harder to get rid of. He knows how much the job's really worth."

⌒ Marked by the Lamb

Shortly after he turned twelve, his grandfather summoned him behind the chicken house to the wet ground where they dug for fishing worms. This time the worm digging was mainly an excuse for them to be alone, because while Grandpa forked over the black earth he said in an offhand yet solemn voice, "You know, Jerry, you've been marked for good."

The boy looked down to see if mud had spattered on his jeans, but he could find nothing. "Marked how, Grandpa?"

The old man plunged the fork again. "You're marked by the Lamb. We're all marked by Him in this family, but you especially. For a special purpose."

Jerry looked off at the hilly field where the sheep grazed while his grandfather explained about his fate. He learned that the family had held a council around the dining table one night after he was in bed. The preacher had driven out from Hickman, and Jerry's uncles had come from up the road. They had listened to Scripture, the preacher had prayed, and the upshot was this offer for him to pledge himself to the ministry of God.

"If you choose the right path, the first step'll be to read the divinity books the preacher left. Later we'll send you to a seminary on profits from the harvests the Lord'll provide. Someday you'll marry a good woman who can direct your choir."

The boy stooped and began piling up handfuls of muck to hide his confusion. He had expected to become another farmer, or a cattle rancher out West. The truth sank in as he sat alone in the parlor that summer, memorizing Scripture and trying not to wrinkle his good wool pants. However, there would be no chance to reconsider. Every time they went fishing together, his grandfather repeated the story of Abraham and Isaac to help him accept his calling.

When he gazed out the parlor window at the ripening wheat now, he felt a distance. If men gathered on the porch after supper to tell about sharp cattle trades or made low smutty jokes the women shouldn't overhear, he kept to a corner so his blushes wouldn't show. His grandfather had been right about him, time proved. What the old man had detected, he'd called the makings of a parson, but it went deeper. The boy wouldn't insist on struggling; he could tolerate a riddle better than most folks.

At school the children mocked: "Preacher Jerry!" The guys he'd once played ball with—Jayjay, Pepper, Rob, and the rest—shook their hands like Holy Rollers and taunted, "Read us a sermon, there's sinners among us!" When they huddled in the yard to discuss the secrets of women, they hooted if he tried to listen. He digested their contempt with eyes lowered. After all, his friends were only helping to safeguard his calling. In fact there might be things the others knew that he should never learn.

The next spring his grandmother, who was always full of mysterious plans, told him, "Stop at the preacher's house after school. You're starting a course of special instruction." Evidently Reverend Broadshears intended to use those sessions with Jerry to practice his sermons. As soon as the study door closed behind them, the old man reared up on his toes and began flinging his arms in circles above Jerry's head. "Where does sin come from, my son? What's the secret of it? Does it breed in the rivers or the hills, or is it a weed in the soul of Man?"

Jerry's mind shifted desperately, trying to form a reply. Luckily the preacher wasn't used to being interrupted. Fixing him with stark, bloodshot eyes, old Broadshears went on, "Faith is a mystery, who can know it? Those of the Elect, why were they singled out?" The boy could only bend under the barrage; the ringing in his ears drove out every thought. "Ours is not to reason why!" pealed the answer, as the preacher thrust open the door to call for a cup of tea.

Jerry was relieved that half the time his tormenter was away on sick calls when he knocked. Consequently he wasn't missed one afternoon when he hurried past the parsonage and ducked into the town park, where he sat on the bandstand steps to gather courage for another of those bewildering interviews. Hopelessness gnawed at him. He wasn't making progress at religion like he did in his subjects at school. Half the questions had no solutions, and the other half were paradoxes, which meant they went the opposite of whichever way he guessed.

He leaned into the bandstand's shadow and watched for spies from the church who would know he was hiding out. Across the green, youngsters were clambering onto a merry-go-round, while fleecy clouds grazed over the sky. Jerry remembered the woolly-haired preacher shaking hands in the churchyard after Sunday services. The parishioners murmured their hellos respectfully, then drew apart under the trees to gossip. After the line had passed him by, the old man let his speckled hand fall. He turned around inside his vast black suit and climbed the church steps alone. The chattering in the yard grew louder after he disappeared.

Jerry strained his body this way and that on the peeling band-stand step, alarmed at his heart's pounding. He had finally discovered one truth, at least: in all that stirring park, nobody cared what he did.

Nor did the preacher telephone the farmhouse in the following days to ask why he'd stopped appearing for his lessons. The boy felt a burden slipping away. Now he circled the town every after-noon until it was time to show his face at home, his mind blessedly empty of verses and riddles.

He'd never gotten to know Hickman before. The life there made more sense than the irregular fields his grandfather plowed, or the church. He felt almost at ease among those rows of white ginger-breaded houses, floating at the back of deep lawns. If he lingered until five o'clock, he could catch the men returning from work. One by one, in business suits or overalls, carrying a lunch box or a newspaper, they walked up to young wives waiting beside the screen doors. Often when the men passed him on the sidewalk, they nodded as if he belonged there too. "Evening, son." "About time for your supper, isn't it?" The warmth in his chest assured him that he was on the verge of a second, better choice. Then he wondered how you got to live in town if you didn't go in for the church.

He enrolled in correspondence courses, which he completed in his bedroom late at night. As he walked the streets after school he chanted a maxim: "If a decision is right, nobody will oppose it." Every few months, he dreamed a certain dream. He was working behind a counter in one of the downtown stores. First he gave directions to the sales staff, who saluted smartly and trotted up and down ladders. Then the customers lined up before him, eager to pay for packages the clerks had wrapped in brown paper.

Drawn in by the beauty of the picture, maybe he forgot an important point. During graduation week he simply announced to his grandparents, "In my heart I'm sure. I won't head for the seminary, I'll study accounting at the state college and see where it leads."

Doors slammed all over the farmhouse at that, and unholy curses were shouted. But the size of the miscalculation only dawned on him the next Sunday when his grandparents took seats down by the pulpit and left him sitting alone in the family pew. "Has the leopard changed its spots?" old Broadshears thundered at the height of his sermon. The next week when Grandpa was calm enough to talk, he led the boy behind the chicken house and said, "That money was saved to make a parson. The Lord won't pay for any business courses." Jerry couldn't enroll in college unless he scraped up the tuition by himself.

Just as his grandfather was thinking about putting him to work in the fields to earn his dinners, he heard about a job at the Penney's store in Hickman. He was glad to get it and escape the farmhouse every morning, even though he had to walk to work. The town was four miles away, uphill and down, but Grandpa said, "I'm not lending the car just so you can sell dry goods."

The trick about the Penney's job was that he loved it. He fetched down boxes and swept out the storeroom, and he ate lunch with a pair of clerks who explained how to handle the customers. "If a lady's wearing anything new, tell her how nice she looks. If it's a man, tell him how smart he is for liking what you show him."

Jerry nodded. After a month he knew he'd found his place, even though Grandpa still turned his face away at the supper table, and Grandma's eyes wandered from man to boy as if she was trying to decide between them. On his hikes into town he took strength from repeating, "After I bring a wife back from college and move into a house on Pine or Second Street, everything will fall into place." Meanwhile his chief disappointment was that he couldn't save money fast enough to start college the first year.

Then he read an ad for a small grocery store over at Kidder, a village three miles beyond Hickman. An agent drove him out to inspect the business one evening. The building sat at the main intersection, its plate-glass window facing the south hill. The store-keeper had just died, so the building was padlocked. A stink of vegetables hit Jerry's face when the agent opened the door. Inside, half-empty barrels surrounded the counter, while in back was another room where he could unroll a mattress on the floor.

"How much you got for a down payment?" the agent asked confidentially and then gave a laugh. "Why, that's just the amount they're asking!"

Jerry took this coincidence for another sign.

He tried to explain the deal to his grandfather. "In two years I could save all my college expenses and make a profit on the resale of the building to boot. Working in Penney's is great, but it's not leading anywhere real fast. Mister Blister was thirty-five before he got raised to assistant manager." Finally, when he saw that the family would offer no help, he went alone to the agent and swore he was twenty-one. He signed the papers, panting a little. After that there was nothing to do but gather his clothes and move into the store, drunk on hope.

He thought Kidder looked almost like Hickman, but soon he noticed how fingers of pastureland poked deep into the town's center. Field mice nested in ditches, and there were no sidewalks for his late-night strolls, just the rutted, snaky gravel roads.

At first he had only the mouser, Biff, for company, but after he'd met everybody in the place, he didn't feel too lonely. Only, folks in Kidder had a sly way that surprised him. They acted nothing like the Penney's customers in Hickman or the buyers in his correspondence course booklets. What's more, there was no Mister Blister around to ask for advice.

"My neighbor been in here today?" the stooped gray-haired woman before the counter would ask.

"Mrs. Dicey? Haven't seen her," he would reply brightly, ready to reach down cans or scoop flour into a sack.

"Guess that means she didn't leave no half-dollar for me on the tab?" the woman would say, pulling her shawl tighter.

His face would fall. "Nobody's left money for you, Mrs. Porter. Do you want any groceries today?"

The old woman would lean her hip against a barrel. "I'd like a little bacon, well trimmed." He would turn to his meat safe. "But I surely can't afford any if my neighbor didn't leave the half-dollar she owes. I'll have to go home and wait."

He would frown, wondering what the woman was getting at. But one thing was clear: he couldn't let her lose the habit of buying from him. The Friendly Market had just opened on the edge of Hickman, a ten-minute drive away. "You could take the bacon on credit," he'd offer. "You can pay me when you get what you're owed."

To forget the customers' peculiar grins, he read an accounting textbook by night. He never touched a drop, but drove the battered truck he'd bought to his grandparents' church every week, where he sat by himself instead of in the family pew.

Was the bloom nearly off the rose by the time his old friend Jay-jay stopped at the store for a bottle of pop one Saturday? He hadn't seen Jayjay since high school. "Hey, Jerry! You gave up the church for this?" the other laughed when he saw the chubby, pale young man behind the barrels.

Jayjay had been trying out his hot rod that morning on the curving back roads. He hadn't gone away to college either—he'd taken a job sweeping out the Flying Horse Garage. His snazzy Merc ate up a lot of cash though, and he ran with a fast crowd on weekends, so he listened closely when Jerry urged, "You could mind the store when I'm away. You could throw your mattress across from mine and save on rent too."

The thin-faced, copper-haired youth looked over the back room through narrowed eyes. "Is that cat the only thing you got to warm your bed?" he cracked. "At least a fellow wouldn't starve," he allowed, thrusting his chin among the groceries. On Sunday he drove over from Hickman with all his clothes.

Jayjay was sorry the war had ended before he'd gotten a chance to see the world. "And you know why?" he winked.

Jerry smiled and shrugged; he didn't know.

"Those Italian gals, they loved the GIs. My brother had two in Rome, one for mornings, the other for afternoons. Broke their hearts when the army shipped him home."

Now when Jerry snuggled into his mattress and listened to his friend spinning stories in the dark, he thought of Jonathan and David on a hunting trip under a cobalt sky. Everything seemed possible again: earning his way to college, marrying some generous girl, and settling down on one of those perfect Hickman streets.

On Saturdays Jayjay minded the store while Jerry drove his truck to the grocery warehouse in St. Joe. He took his time there, cruising past the blocks of freshly painted houses, studying the women who weeded flower beds while their husbands pushed mowers across the lawns. What everyone was doing on those well-ordered plots looked perfectly clear.

Back in Kidder he didn't notice any change until one evening Jayjay said, "This town's a slow place." He ate his dinner out of Jerry's stock and left empty cans on the counter. He turned over the spoon inside his mouth while he thought. "There's not a single good-looking gal that comes in this store. It's only housewives and a couple of old men wanting smokes, then at suppertime a few kids stop to buy whatever their mamas forgot."

Jerry had been watching Jayjay work at the baked beans, trying to remember how many cans of beans he'd moved that month. They sold well and he wished Jayjay would eat something else, but he didn't like to spoil things by mentioning it.

"There's Joy," he said.

"Joy who?" Jayjay looked at him shrewdly.

"Joy with the long hair, that lives at the first turning south of here. Mott's their last name. Mostly the mother comes in, but sometimes they send the eldest daughter."

Jayjay grinned. "How old is Joy?"

"At least twenty-five," Jerry confessed. He blushed to see his friend's frown. He tried to make the woman sound more interesting by adding, "When she comes, she likes to linger. She's kind of slow and strange."

"She's sweet on you," Jayjay said. He set down the empty can and picked out an orange for dessert, but he watched Jerry all the while.

"I expect it's just that the housework's hard on her. They got eight other kids to be cleaned up after. She's probably glad of a rest when she comes in here."

"You been holding out on me," Jayjay laughed suddenly. "You got your love nest while I'm working at the garage, and you weren't going to tell if I hadn't asked."

That hint started Jerry thinking. There might be closer wives for him than away at college. All the next week he paced behind the counter, waiting for Joy to come into the store.

People talked about her in Hickman for years after that: she was a waitress in all the cafés. Her chestnut hair was her beauty feature, straight and thick as a horse's tail. It swished when she tossed her neck. Clothes never looked right on her, though—her slip always wanted to show.

She had a rich laugh. "I'm a quarter Comanche," she told him when he started escorting her around the gravel roads at night. "I left my tomahawk home this time, so you're safe for now."

The women who came in the store winked at him. "I saw you two out sashaying last night." The old men were blunter. "Your new girlfriend isn't much of a looker!" The attention pleased him. Living with Jayjay had taught him how to interpret those jokes. He felt like part of Kidder at last, and part of something bigger that was moving with him in its arms.

On a couple of evenings Joy wandered over to sit beside him on the store's front step and count the stars. Jayjay stayed inside. Jerry figured that his friend was spying out the plate-glass window to see how far they'd go, but he didn't have time to worry about that. He was having enough trouble keeping up with Joy's conversation.

"I don't know why Mama wanted to go and have nine of us, do you?" she laughed, as if she was trying to make a joke out of a grudge she'd been nursing. "Couldn't she see the trouble she was bringing on?"

He didn't know how to answer a question like that. Joy's resentment seemed needless. He didn't mind that she came from a swarming, messy household or that she was another farm child like himself. He felt close to her once he understood that she planned on moving to a big town as quick as she could. "I'm going to college in a couple of years," he confided in return. "Kidder's only a stepping-stone for me."

He still said college was two years away, even though he'd been in the grocery business for nine months. He was managing his stock better, but most of his customers owed small sums. After he paid Jayjay for minding the store every week, there wasn't much left to put in the bank. He usually let his stash accumulate in a Folger's can for a month before depositing it, and then he'd count over the coins at night, wondering if there was some lesson he still hadn't learned.

Jayjay might ask to borrow a dollar if he had a date or needed to buy a part for his car. He would stick his hand in the cash register on his way out the door and call, "Pay you back next week."

Jayjay was treating him a lot cooler since he'd seen Joy. His respect seemed to slip a notch once he understood that Jerry could get interested in a woman like that.

"Mouth like a side of beef!" Jayjay flashed his tongue. "Got a bay window in front and broad in the beam! Sure, she'd love to trap you if she could. Nearly thirty and never been kissed, been passed up by all the guys her age. How else will she get off that farm, unless you marry her?"

Jerry had never had a girlfriend in high school, while Jayjay'd found a new one twice a year. Consequently Jerry didn't entirely trust his own choice. Still, he seemed to recognize some truth in Joy that was deeper than anything in the smart college girls he'd been dreaming of.

He tried to put the feeling into words while Jayjay spooned his supper out of a tin can. "She's had a hard time, but she's still hopeful. I think that's a good trait, don't you?"

Jayjay gave it up and grinned. "I need a couple dollars for tonight, OK? I'll pay you Friday."

Jayjay left him alone most evenings now, so it was harder to take Joy out for a stroll. Then he wondered how many nights it had been since she'd come over to sit beside him on the step. But just as he was beginning to feel neglected, she ambled in one afternoon with her grocery list and asked where he'd been keeping himself. She smiled at his excuse, though she offered none of her own. "Is that all? I thought you were a two-timer like the rest."

Remarks like that one reminded him how little he knew about her, and how curious he was to learn more. On an impulse he asked, "Come with me to St. Joe this Saturday?" He thought she might enjoy looking at a real city for a change, since talking about their plans for escaping Kidder had always brought them closer.

She made clear that he'd guessed right to invite her along. Her laugh made up for all his evenings by himself.

It was a beautiful trip. They spun down the highway at fifty, and they didn't go straight to the grocery warehouse. First he took her sightseeing along his favorite St. Joe streets, where the wedding-cake houses sat back from the sidewalk in rows. Joy was so intoxicated with all she saw that maybe she let herself go further than she'd planned. She'd never seen this part of the city before; she'd only visited the stockyards with her father once and eaten in a filthy restaurant where the smell of manure hung thick.

"We could live over there, or there!" she pointed as the pickup eased along the boulevard. "We'd have a cook, and a butler to pour you out a big whiskey when you got home from work."

He thought he'd never seen the place before that afternoon. Her delight made it fresh. On the way home she bent across the seat and kissed his cheek, then sat chuckling to see how red he turned.

"This day's been the crown of my whole life," she sighed as they drove up before Jerry's store. "I guess I can stand living with Mama awhile longer, after those sights to cheer me up."

If that exaggeration was a hint, modesty kept him from seeing how to follow it up. He needed for Joy to tell him what came next, but she was looking out at the empty crossroads, her smile frozen.

The best he could do was jump down and run to help her from the truck. She laughed at his eager face and took his hand. But whatever moment they were on the verge of evaporated when Jay-jay appeared on the front step to help unload the boxes. Instead of coming inside for a bottle of pop, Joy disengaged herself and walked off toward home.

Afterward Jerry thought about that moment, with her swishing up the road in her heavy-bodied way and him laughing back encouragingly when she turned around for another good-bye. She echoed his laugh from a distance, while on the far side of the truck Jayjay was laughing too. He thought and thought: for Joy had seemed to be laughing not only at him, but beyond him at Jayjay. Meanwhile Jayjay was laughing at him too, but his friend also seemed to be laughing past him, toward Joy. Were the two of them mocking each other, or had Jayjay cracked some joke he hadn't heard?

The next week he had to mind the store every evening and couldn't walk out to call for his girlfriend. She never came back to sit on the step like she'd said she might, either. That was frustrating as heck, because he knew they were close to something big. He sent her a message by a kid who stopped in to buy a popsicle, but when he finally made it down to her house late that night, all the lights were out, so he didn't like to knock.

At last it got curious how much he was being left alone. Jay-jay had practically disappeared. Jerry was usually asleep when his friend stumbled in to stretch out on the other mattress; he didn't hang around for breakfast anymore, either. Meanwhile the only one of Joy's family who came in the store was a lean, grubby boy. Until lately the Motts had run up their bill and paid installments every few weeks, but now the boy handed over cash each time. When Jerry asked how his sister was, the kid mumbled, "Don't know."

The next Saturday, because it seemed the straightforward thing to do, Jerry stopped the truck at Joy's house on his way to St. Joe. The mother faced him behind the tattered screen door, her body spread as if to block his view. Inside, the cries of children and the tumbling of chairs ceased; he couldn't interpret the sound of feet pounding on the stairs.

"She's gone for the day," Mrs. Mott said, her eyes aimed at his chin.

"I'll stop by again on my way home."

"Won't be back till late, I don't know when."

"Tell her I called, then. I'll call again tomorrow."

Alone in the truck, he told himself that she had finally hitched into Hickman to look for a job that was better than scrubbing and cooking at home. She had wanted to surprise him with the news. He saw at once that this might be the first step toward the two of them moving to the big town together. His blood raced and he pressed the pedal to the floor.

Late that day when he returned to the store, eager to tell someone what he suspected Joy had done, he found Jayjay in the back room soaping his skinny torso over a bucket. Luckily there were no customers in front. "Got a big night ahead," Jayjay grinned. "You're just in time to see me leave. Can you unload those groceries by yourself?"

He looked as if he was high on some expectation of his own. He swung past Jerry, pulling on a white shirt, tying a tie. His jangly laugh made it impossible to talk. "I borrowed some cash for the weekend!" he called. Outside, he climbed into the hot rod, and the engine roared.

Alone again, Jerry sighed. Idly he punched open the cash register to see how much his friend had taken this time. He couldn't believe his eyes. All the compartments were empty: no coins, no bills. He always began the morning with three dollars there, so Jayjay'd helped himself to that much plus Saturday's receipts: probably six or seven dollars more. Then he got a clutch in his belly. He ran to the back room and groped on the shelf for the coffee can. As he brought it down, he knew it felt too light. It had held seventeen dollars in quarters and halves.

His eyes darted over the room. Jayjay's mattress was gone and his pile of clothes was missing from the corner, where the cat was sniffing. He had cleaned out of Kidder entirely, then.

The next week Jerry served his customers as usual, but he didn't encourage them to linger. In the evenings he sat behind the counter with the light out, trying not to think. He couldn't bring himself to telephone Jayjay's family: he would've felt ashamed to worry them. But the worst part was not having Joy to share the disaster. Whenever he walked down to the Mott place, the mother appeared, blocking the door. "She's out, I'm not sure when she'll be back." His hopes for his girlfriend had begun to unsettle too. He had run out of guesses about her by that time.

Then on Friday he heard a familiar roar outside the store and Jayjay breezed through the door. His sharp nose stuck in the air and car keys swung from a finger as usual, but his eyes shifted and dodged.

"You're back!" Jerry breathed.

Jayjay tried to whistle, sucked air and blurted out, "I wonder if we could make that money a sort of a long-term loan?"

"Maybe part of it, if things are tight," Jerry said. "Can you pay any at all today?"

Jayjay broke his stare, then sniffed. "You still don't know much, do you, pal?"

Jerry had to shake his head.

"I quit the garage and got a real job. Fifty-four hours a week in Penney's storeroom. Sweeping out the Flying Horse didn't bring in enough, now that I have responsibilities."

"Is your mom sick again, Jayjay? I thought you were free and clear."

"You poor stupe!" At last the old grin flashed. "Don't you even know I had to go and marry her? That's why I needed so much. She wanted a corsage, and the preacher took two bucks, then two nights at the honeymoon hotel in St. Joe. You do something like this, you got to do it right."

Jerry swallowed, trying to comprehend. "That's great, Jayjay. I didn't know you were getting married. Who's the lucky girl?"

The silence crackled between them until at last Jerry reddened and ducked his head. "But you made fun of her. She never even mentioned you when we were alone."

"Didn't say I liked her, only said I had to marry her," Jayjay smiled sourly. "Sometimes a man gets sucked in and has to do the honorable thing. I didn't lie to you much."

Jerry forced himself to raise his eyes. "You don't mean you *had* to, do you? You *wanted* to."

"Why, the proof was riding in front of her plain as day!" Jay-jay shouted, patience suddenly gone. "Everybody in Kidder saw it except you. The women turned their faces away when she walked by—not that she cared what they thought, but her dad cared plenty. He knocked me down right outside the store, kept making threats till I promised. I bet you never even heard the shouting, did you, pal?"

Jerry's color deepened, but he hung on, insisting, "Why did you let me go out walking with her, though, joking like you thought we were courting?"

He stared into Jayjay's knotted face, where pain and arrogance and pity were at war, until he really did understand at last. "You were hoping I'd solve your problem for you," he said. "Only I didn't work fast enough."

"Everybody in Kidder knew!" Jayjay flung out again. "If you couldn't see to protect yourself, it'd be your own damn fault."

After all, Jayjay had done the honorable thing. He'd come back to apologize and had ended by shifting the load from his own shoulders onto his friend's, probably easier than he'd hoped. There was no use mentioning the money again, since it was spent. The screen door slammed and the hot rod roared up, then the sound died away.

Jerry stood rigid while his mind searched the web of Jayjay's story to find all the little truths that were caught in it. Prickles crept over his flesh. When two boys ran in for popsicles, he stared at them so crookedly that they backed out the door without getting what they'd come for.

His shock wasn't just the loss of a woman he hadn't known too well, or the disgrace of learning that the whole town had been in on the joke. He didn't blame Kidder, or Jayjay, or Joy. Yet how could he have seen something coming that he'd never in his life been taught to expect?

As if to escape that mystery, he listed the store with an agent the next week and sold it to Tommy Barker, who owned the Friendly Market—a round cheery man who planned to install his son in the place so the boy could learn groceries on his own. All Jerry's profit went for the agent's fee. Then he hit the road for a couple of years. He hitched as far as Chicago, rode a barge to New Orleans. He saw the Great Salt Lake before he stopped. He took any kind of day labor in order to eat and slept alone in barn lofts or the cheapest hotels. His hands roughened and his face grew lean and sunburnt. "My education!" he smiled when he told about those days. "What I never had before."

When he finally swung down from a boxcar and hiked out the familiar gravel road to the farmhouse, his grandparents listened closely to all his stories. They were trying hard to understand why he had failed to settle down in one of those fine cities he described. At last the grandmother guessed that some instinct about home must have been moving in his belly, drawing him back to climb on the tractor where he'd never sat before. Soon he was plowing furrows up and down the hillsides, battling grasshoppers under the swollen sun. But what fear throbbed in the grandmother's heart, seeing him still wifeless and no closer to a vocation than ever! What passion darkened the grandfather's face as he surrendered those fields to his heir!

The old man stepped aside not because he felt too broken-down to work, but because he was still partly in awe of his grandson's character. He understood that after such careful rearing, the young man had turned out too honest for business or even the church. He imagined Jerry had come to prefer the farm to any of those sparkling cities he'd seen because the land wears its crookedness on its face, for anyone to recognize. After all, the grandfather told himself, there might be honor in such a failure too.

Days finally came, though, when the old man choked back tears of rage, staring at the yellow hillside where his boy was driving the harvester round and round a diminishing stand of wheat. By this time the grandmother had died, and the old man's nerves had withered. The smallest things irritated him now: the way Jerry never turned his head if a car honked from the road, and seemed not to notice the dog that was flushing rats out of the stubble beside him.

Everything the old man had done in past years, even his mighty shows of anger, he had done out of love. But in those last parched harvest days the effort appeared wasted. So far as he could tell, all his conniving had produced a solitariness that went so near to purity it became a crippling. He expected that on the day he died, Jerry would walk into the fields to work as usual, as if ordinary grief was beneath him. When he asked about this at supper, his voice quivering with self-pity, the young man replied stiffly that death was a paradox too deep to be resolved. Then he seemed to remember that there was no more risk to be faced, at least where the old man was concerned. He began chewing again, and soon between bites he agreed that what his grandfather had said was probably so.

⌒ The Partridge Place

The cracked, wheezy voice inside the telephone receiver told Stan, "Dwight Osgood recommended you as a real go-getter!" Evidently Stan had been the listing agent on an eighty-acre parcel that Dwight had inspected once but decided not to buy.

"What's more," the voice rasped, "I used to see you at the Pentecostal church!" That must have been while Stan was dating his first wife, Wanda, who later became the Wild-Eyed Lunatic in stories he told at the Red Neck Tavern.

"On top of which, your wife's my cousin twice removed!" This was probably Stan's second wife, Eleanor, who was divorcing him and lived with her parents. She had relatives scattered over the county like grasshoppers.

The voice on the phone exploded in a cough, then continued through a bubble of phlegm. "No trouble for you to sell my farm, would there be? Beautiful property, only it lies off the highway so it'll take advertising. Can you look it over today?"

Stan poured a whiskey with his free hand. He didn't feel like starting the Chevy on an afternoon when brown leaves were hurling themselves against his office window. He promised Friday and hung up so he could use both hands to recap the bottle.

Friday morning was marred by headache, so he switched on the radio and napped at his desk. After lunch he felt the car key in his pocket and admitted that the geezer would do better listing his place with Tarrance and Sons. The Tarrance boys had glad hands and smiley teeth bespeaking a faith in commerce that Stan had lost. "If anybody could sell a farm in this godforsaken neck of the woods, it'd be them."

As he said this aloud, the phone began to ring. The high cracked voice pronounced its name. "This is Partridge, son of Vernon. Husband of Thelma. That called Wednesday. I put off an errand to wait for you."

Stan cleared his throat preparatory to recommending the Tarrances. The voice broke in: "I guess anybody that moves as fast as you must miss a date now and again. Can you make it yet today?"

Stan ran a hand through his hair. How could he confess that he had decided to drink his liver to blazes, and he only came to the office to avoid questions from his landlady? Because he couldn't think of anything else, he muttered that he'd be there within an hour.

When he leaned back to gather strength, he fell asleep at once. He dreamed of his son, Skipper, that his second wife was keeping from him. The boy's small brave face made Stan's heart bleed with yearning. A lawyer had warned him that the judge would be on Eleanor's side. His chest sank under the weight of the dream, as he and the wife—her face scored with X's and V's—pulled chunks from each other's scalps in a fit of spleen.

He awoke after dark, his spine crucified by the spoked back of the chair. He realized at once that he had missed another date with Partridge, but this time he felt only relief. Now the gaffer would see how undependable he was and would let him sink in peace.

The next morning as he fumbled to unlock the office, he caught sight of a skinny pair of overalls topped by a Stetson, headed down the block with a wide-swinging hobble. Stan panicked, realizing that Partridge had come to force the listing on him. He ducked into the dry-goods store next door and hid among the greeting cards. His hands were shaking so badly that after a minute he couldn't even think why the sight of the old man had shocked him so.

When he poked his nose into the gusty street again to see if the coast was clear, he found two puckery red eyes beneath a wide-brimmed hat aimed at him from the curb. He gave a yelp and lurched off beyond the old farmer's reach. Around the corner he banged into the door of the Red Neck, which Henry the bartender was swinging open for the day. Henry waved him inside with a frown.

Settled on a stool in the dimness, Stan shuffled off his coat and called for beer. He downed half a dozen while Henry read in the paper about Eisenhower's golf game. At last his shoulders sagged and he sighed: the day might still turn out all right. For reassurance he let his mind run back along familiar tracks to the nights he had spent drinking with the boys in Korea. He took his time, savoring the images. The black-haired girls in the bars had smelled of incense and gingery soap. He'd made them giggle by tapping out a jazzy beat on the table with his fingers. When he and the boys finally piled in the Jeep again, a small red shrine high up on a green hill was just beginning to catch the sun.

Stan was facing the vinyl booth where he and the first wife, Wanda, used to sit before the war. She'd made him nervous, playing with matches until she burned the bar menus. Once her curly hair had caught fire because she was laughing so hard at the way Stan kept lunging to snuff out her light.

The day he got home from overseas, he'd caught her in their kitchen making out with Matt Dexter against the sink. When she saw him walk in, wearing the uniform he'd put on to impress her, she dropped her jaw, then laughed. "Oh God, Stan! I'm sorry, but you might as well know!" Sometimes after that it seemed like he'd brought the war back to Missouri with him in his duffel bag. His hometown looked shriveled now. The houses were peeling; giant trees lay uprooted by storms. He could never tell when a client or an old school buddy might begin, "Sorry, fella, but you might as well know. . . ."

When the Red Neck's door opened a second time, the breeze carried a whiff of dung. Stan watched a dark figure perch two stools down. A raspy voice called for a long neck. Then the place fell quiet and Stan ordered another before he felt a hat brim brush his hair.

"I recognized you the minute I come in. I figured if the mountain won't come to Mohammed, Mohammed'll have to find the mountain. Finish that drink so I can run you out to the farm."

"Call the Tarrances," Stan mumbled. "I'm closing up shop."

Partridge's rough lips tickled his ear. "I need the cash so I can keep the wife in painkillers. I don't even have time to milk, since I got to nurse her. The kids have moved away, and none of them can help now. Had to pay a neighbor to bring the harvest in this year, and a third of it's still lying out in the field. Come on, I'll show you."

Stan blinked, fighting for distance. In the shadows Partridge's skin looked as if his sunburn had begun to rot. The lines in his face were softening like scratches through mud. Against Stan's will something like pity hurt his throat, and he found himself rising from the stool to stumble out into the chilly sunlight. Climbing in the old man's pickup cab, he promised himself that he would only inspect the land as a courtesy; he would not meet the wife.

Partridge's fields stretched up steep limestone hills, where cattle turned their haunches against a devastating north wind. Out here the autumn seemed farther advanced than in town. The barn leaned away from a circle of ramshackle sheds, and an angry mule brayed in the yard. Stan could not imagine selling the place to anyone who saw it in daylight. He resisted going in the house at first, but he succumbed when a shade of pleading fell across Partridge's mouth.

The rooms stank of medicine. Then in the half-light Stan caught sight of the invalid, rigid on a cot beside the stove. Blood rose in his cheeks and he murmured a thick hello. Mrs. Partridge seemed attentive to something going on inside her, and her taut face did not alter at his greeting. He considered: Suppose you lived with a woman not just a year, but until you understood her, and then you had to watch every minute of her dying.

When the old man asked, on the drive back to town, "How much could the place bring?" Stan replied, "Twenty-five"—a figure that expressed all his bitter hopelessness.

Partridge nodded. "Let's sign a paper then, so you can get to work."

The foolish optimism embarrassed Stan. But as he gazed out the pickup window at the passing fields, gray and dreary beneath the weak sun, he felt a compulsion rising in his chest. He hated to think of Partridge's children refusing to come home when the mother needed nursing. ("Sorry, Dad, but you might as well know. . . .") He wanted to offer the old man some comfort against the snows that were coming, though he wasn't sure yet what he had to give.

Shrugging off a headache, he drove to the office early Monday to compose advertising. He placed a notice in the local paper and ordered a hundred posters, which he planned to tack to utility poles. He cast these ads to disguise the fact that it was the Partridge place he wanted to sell. Anybody who saw that name would probably laugh, already aware of the rotten barn and the narrow house with its blackened walls. Stan's only hope was to trick some farmer who wanted space to feed an extra herd—somebody who didn't need the buildings at all—into inquiring. Then it would be his job to talk faster than the fellow could remember what was wrong with Partridge's hills.

Hammering up posters the next week under a ragged, wind-swept sky only pricked his restlessness. Afterward he paced the office or glared up and down Main Street. Instead of brooding about his two wives and Skipper and Korea, his mind ran along the rolling country lanes to the gaunt old woman lying on her cot, and the cattle that looked as if they would not survive a winter of Partridge's neglect.

Drinking didn't improve his outlook. The Red Neck's gloom reminded him of military coffins he had seen once being loaded through the black mouth of a cargo plane. Behind the bar, Henry's face made him think how little the world cared for suffering. He knew well enough that real estate was only a bunch of accidents heaped up to look like a business. That meant there was no use putting your heart in it. Still the anguish grew until one morning he ran to the bank and withdrew his last forty dollars. Then he drove the thirty miles to St. Joe and placed an ad in the *Gazette*'s real estate section, to run until further notice.

Gradually all the publicity woke people up. The next weekend a couple of folks invited him to inspect a house or a vacant lot, just to see what price they might fetch. Because of his distress,

Stan was eager for distractions. He responded to the calls at once, shook hands all around, and ended by listing four properties in two weeks. However, he did not expect these places to sell. There were never many buyers this late in the season, and besides, even the Tarrance boys weren't booming like they had been right after the war. Woody Tarrance hadn't bought a new Buick in three years. Stan was only putting in his time, praying for a call about the farm he really wanted to move.

Then on a drizzly late-October day with no promise in the air, something did sell. It was not Partridge's farm—it was only a miserable three-room bungalow behind the movie house with a garage slanting into the alley. A newlywed couple bought it for $3,550. At first the moldering shingles and broken sidewalk discouraged them. Stan leaned against his Chevy while they poked around, confident that they had no intentions. When the freckle-faced groom remarked, "The place sure needs fixing," Stan shrugged.

"The wife'll be home alone till the kids start coming. Buy her a can of paint and some nails. You'd be surprised."

The youth nodded soberly and backed off to confer with his bride. Stan watched in bewilderment as their faces grew animated and the young man began running around the yard, pointing at the roof line. In ten minutes the woman strode over to say, "Thanks for showing us such an opportunity!"

His heart thundered at the way he had put something over without even trying. With the commission he decided to extend the lease on his office, thinking that after all, miracles happen. Somebody might inquire about the Partridge place if he gave it time.

As if to encourage this belief, a hunger for property seemed to sweep the county overnight. Stan listed two spreads on the fat bank of the river, and within a week he sold one of them to a retired circuit judge. Then a couple of men sitting in Fern's Café said the farm economy was finally looking up, and pretty soon Stan moved another bungalow and a filling station that had sat vacant since the war. Every time he walked into the office now, the phone was ringing.

When he met a new prospect, he mentioned the Partridge place first thing. He had practiced his pitch until it sounded half-convincing: he enlarged the house, smoothed the hills, and moved the farm a mile closer to town. Unfortunately his clients always had different requirements. When he saw that Partridge's farm wasn't for them, his interest dropped and he drove them to look at his other listings almost sullenly.

Objectively, he had to admit that these buyers were offering him an astounding change of luck, but he couldn't take them seriously. Their motives for acquiring property sounded trivial—schemes to increase their profits or gain some pointless comfort. Consequently he left them to convince themselves. If someone asked a question, he made a face. "If the well needs cleaning, you'll have to do it yourself, so what's the point of bringing it up?"

His indifference stunned the clients, who often flushed at his answers. The effect on them was surprising, though. They interpreted his attitude as a sign that his listings must possess some subtle advantage that ordinary folks couldn't appreciate. They reached for their pens to sign the contract while he was still grinding out his cigarette. Once Buddy Tarrance, driving past him on Main Street, shouted, "Where you finding these crazy buyers? Don't they know farming's on the skids?"

The week after Thanksgiving, in the midst of typing a transfer of deed, Stan felt so bored that he stepped outside to breathe frost. Still not knowing where he was headed, he started the Chevy and whizzed over to Eleanor's parents' house. Through the storm door his wife stared at his new blue suit. "You dating or something?" she asked.

He laughed at her suspicion. "I'm selling tons of property. Can I come in?"

She grimaced but stepped aside. In the hall hung a photograph of their wedding party: four unhappy adults, one of them standing at attention in a woolly uniform. Eleanor had taken him on a quick rebound against her family's advice.

"Where's Skip?" he asked, glancing around.

"Where would he be at two in the afternoon? He's in school. You're not going to see him anyhow. You're not safe." Her voice sounded mostly like sleepless nights, he thought; her anger must have nearly drained away.

"I'm as safe as anybody. I'm making money hand over fist. The problem was, I used to try too hard. Now the buyers are selling themselves."

She gave a sarcastic laugh. "You're just having your little string of luck. Later it'll be like the old days."

The cross above her eyebrows was permanently etched. But she was still putting that wave in her hair. "Maybe it's because I stopped drinking that my ability's coming out. You should think over your options, Eleanor."

She raised her eyes from his suit distrustfully. "Let's see if the cure takes."

"I want to see the boy. I'll be back Saturday to pick him up for overnight. You hear?"

Every week he drove out to assure Partridge that he was shaking heaven and earth to sell the farm. His voice rose as he paced the yard and brought out the old lies. "I've got a good feeling in my bones about this place! The right buyer always turns up in the spring!" Then he blushed, remembering the woman inside the farmhouse who would see eternity before the new year. These visits would have been unbearable if Partridge had appeared to listen, but he only leaned against a fence, gazing at the road as if Stan's problems were not important. Now that he had picked his agent, he seemed prepared to wait. Still, Stan always drove back to town depressed by doubt. He had begun to suspect that no matter how many properties he sold, he would never move the Partridge farm. When he stood on the land, he felt something about it beyond the reach of luck.

Skipper was watching cartoons on Saturday and didn't notice his father walk in. But at the sound of Stan's voice the little body stiffened and dashed across the floor to leap into his arms. The boy made no cry; it was his palpitating chest that showed how hard he had been hoping for this loveless split to end. Stan pressed his mouth against his son's cheek. Skipper looked like his father felt, though Stan was a big galoot with huge pores and uncombable black hair, so that women sometimes laughed, "What a he-man!" But inside, his fibers were as tender as this child's.

Nobody spoke as Eleanor zipped Skipper's coat and handed

over a change of underclothes. Looking after them from the porch, though, she regained some perspective. "Bring that boy back clean!" she called.

Skipper slept on the sofa in Stan's apartment. On Sunday morning they ate ham and eggs at a café and then, despite the lowering threat of snow, father and son hiked out a country road. When Skipper stumbled, Stan scooped him up and set him behind his neck, so that the boy's shoes dangled against his chest. Stan pointed out the farms as they passed. "In the war your daddy saw Oriental people plowing the same scrap of land their families had owned for a thousand years. It's not like this country, where a place changes hands every generation. There'd be no work at all for a fellow like me over there."

Skipper said nothing all weekend except "Please" and "Thank you," as if he wanted to control his risks. But every time his father spoke, the boy's breathing quickened, as if he was hoarding up the words.

That afternoon Stan drove out to see Partridge as usual, with Skipper perched on the car seat beside him. The old man tousled the boy's head so violently that he ran away into a nearby field and began hurling clods at fence posts while the grown-ups talked. Stan suppressed an urge to call his son back. At that moment he felt like pulling off the old man's mountainous nose, which resembled a lump of clay, so that Skipper could play with it—as if that would help the boy to understand the tie that bound them here.

Circling the barnyard, Stan shouted and gestured, trying once more to explain to his client how the real estate market could turn your way on a dime. Today when his voice broke, Partridge said mildly, "You can't rush it. When your chance comes, you'll do OK."

At twilight the old man invited father and son into the kitchen and served up biscuits and pork gravy that was clotted with flour. Skipper watched his father eat before raising a fork. It was the first time the boy had tasted coffee, and Stan stirred in five spoons of sugar for him. Just inside the next room, Mrs. Partridge lay on a cot. Partridge never mentioned her, but at the end of the meal he took the ladle and basted her lips with gravy, then wiped most of it away with a rag he carried at his belt.

On the drive home Stan shocked his son by bursting into tears. The boy quickly turned his face to the window, but his father's voice filled the car. "How can the old man bring me luck and can't bring himself any? Did I shrug off the plague that was on my shoulders and it got stuck to him instead?"

The next week Stan read in the local paper that Mrs. Partridge had died. That afternoon he closed his office and drove to the Pentecostal church for the funeral. Two recent clients nodded to him from the back pews, but he cursed them because they had bought other properties instead of Partridge's. He spotted the old man's naked head up in front before the casket. Stretched beside him was a row of strangers with glossy hair and gleaming pink ears. These must be the children, Stan thought—the ones who had deserted the farm. He sat directly behind them in order to glower at their white collars. Next to them the old man, with high shoulders and rutted neck, looked like an emblem of steadfastness. Then Stan noticed a red lump on his noggin the size of a duck egg. He wondered if the corpse had hit Partridge on its way out of the farmhouse, or if the old man had banged himself in grief. But when Partridge passed up the aisle behind the pallbearers, his face wore a surprisingly angelic look, as if he had transcended pain.

In the cemetery Stan huddled among the other mourners, watching the casket descend on ropes beneath a dripping sky. When the little crowd hurried back along the wet path to the row of parked cars, he faced Partridge alone across the grave. The old man held his Stetson in one hand despite the rain that splattered his head. Abandoned again by his children, he was waiting for the diggers, who had disappeared inside a shed. Stan reached out an arm and cried, "I'll work twice as hard! It'll sell within the month or I'll kill myself!"

Partridge nodded to acknowledge the feeling. "She was born to die. I'll follow soon enough. Once I'm gone, the only land I'll care about will be the heap of it over my head."

"No, I'll really sell it! You've got to believe!"

The old man's eyes narrowed, as if his shrewdness was returning. "Maybe I don't need the farm sold any longer. It'll be a good enough spot to end my days."

Stan jerked back his hand. "You'll be happier in the nursing home in town. Besides, I've got your signature on the agreement. Don't worry, I'll move it for you all right."

He fled the cemetery on foot, his new shoes pulling up rounds of mud that scattered behind him. That night when he recovered his presence of mind, he had to walk back to retrieve the Chevy under the waves of a sleet storm. Saturday when he stopped at Eleanor's to pick up Skipper for another weekend, he snatched the boy to his chest as if defying flesh and blood to fail him.

Eleanor's parents bustled out of the room when Stan entered. Evidently they wanted to leave husband and wife alone to patch things up. He had prosperity written all over him now, and his in-laws were probably afraid he would think he could do better than their daughter. Stan observed their departure without despising it. They had him locked up, whether they knew it or not. Eleanor's yellow hair had dulled and her waist had thickened, but she could hold things together for him well enough. What's more, she would never be in a position to say the words he hated: *Sorry, honey, but you might as well know. . . .*

That afternoon in the office Skipper arranged a bunker out of wooden chairs, the way Stan had showed him they'd done it in Korea. Then he hid in the center to spy on his father. Stan sat at his desk sorting papers while dance music played on the radio. These distractions did not entirely prevent him from remembering the Partridge farm, which lay five miles from town under a deepening snowfall. Shut inside with the kerosene stove, neither father nor son noticed the black DeSoto pull up before the window, or the dark-hatted, dark-suited stranger who became covered in snow-flakes as he traced the lettering on Stan's door. The man walked in without knocking.

Stan and Skipper looked up together, almost frightened by the broad oily face and the yellow pigs' eyes that shifted behind it. The man spoke in a quick, guttural accent that sounded like some of the immigrant men Stan had met in the army. "I saw them ads on the poles driving into town. Let's see this farm you're so hot to sell."

Stan could not believe the words and asked the stranger to re-peat. Then he called, "Come on, Skip, we're going for a drive!" No one mentioned that drifts were piling up in Main Street, or that the farm lay on a narrow lane that might be blocked. Instead Stan smacked his son's hands away when he saw him having trouble pulling on his boots. He grabbed the boy and followed the stranger outdoors.

"I got chains," the man said. Inside, the DeSoto smelled of leather upholstery and cigars.

Stan shoved Skipper into the back seat and tried to calm his heart so that he could introduce his sales pitch. "You ever farm around here?" he asked. "What business are you in?"

The stranger dismissed these questions with a grin. "I'm on my way to Kansas City to collect some cash, and I'll need a place to park it, that's all. They tell me farmland's hit bottom and it's bound to go up. You agree?"

"Absolutely!" Stan replied and fell silent, thinking: This fellow's willing to buy something he knows nothing about. They're sharp with one another where he comes from, but out here, don't I have the edge? He also thought: With cash, Partridge can move anywhere he wants. If he doesn't like the local nursing home, he can look in St. Joe or K.C. Stan decided at that moment to forgive Partridge his sales commission. He would hire a truck and help the old man load any furniture he wanted to take along.

Meanwhile the stranger barreled through the snowy lanes. They rolled up before the farmhouse just as Partridge was hobbling down to the pigsty with the evening slops. Stan's eyes brightened: he felt he was bringing good news just in time. Then it struck him how ridiculous the old fellow looked, with a quilt draped over his head for protection against the storm. Suddenly he was afraid for Partridge to meet the prospect and wondered if he might introduce him as a hired hand.

They sank above their trouser cuffs when they stepped from the car. Stan turned Skipper over to Partridge, who led the boy inside the house without offering to shake hands. However, the stranger seemed dismayed by nothing: not wetness, cold, gloom, or even the dissolving face of the old man and the small boy's flailing arms. He pushed off cheerfully to inspect the barn, then plunged out toward the fields. He led Stan through the blowing whiteness, until after an hour they reached the railroad track that separated Partridge from the next county.

Stan wanted to point out the farm's good features along the way, but he could barely keep up with the other's strides. Finally the stranger caught sight of the train embankment looming in the thick air. "Hey, this must be the main line from Chicago through to the Coast! I'll bet I've ridden past here a dozen times in the dining car! Well, what do you know!"

Laughing, the man tugged his hat lower against the wind and began trudging back. At the end Stan trailed ten yards behind, shocked at how much cold his new suit let through to the skin. He wondered if he would remember his pitch when they got inside the house, or if the stranger had knocked it out of him entirely.

When Partridge opened the kitchen door, the stranger only glanced inside. "Get the kid," he called as Stan came up. "We can talk business on the road."

Stan winked at Partridge, hoping to rouse a good-bye from him to encourage the prospect. But the old man was moving toward his rocking chair, so Stan grabbed Skipper, who held himself stubbornly away from his father's face, and hurried out to shove the boy into the rear seat like a doll.

On the drive to town, Stan's mind buzzed so badly that he could not open his mouth. He was furious with Partridge for acting indifferent toward the prospect. He was also distracted by the thought of his son. He decided to apologize to the boy for the rough handling as soon as they were alone. He would tell him that sometimes you have to sacrifice family for business, but that it has nothing to do with love. Mostly, though, he kept glancing at the stranger—who was whistling as he steered through the blizzard—and tried to review in his mind the seven surefire steps for closing a real estate deal.

Suddenly over the whirring of tire chains the stranger asked, "How much the old geezer want?"

Stan choked before answering. "Asking twenty-five, but the price is soft. I'd offer twenty-one if I was you."

"Twelve," the man said at once. He pulled up sharply before Stan's office, so that they nearly banged their heads and Stan heard a thud from the back.

"What say?" Stan asked, incredulous. But then joy sang along his nerves. He realized that price didn't matter at all.

The man turned on him and spoke exactly like a sergeant who instructs a platoon to take a hit. "I'll be driving through here late next week. Have the papers ready and I'll pay on the spot. Remember, no lawyers: I only deal with you."

Stan nodded and bent to lift his son from the floor, not daring to risk his voice again. He nodded once more as the DeSoto disappeared in the cloud of snow.

Afterward in the apartment he sat across from the sleeping boy, analyzing the deal. Naturally it was a low price. What could Partridge expect, looking like death when a prospect called? Anyway, Stan wouldn't let a blizzard stop him now. He'd drop Skipper off at Eleanor's the next morning and drive out to present the offer. He only hoped his wife didn't notice the bruise on the boy's forehead, or she might accuse Stan of drinking again.

Sunday dawned clear and heart-stoppingly cold. The Chevy crunched along the lane in tracks left by a single fast car. Stan found Partridge crouched over a pig in the snowy barnyard. The old man was dosing the animal with green medicine from a bottle. "Twelve's too low," he shouted without looking up. The pig was wriggling furiously, its squeals broken by the fluid pouring down its throat.

Stan shook his gloved fist. "I've sold a dozen other listings, but yours hasn't drawn a single looker till now! Twelve's the only offer we'll get!"

Partridge released the animal and stuck a hand against his back to straighten up. His eyes were teary with rheum and his putty-like skin had gone blue. Yet he faced Stan with legs apart. "Last fall you said twenty-five was a conservative figure."

"We were testing the waters," Stan replied, controlling his temper. "I set it high because I wanted to cheer you up."

"No, you were right then. It's now I'm having doubts about you."

There was no question: the old man was a curse to himself. Why did he care what price he got? His joints must be hurting savagely today. Once he sold the land, he could move into a room with blazing radiators and rest his bones. But maybe his brain had begun to decay. He had seemed like a reasonable fellow last fall.

As if reading Stan's thoughts, Partridge cried, "As long as I live,

I want what's fair! That's more important than comfort or quickness!"

Stan grabbed the madman's shoulders. He shook him so hard the brittle body crackled. "Don't you see, the market has spoken! What's more, this offer is pure luck! The stranger could've taken the federal highway and missed those posters I nailed up! Then we wouldn't have anything to discuss!"

"Watch out, I might take back my listing and give it to the Tarrance boys!" the old man jeered. He set out for the house alone, leaving Stan exhaling frost.

In the car, Stan let out a battery of curses. When he'd quieted down, he resolved to see Partridge every day for a week. You could probably sell property the same way you fought a war, he decided. You could pound the other side again and again, until they had no choice but to sign whatever papers you'd brought along.

Regrettably, his other business was flourishing so that for five days he couldn't find a free hour. Despite the frozen roads, people kept phoning or knocking at the office, determined to buy or sell. He called Eleanor on Friday night to complain that he had been forced to move three properties since Monday. As a reward, she invited him over to tuck Skipper into bed. The boy had been acting cranky all evening, she said, and besides, she'd baked a custard pie.

The next morning Stan sat at his desk fighting off exhaustion so that he could type the contract he would need to transact the Partridge place. Then he swung by to pick up Skipper for the weekend and made a beeline for the farm. He feared the stranger might return that afternoon. He did not know what he would do if Partridge still refused to sell.

"Maybe it's good I let it rest a few days," he told Skipper in the car. The boy listened with his brow furrowed as if considering what advice to give. "Partridge has had time to regret his loss. I expect he'll sign the minute he sees me."

Turning a corner at the base of the last hill, Stan glimpsed something black heaving from side to side in the lane. He was so preoccupied with arguments against the old man that at first he could not focus on the hulk blocking his way. Then he braked violently, nosing the car into a snow-clogged ditch. Still the black thing came on solemnly. It was the local undertaker, Ezra Whittaker, at the wheel of his hearse. He was leading a procession of three cars toward town. Through Stan's mind flashed the thought: Partridge must have died! There was nobody left to see that it got in the paper. Now the children have come back to bury him, just three weeks after they plugged the old lady.

After the last car passed, the only sounds inside the Chevy were the quick moist breathing of the boy and the tremendous heaving of Stan's lungs. Finally he said, "When the family comes back from the cemetery for the last meal, I'll deliver the offer to them. None of them wants the place—he told me so fifty times. I'll wrap up the deal in half an hour, now that the old heathen's out of the way."

He rocked the car to free it from the ditch. When the front wheels broke out, he braked to prevent the back tires from going off the other edge. Skipper clutched the arm rest, but Stan's mind was still circling the dead. "He was an old man that never asked if he could do better." He turned the Chevy in at the gate. "God knows if he even thought the place would sell! Maybe he only put it on the market so he could tell his wife he'd done it."

Before them the weathered barn, the sheds, and a tumbledown pigsty were flung in a circle. The desolate house bowed beneath a load of snow. It looked as if the storm had hit worse here than anyplace else in the county. "Twelve!" Stan muttered. "Twelve will be a miracle, if the fellow pays it. If he drives by in daylight before he comes to see me, he might offer ten! Or cancel the deal entirely. Why not? He hasn't signed anything."

To pass the time while they waited, he thought he would make up with his son for the way he'd treated him the weekend before. "Maybe next Saturday we'll hop over to St. Joe and test-drive a new car. Which would you like—a Buick or a DeSoto?"

The boy stared at him intently, but did not reply. Wanting to force a word from him, Stan tried another subject. "I think your mama's coming back to live with me. Then we'll look for a house where you can have a room to yourself. Will you be glad of that?"

In a flash Skipper reached over to clasp two fingers of Stan's glove. So it was going to turn out all right for them, Stan saw. Last fall he had finally straightened up and put the war behind him, and in the new year he would be forgiven and loved.

He wiggled his fingers to free them from his son's grip. The glove slipped off, and the child took the soft leather into his lap to examine it.

Stan felt certain that when he got to town, the stranger would be waiting. He kept glancing at his watch because he didn't entirely trust the Partridges to return. A local family would want to have a last meal at the old place, but maybe they didn't think like locals anymore.

Or else they would show up, but the stranger wouldn't.

Or he would sell the farm and that would be the end of it: the end of good luck, and love, and everything.

If he sold this place, the Tarrance boys would envy him for the rest of their days.

Those were his main thoughts, watching the sky change from gray to gray and watching his son measure the big man's glove against the stretch of his small white hand.

～ The Blue Light

When Alcee gripped the doorknob and pushed inside the farmhouse, still staggering after his bliss, the hall rug reached out at once and threw him against a table. The table, seeing its chance, knocked him nose first into a wall. Meanwhile in the corners of the house, the remains of a deep bluish halo were being smothered up in gray. Instinctively Alcee pressed his shoulder hard against the wall and blinked in order to collect himself.

From the parlor he detected sharp mechanical voices, their flights punctuated by explosions of laughter. A parade of silvery shadows flashed over the floor beside him. The television's been running all this time! he thought, amazed. Peering into the room, he saw the familiar backs of three dark heads ranged in front of the bright screen. Annoyance flooded through him as he understood how the last wisps of his trance were being scattered. He quickly turned away and mounted the stairs. Waves of applause beat after him like tempestuous wings.

He shut the bedroom door firmly and gave a great sigh before pulling off his overalls. Dull memory had returned. He knew that his wife would not come to bed until ten o'clock because on Wednesdays she watched "The Best of Broadway" after she sent Harder and Emmaline to their rooms.

Wearily he sank onto the mattress and closed his eyes. There in the blackness shone a lingering pinprick of blue.

However, his stomach had begun its usual nighttime churning, and he found that he could not rekindle the glow. After an instant he gave up the attempt and reached to scratch his legs. Idly he tried to recall the last time he and Sarah had sneaked upstairs after supper to lie together for an hour under the covers. Had they done it even once since he had lugged the television back from town and installed it on its throne? His wife had stood at his elbow in the appliance store insisting, "All the other houses on our road have got one by now. How will the kids keep up in school unless they know what's going on?"

Every day the machine mocked at him in brass: "Motorola!"

He lay with his hands pressed against his rumbling belly, brooding over stories Sarah and the children had told at supper about their favorite programs. His wife would square her strong shoulders and aim her fork at his chest as she described the Cuban band leader's wife, Lucy. "I read in a magazine that she's got red hair—that's what gives her confidence. She can always nail Ricky or the Mertzes with a remark." Alcee appreciated well enough how a shrug from a red-headed woman could take your breath away. But even as Sarah rose to clear the dirty plates, he'd realized that the frosty black and blue stick figure on the screen didn't possess any of the richness he'd just enjoyed in his wife's story. It was Sarah's peaked eyebrows and the devastating slide to her voice—sarcastic after years of farm work—that had momentarily made the stick figure named Lucy seem real.

Alcee'd felt the TV characters come to life again whenever he stopped by Nance's Café on his way home from town. The men who drank coffee around Nance's counter behaved as if they'd discovered a pack of wild-eyed gypsies camping behind the train depot and had gotten so drawn into studying those gypsies' foreign ways that they couldn't stop mimicking them. Alcee almost believed in the gypsies when his oldest acquaintances, Slick Thomas and Boodge Morris, threw their bodies around on the counter stools and exchanged wisecracks that George and Gracie or Jack Benny and Rochester had traded the night before. He actually got a kick out of watching Boodge snake his long arms the way Garry Moore did when he launched into his double-jointed dance routine. But even as he laughed, Alcee would recall the sterile image he had glimpsed through the parlor door on his way upstairs to bed.

Garry Moore's nothing but a toy! he thought as he lay in bed alone, while beneath his folded hands his stomach roiled and gurgled. How can they care about him when he's only six inches high and his face is made of tiny lines zinging through the air from who knows where?

Suddenly he wondered if the indigestion that had been persecuting him that spring could be caused by all the talk about the TV he was forced to hear. Until that minute he had feared the upsets might be brought on by the extraordinary blue light that kept appearing when he was alone in the fields or down at the barn. He grinned to think that, after all, his trouble was probably something ordinary, something that could be easily cured. When the grinding in his guts didn't stop that night, he decided almost cheerfully to call on Doc Griswald the next time he drove to town. The doc might banish the heartburn just by showing some sympathy for a man who was being pestered to death by a household machine.

The doc, a reedy old man wrapped in a frayed linen coat, stood with his arms folded the next afternoon while Alcee described his symptoms. In the shadows of the examining room the doc's watery face seemed to invite confidences, and soon Alcee found himself being swept along by a flood of pent-up feelings. "I never really believed the blue light that's been visiting me could be twisting my insides in such knots. It doesn't behave like a thing that'd do you harm, even when it flings you up in the sky so fast your gorge rises and you forget where you came from. You just want to keep hanging there, with your mind a blank and the warmth making your nerves tingle, but finally you can't hold on any longer, and then you drop back like you was a feather settling to earth. But none of that feels like sickness: it's more as if you'd gotten a gift that might be precious, if only you knew how to use it. The problem is that after the light fades, pretty soon you hear the TV squawking in your ears, and then you can't help feeling peeved at all the stupidity."

The doc bent close to scrutinize his face, then began hawking so loudly that Alcee broke off, reddening. He wondered if he had told more than he realized and violated some taboo. He cast about for a way to persuade the doc that the interest he took in the blue light was perfectly reasonable. "Remember the story folks used to tell about Old Man Honeycutt? About the day he was looking over a garden he'd planted, with the spring growth sprouting up around a scarecrow that had stood there for many a year—and everything was the same as always, until a breeze ruffled that scarecrow's coat, and the next thing you know, the creature raises his hat and tips old Honeycutt a wink. Whether it was the sunlight playing tricks or it was the bootleg the fellow drank doesn't matter. The point is, after that morning Honeycutt could never see anything in his garden but the scarecrow—wondering what the creature thought about all day, and what stunt he might pull next. They say Honeycutt went to his grave still chuckling over some things that scarecrow said while the two of them were alone."

Alcee sat back, pleased with his luck in recalling the old tale. It seemed to put his blue light in a safe place by connecting it with a long line of spiritual hobbies. The story meant that such distractions should be tolerated with laughter and a touch of envy.

The doc spat carefully into a handkerchief and stuffed it back in his pocket fold by fold. His frown seemed to indicate that he was waiting for the air to clear of Old Man Honeycutt's ghost before he announced his diagnosis of Alcee's stomach trouble.

"Never mind those comedies and musicals your wife goes in for," the doc said abruptly. "The shows for a fellow like yourself are the police detectives." The doc's brittle limbs came to life and moisture gathered in his eyes as he described the squad cars driven by the television heroes, and the tricks that made the plots suspenseful. His body curled with menace as he hummed a snatch of theme music, trying to convey to his patient the thrill of big city crime.

Alcee's shoulders collapsed in annoyance. "I tried 'Dragnet' when we first got the set. I couldn't sit through it to the end."

The doc stared at the vision chart above Alcee's head as he digested this confession. "Of course, there's no harm in hating television. Your eyes'll probably outlast the rest of ours. The problem is that nobody can live in the real world forever without a vacation. Since the TV doesn't strike your fancy, your subconscious brain's been calling up these funny blue lights for kicks. It's up here"—tapping his forehead—"that's setting your stomach off."

Alcee shifted on the metal stool. "Is there a pill I should take?"

"Why don't you pour a drink sometimes? Or take the family on a trip? I drove the wife to Florida in the Mercury last winter and the air did us a world of good."

Alcee waited to see if there would be any more advice. "Who'd work the farm if I took off now?" he asked finally. "We've got six new calves this spring, for one thing."

On his drive back from town, the sky was dotted with puffs of wool. He found his mind drifting from the doc—who was an idiot—to his worries about his son. Harder had just declared that he would never be a farmer, and if his father's land was left to him in a will, he would trade it instantly for a bus ticket to any Major League city. The boy was playing second base for the high school team that year and stayed for practice every afternoon. Usually he got home too late to help with the milking. On weekends he moped around the barnyard, complaining, "Right now the rest of the team's drinking Cokes at the drugstore, and I'm stuck at the end of a dirt road shoveling manure!"

Alcee glanced at the steady march of clouds above the wind-shield to see if anything was moving among them today, but so far there was no sign. His mind dropped back and began pondering the way Harder had been taken in by the Saturday "Baseball Game of the Week." The broadcast was mostly a fraud, as far as Alcee could see. The batters pointed their tiny heads toward a flicker that must be the ball and swung their little sticks. They rounded the bases on miniature legs so fast that the picture tube cut them off at the knees.

"You can't eat sports," Alcee had lectured the boy, because that was the way people usually talked. His deeper thought was that Harder had probably never seen anything like the blue light, so he couldn't imagine all the different forms the universe might take on. Of course, if a person thought the TV was the most magical thing going, he was bound to make bad choices. Alcee's gut knotted up every time they spoke because he couldn't see how to raise the real issue in terms his son would understand.

In reply, Harder would grimace. "Dad, you're talking like a hayseed again."

Alcee got no help from Sarah in these disputes. "It's natural for a boy to dream about a televised audience," she explained as if he was simple.

Unfortunately this argument was only the start of the trouble that had reared up between husband and wife. That noon when Alcee had tried to slip away to the doctor's office unnoticed, Sarah had called from the kitchen, "Where you headed so soon after lunch?" Before he knew it, he was entangled in an explanation that led them in ever-tighter circles to the blue light.

"I didn't tell you about it before because it seemed too strange to put into words. Not that I was ashamed or scared exactly, but this thing's as different from the TV as you can imagine."

Sarah watched his mouth moving until she understood what he meant by a light. "We've had a string of stormy days," she offered. "Maybe you mistook a thundercloud for something else?"

When he shook his head, she threw up her hands. "Then go see an eye specialist in St. Joe if you have to. But we both know that light's only tormenting you because you're getting to be so stubborn." She showed more interest in his stomach pains than in his hallucinations. Indigestion might reflect on her cooking.

"I could give you boiled potatoes instead of fried. But in exchange I want you to relax with a program every night. We'll let you pick any one you want."

When he'd scowled and turned away, she'd followed him out to the truck, waving a spatula. "There's nothing immoral about TV, you know! The parson mentions Ed Sullivan in his sermons all the time."

Alcee felt his stomach turn over again when he remembered the sting in his wife's voice. His earlier instinct must have been right: he had overstepped an invisible line by mentioning the blue light to her and the doc. Maybe in the old days grown-ups could talk to one another about their private mysteries, but television had evidently changed things.

As he swung the truck into the driveway, his daughter Emmaline came skipping down the lawn with her arms stretched wide. He smiled in relief at the sight of those knobby knees and the trailing yellow hair. Until today the girl had been the only person he'd told about the blue light. He trusted her because, for one thing, she would wander away from the TV if the programs were too old for her, or when she got drowsy. Then Sarah would call him, and he would carry his darling upstairs to her bed. However, even Emmaline was stolen from him on Saturday mornings by the cartoons and puppet shows.

Now she tugged at the door and dragged her father out of the truck cab into the long grass. The next minute she was climbing on his rib cage, crowing at his mock groans and flailing arms. They rolled over together until somewhere among the sprouting foxtails he lost his cap. Finally when they had quieted down and were sitting on the cistern cover, she began to chant her favorite questions of that season.

"What shape is it, Daddy? Is it bright like the sun? How high does it float above the ground? Does it make any noise—like a rocket?"

"What's most beautiful is the colors," he repeated as if reading a fairy story. "There's all different shades of blue, you know. Aquamarine, and turquoise, and robin's egg, and indigo, and sky-blue. At different times it's been every one and more besides."

She puffed her cheeks, speculating. "Why don't you call it right now and we'll see if it'll come!"

"Oh, it's bad enough I'm seeing it alone!" he joked. "What if it eats little girls?"

She laughed, unafraid, and tilted her head. "Why does it visit you, of all the people in the world?"

"I thought you might tell me that." He winked, and in light-hearted excitement he ventured, "Maybe you saw something like it yourself one time or another?"

She looked surprised. "No." After a second she began to clap her hands and sang, "Daddy's light! Daddy's light!"

His face opened with pleasure. Emmaline had reassured him: the light was his particular friend, which a sensitive person might envy.

"It's probably Martians who want to find out how we live," the child observed when she grew tired of clapping. "I saw that on 'Space Invaders.'"

His lips straightened at once. "You could be right. If there *are* creatures from outer space, this is how they'd operate."

After that day, when he let his mind run free, a ridiculous new worry gnawed at his gut. Emmaline's teasing had put him in mind of little blue men with goggly eyes who would chase him over his own fields, intent on stuffing him into an iridescent gunnysack.

Harder soon heard about his father's strange light from Sarah, and the boy enjoyed needling him about it at supper. Alcee knew better, but the genie was out of the bottle now, and he fell into his son's traps every time.

"Maybe you're picking up TV signals with the button on your cap. Maybe you're getting pieces of the test pattern all scrambled up in blue!"

"That could be it!" Alcee cried to his wife, who was carrying a platter of fried chicken to the table. "I could be picking up TV!"

"This Is Your Life, Dad!" Harder's voice dripped sarcasm. "You won't watch it indoors, so it follows you around while you do your chores."

Alcee felt a sudden twinge below his ribs. "But the signal wouldn't operate through my cap, would it?. The light's usually somewhere way out in front of me."

The boy appeared to consider seriously. "We don't watch the antenna on our roof, either. The signal's carried downstairs by a wire."

"That's right," Alcee agreed more cautiously. "My cap button could be grabbing the light and throwing it over where I can see."

"Then leave your cap at home when you go outdoors," Sarah said in a voice flat enough to level mountains.

He paused before picking up a drumstick, and his wife and son turned their eyes away as if embarrassed by what he might say next. But he had remembered something he thought they needed to know. "Actually I've seen it without my cap on. In the tool room, one of the first times. It was afternoon, but the sky outside was overcast and the bulb had burned out, so I had to feel my way. All at once I saw the workbench clearly, and I knew the room was getting brighter. I turned around, and there in the doorway was just the strangest blue shimmering. That was the closest it's come to me. I felt sure the thing had been searching for me in the dark, and when it found me it flared up almost as if it was glad."

In the fields now Alcee glanced over his shoulder at a bird's cry or a shiver passing across the young wheat. He shrank from working outdoors at dawn or twilight, even though he knew the blue light was no more likely to appear then than at noon. Out of the corner of an eye he watched the firmament for any sign: an oddly shaped cloud, or a fan of scattering doves.

What made his fear crystallize was noticing that for a couple of weeks, the light had not appeared. When it comes the next time, he thought, it'll have had a good long while to gather strength. If I see it again, I'll know it's serious. It could be crouching on the other side of that hill right now, hoping I'll drive the tractor close enough to get nabbed.

In the nights he clutched his stomach, tortured by shooting pains. He groaned when Sarah slipped under the sheet, but she refused to acknowledge that he was in agony.

"You're parading that story about the blue light around town just to get attention. People are starting to whisper, like I married a man in the circus. You better stop talking before we're disgraced."

He knew it had been a mistake to take the men in Nance's Café into his confidence. He had only dropped a few hints to them once in order to blow off steam after Sarah and Harder had been baiting him. The men had told their wives that Alcee was seeing spots, and the women had passed the story along. Apparently none of his neighbors had had any experience that could help them understand what he was going through.

"Actually, I don't see hide nor hair of the thing anymore," he assured Sarah in the dark, trying to ignore the cruel pinch above his navel.

"Then why are you still acting so peculiar? You sure as heck weren't like this when you married me. If you die now and leave me with two kids to raise—"

The mention of his death reverberated as if to confirm all his dread. He resolved at that moment that he could no longer put off speaking with Reverend Tullible. The next morning while he drove the tractor back and forth across the cornfield and the wind piled up stacks of cumulus overhead, he tried to think how he might frame his trouble in religious terms. He wanted to avoid blasphemy if he could, but he was sailing without a compass now, and he didn't know if the parson would be offended by a story about a blue light.

When the pink-skinned old gentleman answered Alcee's knock that afternoon, a tightness around his mouth indicated at once that he had already heard about the light from several members of the congregation. Still, duty required him to invite Alcee into the parsonage. They sat by an open window that offered a square of turbulent sky.

"Tell me in your own words," the parson invited, though Alcee felt reluctance behind the velvety voice. "I'm sure those other folks must have misheard what you meant."

"I've been wondering if it's angels," Alcee began, hoping to please. But when he saw the parson fingering his tie, he shot off in another direction. "Can it be a warning, do you think? Did I sin somehow, not like other men, but so God thought He had to get in touch with me quick?"

The parson raised his head, as if obligated to make a try. "There's no record of blue spirits in the Bible that I recall. The colors associated with the devil are red and black. God the Father, if I was to pick a color for Him, I'd say He's the whitest of whites but also a pure brilliant gold. The Holy Spirit would be dove-gray, of course. So if you're seeing blue, it could be some unfamiliar part of His creation, but that's all. It's neither higher nor worse than that."

Alcee bent forward, trying to ignore the tumult in his belly. "What color would Jesus Himself be?"

"Flesh color like you and me."

He nodded. Still, it was no comfort to hear that the light wasn't God or the devil. It could kill a man for all that.

"Might it be a miracle of any sort?"

"Now we're a lot more careful about calling things by that name than our friends the Roman Catholics," Tullible replied. "Not that we don't believe in miracles, because we do. But if you remember what size you are in comparison with the universe, you'll see that the chance of having your own private one to contend with is mighty small."

Alcee saw that the parson thought the blue light was a hoax.

"Prayer, of course," Tullible continued, pushing up from his chair to follow Alcee, who was making for the door. "And if you could take your mind off this curse. Do you watch Ed Sullivan, I wonder? Those acts he shows are so innocent a child could enjoy them and go straight to the Lord's arms!"

In the farmhouses along Alcee's road, television parties were popular on Sunday nights. The hostesses served pies and sheet cakes while the guests watched a lineup of favorite shows. Everyone laughed in the same places, but nobody spoke except during commercial breaks.

Alcee drove his family to the McCorkles' house two evenings after he fled from the parson. He had begun to wonder if there'd ever been such a thing as the blue light, since no one but Emmaline seemed able to imagine it. He doubted that he could become entirely like his neighbors again, after going through whatever it was that he'd been through; but suppose they were right about how the world stood, even so? Well then, he might at least take a step or two in their direction, he urged himself desperately. The McCorkles' party would be a fair test.

He greeted his hosts shyly, aware that they had heard a mocking tale about him lately, and sat alone by the door while the other guests shook hands. Everybody was laughing at Slick Thomas, who wore a porkpie hat to look like Arthur Godfrey. When the talking hushed and the flickering tube came on, Alcee bent forward gingerly. He heard the usual tinny voices and saw the frosty shadows, and then the first snort of pleasure came from Fred Oppie, who sat on Alcee's right. After that, his mind wandered from the program to the people in the room: to the wrinkles encircling their eyes as they listened to the comedians' jokes, or their hands tensing when the acrobats came on.

Exhausted after an hour, he retreated to the McCorkles' kitchen to stand alone with his thoughts. The desserts were expanding nastily inside his stomach, but he was more disgusted at Harder, who sat in a corner of the living room with his school buddies, Pilcher DaVee and Terry Monoghan. The boys guffawed a second after everyone else in order to ridicule the others' enjoyment, but Alcee saw that they were not disavowing the television at all. They were only keeping a distance from their families, while they took in every movement on the screen with secret fascination.

What hurt Alcee most, though, were the sounds coming from his daughter's throat. Emmaline sat knee to knee with her own friends, trying to imitate the laughter the grown-ups made. She had refused to hear when her father whispered her name. He'd wanted to carry her into the kitchen so they could play pick-up-sticks and forget the others. However, the girl had already made her choice. Her stiff little chest was thrown forward, her face open to the set's enchantment.

Hunched before the McCorkles' refrigerator while a fluorescent light pinged above his head and the TV in the living room played three notes to signify a station break, Alcee pressed his thumbs against his temples and muttered, "Nobody in this county would recognize an angel if it flew down and blinked its eyes. It's like they *prefer* Ed Sullivan, for heaven's sake!"

For a moment the blood pulsed in his brain so wildly that he felt like blocking the screen in the next room with his body and letting out a bellow that would send his neighbors scattering. Just then Edna McCorkle surprised him by coming into the kitchen to fetch the coffeepot. She flashed a bewildered smile in which Alcee detected none of the derision he had come to expect at home. At that instant the glare in the room softened, and his stomach quieted. These were simple people, after all. If they had never seen a blue light, their intentions might still be good. When Edna said, "I'm sorry if you're not enjoying yourself," pulled out a stool for him to sit on, and brought him a magazine from upstairs, he found himself fumbling to assure her, "The marshmallow-prune cake tasted very nice."

On the drive home that night, shame was spread across his cheeks. He knew that he had been perverse to hold a common pleasure like television against anyone. After all, the others were happy; only he was not. He envied his wife's steady breathing beside him in the front seat, and his children's comfortable sighs when they reached their own house for sleep.

The next week as he went about his chores, he brooded not over the mystery of the blue light itself, but over the fact that he had seen it, like so many things, alone. Wasn't that singularity the most important point? The light was merely a proof that God did not mean for any man to keep himself apart. Alcee had tried it, and all he'd gotten for his trouble was a bellyful of gall.

Meanwhile the horizon showed nothing but ordinary sheets of yellow and pink; spring showers passed without meaning over the fields. Even though he was forcing himself to look at the world properly at last, his heart felt drier than he could ever remember. At ten o'clock on Saturday morning he found himself behind the wheel of the truck, barreling down gravel roads with no idea where he might end up. He had racked his brain, but there was no other expert in town to consult. In the mirror he watched white dust scatter behind him on sunshiny gusts, until suddenly a thought seemed to crystallize behind him in the air: despite all his resolutions to the contrary, a part of him still wanted the blue light to return. If he did have a subconscious brain like Doc Griswald said, it must be screaming out its loneliness as a way of persuading the thing to come down from the sky.

He pulled up before Nance's Café because his hands were shaking so badly that he feared he might roll the truck in a ditch. His final hope was that sitting among ordinary people for half an hour might steady his nerves so that he could decide whether to go on or go back.

A dozen men in overalls were exchanging jokes around the horseshoe-shaped counter. The minute he took a stool he regretted stopping, because he saw in the others' eyes a fear that he might force some new confession on them. They greeted him like a halfwit, pronouncing his name but never letting him get a word in. His gaze fell to the coffee mug before him while they wound up their stories and paid their tabs. Today they were calling each other J. Fred Muggs and scratching themselves in the armpits. Finally the last three banged out the door—it was Boodge Morris and the Gabbs brothers—still arguing whether last night's TV newscaster had said Eisenhower would or wouldn't get the farm vote. Before the screen slammed, Boodge glanced back as if to make certain that no one was left for Alcee to torment.

The waitress picked up a tray of dirty mugs and disappeared through the swinging door. Alcee pressed his eyelids together, but the blackness there was complete.

He was startled to hear a spoon hit the countertop on the far side of the horseshoe. He squinted at the shadow by the pie box and saw that somebody remained after all. It was Johnny Delany, with white hair standing straight up from his forehead and crinkly flesh swept into a grin. "Howdy Doody, Buffalo Bob!" Johnny was a retired truck driver and water witch. He told tall tales relentlessly, never waiting to be asked. In a crowd he was a nuisance, though when he sat with a solitary man he might be treated as a friend.

Johnny didn't bother asking Alcee about Sarah or the weather, but immediately started one of his yarns. It was about a man he'd known in the old days who didn't believe in water witching. Alcee hadn't heard this one, so he bent himself to listen. At least it wasn't a story that somebody had gotten off the television. But was it the miracle he had come into Nance's for, after all?

The man in the story had built a farmhouse and then dug all over his yard for a well, but had come up dry every time. Finally he had no choice but to call Johnny for help, even though he cursed him at the same time that he was agreeing to pay him ten dollars to walk over the land with a forked hazel stick. "First thing, I waved the stick over that doubting Thomas's head to rile him with hocus-pocus," Johnny winked. "But once I got down to business, I located water right behind the house. The fella only had to dig fifteen feet to reach it, pure and sweet.

"I didn't charge him a nickel either," the old man chuckled. "It was such good advertising. I knew folks would believe him quicker than they'd believe me, about how the stick works."

When Alcee failed to laugh, Johnny gazed at him cunningly. "You seen that light of yours lately?"

Suddenly the pressure beneath Alcee's ribs eased for the first time in days. He found that he was glad to be asked, even by such a man as this. "Not since April. I'm wondering if it's gone and left me behind."

Johnny whistled, as if he understood how it must feel for a fellow's magic to disappear on him. Alcee stared back at the puckery grin, still wondering if there was any help to be had. "Is there really power in water witching, or is it only a trick anybody could learn?" he asked.

"That's the Sixty-Four-Thousand-Dollar Question, my friend. A witch is sworn not to tell."

"Well then, do you believe there's magic in anything else?"

"Sure, but it depends on what you mean. The TV is a magical invention, for instance. Or the airplane. Even the plow. Think where we'd be without them."

Walking out to the truck, Alcee felt his gut expanding again and loosened his belt a notch. He tried to forget the trash Johnny Delany had spoken by thinking about all the colors he had seen the light take on. He'd always described it to people as blue, but now he admitted that once at dawn it had come as a pale bronze shimmer around the hickory tree beside the garage. Another day on his way to town, he'd seen it moving beside the road, flashing crimson sparks that seemed to burn the air. Then one twilight as he was walking out to shut up the barn, it had thrown off waves of deep orange that fixed themselves in an emerald pinwheel and flew away into the darkening sky. But whenever it exploded in these strange forms, an incandescence at its heart had assured him that it was still his own blue light. The other colors only expressed a passing excitement, or else they were the ordinary world bleeding through.

He opened the door of the truck and heaved himself inside. The noon breeze hinted at the fullness of summer. Soon the sun would reach its most intense degree, the shadows falling their deepest. What if, in that blunt configuration of earth and star, the blue light had no further room to live?

He pulled into the street, houses fell away on both sides and the familiar fields rolled around him. He noticed that the truck was headed toward home. His thoughts quickly strayed into another sorry maze. He wondered if Harder would plead baseball practice as an excuse to avoid helping with the harvest this year, and what Sarah would say if he did? But after a minute he lost the picture of his wife's blistery face, because he saw at the top of the windshield the unusual freshness of the sky. How lucid it was, cloudless, as if inviting him to see through its faint pearliness, beyond and beyond.

He forgot the gas pains Nance's coffee had given him, he forgot where he was driving, because the sky began to absorb him. Disgrace and anger dropped away as he realized that in such a perfect vacancy, the blue light might congeal at any time.

The truck wove from side to side while he craned to catch as much of the heavens as he could. After a minute he braked to a stop and stepped into the road, leaving the engine to idle. Anyone who drove up now would have to pull into the ditch to get around, but Alcee didn't notice. His face was thrown back and he was barely conscious of thinking at all. He was simply spreading his arms to invite the possibility. In former days it had come more easily than wishing.

He drew his hands into fists and squeezed. The universe was growing more enormous as he stumbled farther from the truck. The sun had disappeared in the general brilliance, while the air had softened to a luminous, humid gray. Mightn't the power take on this shade as one more of its disguises? As a test, to see if he wanted it badly enough yet?

"Where are you?" he cried, running far down the road. He felt as if the whole of creation was trembling on the brink. "I know you're there!"